Craving Talon

BOTTLES 69

CRAVING TALON

69 BOTTLES #2

Zoey Derrick

Praise for Claiming Addison and the 69 Bottles Trilogy

"I could go on and on about this book, but I'll leave you here... and the fact that buying a copy of this book should come with a complimentary change of panties..."
5 Stars Shurrn - The Smutsonian

"Holy smokes batman! Where is the fire extinguishers? This final book in this trilogy is scorching hot. Must have significant other around when reading this book!" - Beta Reader on 69 Bottles Trilogy

"Simply AMAZING! Definitely a MUST READ for 2015!" 5 Stars Stephanie - Stephanie's Book Report

Praise for Craving Talon

"Absolute smutty perfection!"
5 Stars Shurrn - The Smutsonian

Acknowledgements

Z-Team: Thank you to my beautiful Street Team. You ladies are the best and I love you for everything you do.

Rachel - My BFF, my Numero Uno Beta Reader. Thank you for always being ready, able and willing to read my raw craziness and for loving every word! P.S. Tell your husband he's welcome!

Mandy and Lorraine: Ladies, without you, this book wouldn't be in everyone's hands. You're amazing at everything you do. Stay Raw!!

To my beautiful Beta Readers: Lisa, Danielle, Vickie, Kali, Liliuokalani and Amy - Thank you for your kindness and willingness to read my mess of a beta copy. Your feedback has been instrumental in creating the story in your hands. Your love of Addison, Talon and Kyle is amazing. Thank you for everything!

To Emily - your words, your encouragement, and your love of my work keeps me going and it keeps me pushing my boundaries. Thank you for being such an inspiration.

For my Fans - Thank you for always wanting more, for reading, and for reviewing my work. Without you I'd have no reason to keep going. Thank you for loving my work.

To Rachel, a.k.a. Parajunkee - Your creativity is an inspiration. Your work is beyond amazing, Thank you for the cover of Claiming Addison and for everything you do to bring my stories to life.

To Stephanie - Thank you for loving my story so much you told every one about it. Your love for Addison, Talon and Kyle inspires me to write more.

To Shannon - Seriously, you're the freakin shiz. No words can say how much I appreciate you and everything you do. I think you have a lot of woman to fight over to stake your full claim on Talon and Kyle!

To All Our Fans! We Love You and We Thank YOU!!

Stop Right There

Now that I have your attention...
If you have NOT read Claiming Addison - 69 Bottles Book #1,
please stop right here.
I want you, the reader, to have the best possible reading
experience and in order to do that, you need to first read Claiming
Addison.
Book 2 - Craving Talon, is a continuation of Claiming Addison.
Starting this series with this book means that you will be lost, you will
not understand what is happening therefore spoiling your reading
experience.

Thank you for taking the time to read this notice. If you've
*already read Claiming Addison, proceed with caution. *Winks**

A WARNING FOR READERS!
I, Zoey Derrick, am not responsible for the following:
Husband/Boyfriend/Significant Other Breaking.
The cost of batteries required for reading this book.
Broken Vibrators.
Loss of sleep
Or
Panty washing.

Read One Handed!
XXOO! Enjoy Craving Talon!
Zoey

chapter 1

addison

Sandwiched between a sexy as hell rock god and his equally sexy and sweet manager...yup, that's where I sit right now. We're on our way to a dinner party. In a Suburban, packed with the members of the band, 69 Bottles, along with their manager, and four – yes, I said four - members of their bodyguard staff. I feel bad for Dex - the band's drummer; Eric, also known as Peacock - the band's bassist and Calvin, better known as Mouse - the band's lead guitarist - because the three of them are sandwiched more than I am between Talon and Kyle.

They're big guys and well, it's a Suburban. In the middle seat behind me, are Beck and Rusty, two of the four body guards, and sitting in the front passenger seat is Leroy, the dude is frickin' huge, and Mills, lead bodyguard extraordinaire, is behind the wheel.

We're on our way to Cami and Tristan Michaels' house for a dinner party that is promised to be not only us, but a few of their friends as well. Which should be great; a chance to be normal, sort of.

Normal is hardly in my vocabulary anymore. Not since five days ago.

Five days ago I stepped onto a tour bus that belongs to America's hottest alternative rock band, 69 Bottles. And five days ago, everything I thought I knew about myself was turned upside down.

I hit that bus with a fierce determination to be professional, do my job, and to have a good time doing it. But what I didn't expect was the hotness that would surround me. There's Dex, the drummer, who's a dick, but still very attractive, living up to the rock god name in every stretch of the imagination possible.

Then there is Mouse. Why do we call him Mouse? Well, for his size he has a tiny ass voice that resembles Mickey Mouse in a strange way. Though when he sings backup for Talon he actually has a very low register. It's kinda strange to hear.

And finally we have Peacock, who is aptly named for his wild hair color choices and his mad mohawk skills. His hair is colored to be hawked, so on nights like this, when it's pulled back, it looks like a mosaic of color. He's very good looking too, a little on the heavier side when compared to the other guys, but he's solid underneath.

Ironically, I've yet to see any of them use the gym, so how they keep their figures is way beyond me.

My hotness meter landed on Talon, the band's lead singer. He's just all around yummy to look at with his shaggy light brown hair and the sexiest, scruffiest beard that is so deliciously perfect it's turned me from ew beard to an OhMyGod beard person. He basically just looks like he hasn't shaved in a week. He keeps it that way and it's fucking delectable. He has these vibrant green eyes that almost seem to glow with their vibrancy. Just thinking about them when he looks at me with sex on his mind makes my entire body vibrate with sexual promise.

On my other side is Kyle, the band's manager, who is equally as sexy as Talon is, but in a much softer kind of way. He's built and tall, not quite as tall as Talon, but close. Kyle has beautiful blue-green eyes that open straight into his soul. Though he isn't an open book, he's incapable of hiding who he is on the inside. He has dirty blond hair that has a little length to it, but he's more of the pretty boy between him and Talon. He keeps his goatee trimmed and he has that small, perfectly shaved line of hair that runs along his very strong, masculine jawline. Tonight he's wearing a dress shirt, boots and jeans. All he needs is a cowboy hat and he'd make the perfect country specimen.

Just this last Sunday morning, waking up in Vegas, Talon, Kyle and I crossed a line that I never intended to cross, but was unable to resist any longer. They refused to make me choose between them, which is a good thing because there is no way that I could have. They're the perfect balance of salty and sweet. Talon's rough around the edges, a little crass at times, and he loves taking control and taking me roughly. Which reminds me of not so long ago when he took me hard, fast and rough. It was the perfect antidote to the shit day I'd had. He pushed me to let go, to surrender my body to him, thus taking my mind off of everything else. It was amazing.

Then you have Kyle, who is the polar opposite of Talon. Though not at all bashful about speaking his mind, he's softer and more controlled and very passionate about me and things in general. I don't think he realizes just how sweet he really is.

With the two of them, it's the perfect balance. Good and evil. Salty and sweet. Loud and quiet. Hard and soft. And I am sandwiched between them. Engulfed with their personal need to be near me, to hold me and to have me.

They've claimed me as theirs and I wouldn't change it for the world. They're proving to be everything I need all rolled up into two nicely kept packages for me to unwrap at any time of my choosing.

chapter 2

We arrive at Cami and Tristan's. Don't ask me where in Phoenix we are because I have no clue whatsoever. Regardless, the house looks massive. Though it is a condo, I can see at least four floors above ground.

I'm leading the charge and ring the doorbell. Tyson, Tristan's bodyguard, answers the door. I find that a little odd, but I don't question it. "Hi, Tyson."

"Good evening, Ms. Beltrand."

I roll my eyes. "Addison, my name is Addison." I give him a playful smile.

"Addison. Sorry, old habits die hard."

"No problem. Tyson, you've met the guys. Talon, Dex, Mouse and Peacock. And this is Kyle." I point to each one as I introduce them.

"Hi guys, come on in." We slide past Tyson and are in an entryway with just a set of stairs leading up. "You guys want to come in too? I assure you they're safe in here, but we have plenty of food to go around." He's talking to Mills and Rusty. I don't hear their reply, but given that Tyson closes the door, I assume the answer was no. "Follow me," he says as he heads up the stairs. Somehow I'm pushed to the front of the pack, like I can save these wild animals from anything. When we reach the top of the stairs I notice an elevator to my right and it's wide open to the left.

Tyson rounds the corner and there are several people milling about, alcohol in hand. Other than Tristan, I only recognize one other face and it's Travis Jackson, a fellow actor friend of Tristan's and Hollywood's second hottest celebrity, behind Tristan of course. And one of Bold's biggest clients.

"Addison," Cami calls from my right. She's coming out of what I think is the kitchen. "Hi Darlin." She gives me a hug and I try hard not to flinch, but damn, it hurts. She pulls back. "What the matter?"

I smile, she will most certainly understand this. "New ink."

Her eyes get wide. "Oh my god, let me see." I hear a collective chuckle coming from behind me and I'm making a mental note to thank the knuckleheads for the outfit. With it hanging loose in the front it doesn't rub in all the wrong places and it makes it easier to show it off. I lift my shirt, careful not to expose my nipples, but it's only going to be any good if she can see the entire thing. As I show her the matching swirls under my breasts I hear her laugh, "oh god, that had to hurt like hell, but they're gorgeous, I love it."

"It did hurt like hell and you never realize how many times someone actually hugs you until you have sore ribs." I laugh.

"Oh, I am well aware of that one. Hey, let me get introductions going." she says with a smile.

"I should've brought 'Hello my name is' stickers," I say and Cami laughs.

"That would have been a great idea. Next time." She winks at me. "Okay, you guys know Tyson, Tristan's bodyguard, among other things, and this is his wife Jolene." Jolene is taller, than I am, with long blond hair and big beautiful eyes. "Jolene, this is Addison."

We shake hands. "Nice to meet you," I say.

"Likewise, I've heard a lot about you."

"Oh dear," I say and Cami laughs.

"Okay, I am going to screw this up." She reaches for Talon's shoulder. "This is Talon." They shake and exchange pleasantries, then she moves on to Mouse, but calls him Calvin, which actually makes Mouse blush. It's freakin cute. Then on to Eric, Dex and finally Kyle. They all exchange greetings and we move on to the next couple in the room. "Addison, this is Mick Bass, you may have heard the name before. He used to work for Bold."

"It sounds familiar but I don't think we've ever met."

He extends his hand and I take it. "I'm with Jolene, I've heard a lot about you, and the guys." Mick releases my hand and then says hello to everyone else then comes back to wrap his arm around the woman standing next to him. She's shorter, about five six, long brown curly hair. "This is my wife, Beau." She's very pretty and very pregnant. She's friendly with me and I can see that given time, she and I could be friends.

We finally move on to Travis and I pray to god I don't make an ass out of myself. Tristan was easy, I'd seen him before, knew about him, but Travis is the enigma locked away in the executive offices. We exchange greetings with him and his girlfriend Naomi who is about as tall as Cami, skinny as a rail and I've seen pictures of her because of her boyfriend.

"And last, but certainly not least we have our good friends Derek and Dacotah Hunter. Derek was just telling me that he and Dacotah were at your Saturday night Vegas show. Addison, did you know that they went looking for you with no luck?"

"Oh my goodness, I'm so sorry. I was only backstage for about ten minutes and went back to my room with a nasty migraine."

Derek smiles. "No worries, we have tickets to one of the New York shows. Cotah is a huge fan, and we'll stop by then." His voice is sultry and very possessive, it's strange, but without knowing better, I'd say he was a very dominant person.

"Excellent, I very much look forward to it." I start talking to his wife. She's absolutely gorgeous with blond hair and beautiful curves. Very confident in herself and comfortable around all the celebrity going ons in this room. We chat and I learn that they have a place in Vegas, atop the Cosmopolitan and they're often there.

The party kicks up, drinks are passed around and the guys are doing what they do best. Mingling with people. Talking about different things and it is nice to see them all engaging with other people and I'm not just talking about Kyle and Talon either.

"I need to have a chat with you," Cami says from behind me. I turn to look at her.

"I had a feeling," I reply to her and she smiles.

"We have about twenty minutes before dinner, but I need to ask your boys something first. Who should I talk to?"

"Oh, um, Talon and Kyle probably."

"Okay, stay here," she says, walking around me to grab them, she brings them back to me, but before they get there, someone comes up behind me.

"How you doin?" I hear Tristan say behind me, I turn to look at him.

"I'm great, yourself?"

He smiles. "I can't complain, it's been a crazy day around here."

"Oh, I don't doubt that. I tried to call Cami this morning, to see if she needed any help. She texted back, said she was good, but that if I needed to escape I was more than welcome."

He laughs. "That's Cami for you."

I smile. "The guys left me alone today. I read some, did just a little bit of work, got some R&R in. It was a good day."

"Glad to hear it. Listen, take this." He hands me a card. "This has my cell phone number on it. Cami is going ballistic regarding you. She's very excited, maybe even desperate to have you on her client list. Before you make any final decisions, talk to me, ask me any questions you might have. I started as nothing and look at me now." He smiles and shrugs. "I can help, but listen to her when you guys go talk. She's very knowledgeable with what she's doing and she won't steer you wrong." He gives me a sad smile. "This business is full of animals that will take anything they can get for as cheap as humanly possible. So make this decision with everything you have and don't make it lightly."

Cami returns with Talon and Kyle. "All good?" she says with a knowing smile.

I smile back. "All good. So what's so important?"

She turns to the guys. "Well, I'm wondering how you'd feel about an impromptu, private concert tonight?"

chapter 3

"Where? Here?" Talon asks, looking around.

Cami laughs. "No. We own a bar, not far from here. We closed up shop tonight, but we were wondering if you'd want to jam, do some acoustic stuff, just have fun."

"We haven't done that in a long time. I'd love to, but let me ask the guys to be sure. We can have our equipment brought over there and my guitar is back at the hotel room."

"We can send someone to get it, I'm sure. Tyson said a couple of your guys are outside."

"Absolutely," Talon says with excitement.

"Oh, and Addison?" I look at her.

"With Talon's permission of course, we'd like to get a recording of you and him singing 'Your Eyes'." Panic, or something close to it wells inside me.

"For personal use?" I ask past the lump in my throat.

"No, I'd like to hand it over to the label," Cami says and the panic escalates.

Talon chimes in, "That was something we wanted to discuss with you tonight. Kyle?"

"Oh, right, they're asking the band and Addison to be in New York early to get an official recording of the song."

Cami gives a knowing smile. "I know, but in the meantime I want to record it, and sell it back to them."

I laugh. "Can you even do that?"

She smiles. "They're the ones who asked me to do it. Look, we have a lot to discuss, hopefully before dinner. Do you want these two to join us?"

I look at both of them. On a personal, I'm sleeping with them level, yes I do. But on a professional level- I turn to Talon. "Would you mind if Kyle comes?"

He smiles. "Not at all." He leans in, gives me a kiss on the cheek and whispers softly into my ear. "Good choice."

"Thanks," I say as Talon goes back to mingling with people and Cami, Kyle and I go to the elevator and step in. "You need an elevator in your house?"

Cami laughs again. "No, but it's easier than the stairs sometimes." We're only in the elevator for all of five seconds (not really, but you know) when the doors open to a hallway. "We're just going to my office. It's quiet and away from prying ears." She turns to Kyle, "Thanks for coming with her. I'm not sure that she needs a manager, but you know what you're doing, so. Though if she wants one..." She shrugs, leaving the thought hanging in the air.

We stop at an open door and she ushers us in. The office is sparse, but yet very Cami with bright colors and a wicked looking tree painted on one wall. I stand, admiring it.

"You like that?" I nod. "That's Beau's work. She does an amazing job, doesn't she?"

"Absolutely." I smile.

"Take a seat you two. I don't do much business in here other than computer work, so forgive the informal setting. Addison, your impromptu performance Sunday night has sparked a wide variety of interests, everything from clothing designers." She shrugs, "I got a lot of those too when Tristan and I got together." She winks. "To record labels. Most are communicating through Trinity at this time. Though we haven't officially signed you to Bold, they came to us because 69 Bottles is with us and they assumed we had something to do with the pairing. Which we did, but not in a singing or musical sense. So, while I am not asking you to sign your life away with Bold, I need to know what you want to do."

She sets two folders down on the desk in front of her and continues, "Inside these folders are two contracts. One," she pats the one on my left. "Is a full contract, giving Bold the right to sell your name and your image to the highest bidder. When we do that you then become a product of the label and no longer an employee of Bold, which means your job with 69 Bottles will terminate."

I don't like where this is going. "What's the other contract?"

"This one is more complicated, but less involved. This one means that Bold doesn't own you, essentially just your voice. It gives me free reign to negotiate for your voice. For example, the recording tonight, should we do it, this contract allows me to sell that recording on your behalf to the label who will then pay Bold, you and the band for their work. It also allows me to negotiate with them for the official recording in New York, as well as any future performances on the tour. It basically only allows Bold to sell anything you do with 69 Bottles and nothing further."

"This is all so confusing," I mutter. "Talon has asked me to perform with him throughout the rest of the tour."

"For free?" Cami asks, there is no malice in the question, but I can see her concern.

"We hadn't talked about it. It's one song and a few lines. It was totally impromptu and I was caught up in the moment of being on stage. Talon was only trying to sing it to me and I was singing back to him." I put my head in my hands. "He liked the sound of my voice, I never imagined it would lead to all this."

Kyle rubs his hand along my back, the gesture is very comforting. "Can I make a suggestion?" he asks and I nod. "Go with the voice contract. Allow Cami to negotiate with the label regarding tonight's recording, the New York recording and anything else in the future that you and Talon might do together. Once the tour is over you can make a decision as to whether or not you want to pursue a full time music career."

"It's so much to take in."

"Look Addison, I don't need you to make any life changing decisions, but it would be wrong of me to not tell you what is in store for tonight and New York's recording."

"This has nothing to do with money," I blurt.

"I think you might change your mind. Tonight's recording comes with a ten million dollar budget that is meant to pay the band, it's agents, plus recording and distribution costs. With what's leftover, twenty-five percent to Bold because we're dealing with both you and 69 Bottles. Sixty percent to 69 Bottles and the remaining fifteen present is yours."

"How much is left over after all of that is paid?" I ask her.

Cami shrugs, "it really depends on what the label spends on their end, but between two and two and half million.

"Three-hundred and fifty thousand dollars for three minutes and forty one seconds?" I squeal in shock.

"That's just for the recording. That's not counting your percent of things like airtime play and performances. The official recording will garner more for you because it will give the label the ability to sell to the consumer as a single."

"And when this is all done, if 69 Bottles decides to not coordinate on future songs, I can just walk away?"

She leans back in her chair, her confidence is palpable. She knows she's winning. "Yes, you can just walk away."

"Can I go back to my job?"

She lets out a small laugh. "If that's what you want to do, then it's all yours. It remains your job if you sign this contract." She puts her hand on the one on my right. "Singing becomes your full time gig if you sign this one."

"Got a pen?" Both Cami and Kyle laugh and Cami hands me a pen. I grab the folder on the right and open it. I glance through it. It's standard stuff, I've seen these contacts before. I pop down to the exclusions category and read...

"The above contract does not include the selling of person or image of person to any outside parties." Or something to that effect.

"I will let you know that we will continue to work with the labels interested in you. You will become a client of Bold so it is in our best interest to protect you and handle this for you. We will not make any decisions and I will wait until the end of the tour to discuss them with you. Sound fair?" I nod.

I sign the contract and place it back on Cami's desk with shaking hands. She is radiating excitement as she signs her name next to mine.

"My first piece of advice," she says softly. "Kick some ass, take some names along the way and," she winks, "talk to Tristan. He's very insightful and he knows what the single star status is like. Talon at least has the band behind him to help shoulder some of that crazy. You would be on your own, and talk to me before you guys decide to do anything outside of 'Your Eyes'. I'll agree to it, regardless, but I need to know so that I can start working on negotiations and prepare for it."

Kyle and I both laugh. "You got it."

She stands, puts her hand out and I take it. "Congratulations," she says.

Kyle wraps his hands around my shoulders and hugs me. "Good job, panda girl."

I happen to catch Cami's eye of approval and I have a feeling before the night's out, she'll know that Kyle isn't the only man with pet names for me.

"Now, let's go eat," she says, escorting us from her office.

"Oh, I almost forgot. Talon has a special announcement for the band. Would you mind if he does it during dinner?"

"Not at all, as long as I can announce what just happened?"

I smile. "Absolutely."

chapter 4

"Dinner was amazing. Thank you, Cami," Talon tells her with sincerity.

"You're most welcome. I don't imagine you're gonna get many home cooked meals these next few weeks."

"No, we won't. So thank you again."

Dex chimes in. "That was fabulous. Thank you."

I smile sweetly at Dex and see a pleading worry in his eyes. I make a mental note to find a chance to talk to him as soon as possible. I need to know how he's doing after the Kate incident.

As we finish up dinner I lean over to Talon's ear. "Cami said go ahead with your announcement."

"Thanks, angel," he says quietly back.

The conversation continues to flow like it did over dinner. Everything from what everyone does, to their home and family life. I settle into their small talk naturally. Derek interests me most and my suspicions surrounding his dominance are confirmed by the way his wife acts around him. There's just a certain way she moves and silently seeks permission for certain things. But they are ridiculously happy and it's infectious.

Beau and Mick are some of the quietest ones and Mick is very attentive to Beau. I gathered from the conversation that she's about six weeks away from her due date and she's excited. But no one seems to know the sex of the baby. Which I find sweet.

Tyson, Travis and Tristan are like three peas in a pod. Bantering and having a good time all on their own, while Jolene, Naomi and Cami are obviously best friends.

Cami looks at me as the conversation kind of dies down and I squeeze Talon's leg and nod. "Again, thank you Cami for the wonderful meal and it is my understanding that we will be heading to a bar shortly?" He looks at me for confirmation and I nod. "Good, okay, so before we go, I wanted to let my guys know something Kyle told me right before we left the hotel."

"Just spill it already," Dex teases him.

"Oh hell, I'm so freakin' excited it's hard to spit it out. 'Your Eyes' has reached the number one spot on Billboard's Top 100."

There's some whooping and hollering from the guys, applause from Cami's guests and several rounds of congratulations. I can tell that the band and even Kyle are over the moon with the news. It's 69 Bottles' first number one hit. Now it's a matter of keeping it there. Which is part of why I agreed to signing Cami's contract.

"Now for some more news," Cami says. "I am honored to announce Bold's newest client. Addison Beltrand."

I blush beat red. "Oh my god, Addie?" Talon grabs my arm. "What did you do?" He's not angry but he's confused.

I smile at his confusion. It's sweet actually. "I signed a contract with Bold that allows Cami to sell my voice. Which means that I can record tonight, in New York and continue on tour with you and it gives Bold the option to sell my image at a future date."

"Are you serious?"

"Uh huh."

He pulls me into his arms hugging me. "Hell yeah."

I can't help but laugh at his excitement and enthusiasm. "We can talk about it more later. But I get to stick around for a while."

I'm met with congratulations and atta girls that last for a little while until I get up to help Cami clean up the dishes. "Leave 'em," she tells me as I start the water in the sink. "I have a housekeeper."

I laugh. "Alrighty then." I turn, leaning on the counter. "I don't think I thanked you properly."

"For what?" she asks surprised.

"The job, signing me, everything."

"Well, the job you earned and you've done a wonderful job so far. The deal with Dex yesterday." She raises an eyebrow at me.

"Oh, I didn't do anything with that. I made the decision to leave it alone once I realized I was getting more airtime than he was. Why wake up a sleeping dog? But we figured out how and why it happened."

"I heard. Not the details, but that some good investigative work solved the problem."

I nod. "Yeah, it was personal against Dex, and Talon is working on the drug aspect with him. He says it was the first time he's touched drugs in four or five years. He's concerned, but everyone is keeping an eye on him. I've noticed since it happened he's mellowed out a lot."

"I can tell. He's like a whole different person than he was in San Diego when I met him the first time. I had a pretty good idea when you guys got here that whatever had happened was pretty serious. Be sure to keep an eye on him. If he has a history of drug abuse..." she lets the thought fall off.

"I think he'll be alright. I also think that once we get back on the bus away from Phoenix, he'll slip into his old way again. I hate to say it, but I kinda miss the old Dex."

She laughs and I join in.

"Hey ladies." Tristan comes into the kitchen. "We're ready to go."

"Perfect," Cami says. "Let me run upstairs real quick and we'll go. Addison, you okay in those shoes?"

"Oh my god, no." I laugh. "I asked Mills to bring me my flip flops."

"Perfect."

Cami disappears leaving me with Tristan. "You've made her night," he says with a smile. "And you made the right choice. For now. Not many people get to experience it first and decide later." He winks, "Also, I can tell that you have a special place in your heart for these guys, I can't picture you walking away from them for your own benefit."

I chuckle. "You seem to know me really well."

He smiles. "Not really, I know your type." His eyes look upward. "She's the same way. Just remember, she's a very personable person, don't hesitate to ask her any questions, stupid or otherwise. And, call me." He pleads with his eyes. "Trust me, I don't want to scare you away, but what I do isn't exactly my first choice either."

"Alright Tristan, I promise. I need to let this soak in a little before I can begin to think straight."

He laughs. "That will take some time. Come on, let's get out of here."

We head into the living area where everyone is waiting around. "We have a Suburban that has a few spots open if anyone wants to ride with us," Kyle says to the group.

"We will," Travis pipes up.

"Awesome," Mouse says. He and Travis have been shooting the shit most of the night so I can't say I'm surprised.

Cami comes back down. "We ready?"

There is a collective yes and nods so we head down the stairs and out the door. Everyone piles into cars and I am sandwiched between Kyle and Talon once again. Talon is bursting with excitement, it's kind of strange. "What's...?" I start to ask, but he cuts me off.

"Oh, I've just been waiting forever to do this," he says as he grabs my head between his hands and he pulls me in for a deep long sensual, panty melting kiss.

"Get a room," Dex chides.

"You think that's bad," Kyle teases, causing both Talon and I to laugh, breaking our kiss. "Try being in the same room, it's kinda hot."

Oh my god, he didn't. Yeah, he did. I can't stop laughing. I feel high both from Talon's kiss and from the fact that everything in my life has changed dramatically in just a few short days. The time seems like it's been months, not days.

"I am so happy for you," Talon tells me.

"It's not just me benefiting from this. The band is too."

He cocks his head in my direction. Mouse and Travis are deep in conversation about something I can't make out, but I've captured Peacock and Dex's attention.

"Cami is going to take tonight's recording back to the label. The price has already been set. The recording will be used for airplay only. The New York recording will be what goes live for sale. Though that is being negotiated, tonight's recording has a ten million dollar price tag on it."

Talon's eyes widen in shock. "Baby, that's amazing."

"I know, considering sixty percent of it's yours, or at least the band's." Talon's mouth drops. "The concert performances are now under Cami's control to negotiate. If or when we decide to do the duet you wrote, that will be worked into the performance negotiations. I'd imagine she'd negotiate to record it in New York also."

Talon just sits back, soaking in what I'm telling him. "I'm proud of you," he says with soft reverence in his eyes.

"This isn't about me. Whatever you want to do with me is your choice. If you don't want me to perform with you, you don't have to let me. Though I am pretty sure the 'Your Eyes' duet recording isn't much of an option anymore. We've already opened that can of worms. But if you don't want me...."

"Shh." He sits up. "I want this, Addison. Believe me, I want this for you, for the band."

"So why are you so sad?"

He leans into me. "I'm afraid of you becoming too big for me," he whispers.

I give him a sad smile. "I haven't agreed to anything outside of what I do with 69 Bottles. Cami is pocketing the label offers until after the tour. Honestly, at this point, I do not see myself making a career out of singing. I even asked her if I could keep my job with Bold and if returning after the tour would be a problem. Talon, I only want to do this because you're insisting I do this with you for the tour. It isn't about the money or the fame; it's about you and the band."

He leans in, hugging me gently. Nestling himself into the crook of my neck. I can hear him inhale. "You're way too good for me, you know that?"

I rub his back. "Nothing, not even me, is too good for you."

He mumbles something into my neck and I can't hear him. I take more comfort in the fact that Kyle is comforting both of us. I feel Talon shift to look at him, though I can't see the exchange, Kyle's hand tightens on my hip. There is some type of exchange between the two of them, but I don't know what it is and that's okay. They need their time too.

The conversation in the car changes when Peacock and Dex join in on Mouse and Travis's conversation. I can feel someone watching me and I wonder idly if it is the quiet Naomi, but I don't turn to look. I'm going to enjoy my moment with my boys.

chapter 5

It's just after eight when we arrive at the bar. The area seems pretty remote, but by gauging the traffic on the road in front of the bar, we're still within the city limits. There is a big sign out front that says "Blu Phoenix" and the building is rather unremarkable from the outside.

The building is long or wide, depending on how you want to describe it, and brown. Cami and Tristan, Tyson and Jolene and Mick and Beau are all waiting for us outside the door and I can see Tristan is unlocking the door.

All the lights are on inside and there are a couple of people moving around. "That's the sound crew. It's going to be far from soundproof but it's all we've got on short notice," Cami says. "These guys are amazing at what they do. They will digitally enhance the recording for better quality."

The atmosphere inside is great. Blues, blacks and chromes make up the décor. On this end, across from the door is a stage. It's small but I imagine it's a bit nostalgic for the guys. They played this scene for years. On the far end from where we came in is a beautiful shiny black high-top bar with chrome stools in front of it. It stretches the entire width of the space.

Beau stands in front of everyone and smacks her hands together. "Bar's open for all the non-pregnant ones. What can I get you guys?"

Beer is immediately ordered by most of the men in the room.

"Oh please, you guys are boring as hell," Beau teases.

"Nope, just practical," Tyson says as Beau heads toward the bar. Mick is hot on her heels. She isn't gonna be able to lift a finger and it's freaking adorable how he follows after her.

"The gear bus is here," Mills says from the doorway.

"Great," Talon says. "Let's get it unloaded."

I'm surprised when Talon, Kyle and the rest of the crew head out the door. I've never seen them set up their own equipment before.

I follow them out and get shooed back inside. I roll my eyes. "You're not helping, not in those." Kyle says looking at my feet. I actually forgot I was wearing the heels still. I turn to look for Mills and find Rusty instead.

"Any luck finding my flip flops?"

He hands me a bag. "Grabbed you a change of clothes too. You might be here a while."

"Thanks," I reply, trying to fight back the weirdness of him finding me clothes. Then again, my suitcase is open on the stand in the room. I go back inside and am quickly followed by the guys. Two of the road crew came with them. Have these guys been on the bus the since our arrival in Phoenix on Sunday? God, I hope not. I vow to ask Kyle about it later.

They go about setting up Dex's drums and a couple of the amps that they use in their setup.

"Alright guys, we have a couple of things for you," one of the sound guys says. "We have a couple of microphones for Talon and Addison. Plus ones that will hook onto the bass and guitars. So once you're all set up, we will get it all hooked up for you. It's our hope that we can cut some of the echo. We've recorded here before, though with a packed house and the sound has been pretty good."

"We could move outside," Cami suggests. "It's set up, would that help with the feedback?"

The sound guy smiles. "It might, but we're already in here. Let's try here first, if I can't get the quality I want, we'll give it a go outside."

Cami nods and Mick shows up with a tray full of beer bottles. I smile, after what Talon told me about where they got their name, it's rather fitting.

"What so funny?" I look to see Jolene standing beside me.

I nod my head in a silent chuckle. "I was thinking about the band's name and where it came from when I saw all those bottles."

"Oh, oh!" she says like she gets it. "Sixty-nine of them?"

I nod and smile. "What I don't get is who decided to count the bottles?"

"I did, love," Dex says as he comes up to take a bottle. "I was ridiculously anal retentive back then, oh and bored too. I decided to count them as I threw them away."

"That's pretty funny actually. I used to do shit like that all the time. I still do, but Tyson doesn't put up with my shit so I've mellowed out some," she says with a laugh and takes a sip of her beer.

"Yo, Dex, getcha ass ova here," Peacock shouts so Dex takes off back to the stage.

"I don't know how you do it," Beau says as she comes to sit at the table with all the beer, propping her feet up on an adjacent chair.

"Do what?"

Beau laughs. "I have a hard enough time keeping up with Tristan and Travis, I can't imagine four of them."

"Try five," I tease, grabbing a beer and taking a sip. "Kyle's just as good or bad as they are, depending on the day. They've been friends for years. And to be honest, this is only just beginning, I don't know if I'm going to last twelve weeks." I take another sip of my beer.

"So are you and Talon...?" Beau wiggles her eyebrows. I nearly spew beer everywhere. She laughs. "I'll take that as a yes. Can't say I blame you though, they're all pretty hot." I look over my shoulder as the guys set up their stuff. Watching them work, yes they're all hot, but my eyes land on Talon and Kyle.

"Yeah, they are," I say with a harlot's groan.

"Seriously, how do you do it?" Jolene asks. I laugh. "I'm a happily married woman but I have trouble around them. Add to that the fact that they're musicians." I watch as she melts but then her eyes drift over to her husband and she melts a little more. "I'm gonna go stand over there." She nods her head in Tyson's direction and Beau and I both laugh.

"Go for it," Beau says.

"How long have they been together?" I ask Beau as Jolene goes to stand near Tyson.

"Um, three years, I think. Jolene, Cami, Naomi and I have been friends for a long time. Cami had some shit happen a few years back and she ran off right before her birthday, which is where she met Tristan. Then Cami and Tristan played matchmaker. Hooking up Tyson and Jolene and Travis and Naomi." Beau laughs. "That was an interesting weekend." She smiles at the memory running through her head.

"You okay, baby?" Mick comes up to Beau, rubbing her shoulders.

"I'm great, just remembering when we went to Tarah for the first time. What was that, three years ago?" she asks him and he nods. She looks back at me. "He's better with that stuff than I am, especially now."

"This your first?" I nod toward her tummy.

She nods running her hand lovingly over the swell. "I just can't wait for it to be over. I'm so ready to meet him or her."

"So you don't know what you're having?"

Both her and Mick laugh. "That's only because whatever it is is very stubborn, every time we try and find out, it closes it's legs on us. So we gave up. We just have six more weeks left."

"Hey, Addison?"

I turn to Kyle. "Yeah, cowboy?" I turn back to Beau and wink.

"We're ready."

I down the rest of my beer. "Where can I toss this?"

"Set it on the table, I'll get it," Mick says with a smile. "Go get 'em."

I set my bottle down just as I hear the string of 'Your Eyes' being played in typical 69 Bottles tuning fashion. I flush as I'm immediately turned on. Though it's never happened to me before, something about tonight…maybe it's the intimacy of the gathering of friends. I notice now that Travis and Naomi have taken over a table opposite where we are now. Behind them are Derek and Dacotah. He has his arms wrapped around her in a very possessive way that sends a thrill through me. Cami and Tristan are helping out with the sound and equipment.

"Alright Adam, let's run this once with me, make any adjustments and then go again, with Addison," Talon says into the mic. You can hear him but it isn't a whole lot louder than if he were to talk normally. That tells me that the vocals are going straight into the recording system, cutting feedback to next to nothing. I feel a little more at ease about doing this now knowing that I might not be heard all that well. Yeah, right.

"Got it," Adam says.

"Addie, come here," Talon calls and I walk toward him, thankful I haven't taken my pumps off yet. I can see the lusty look show up in his eyes and I stop a few feet away from him and then the band kicks up after Dex's count off.

Your eyes
Are like nothing I've ever known
Nothing I've ever seen
They bring me here
They bring me home
Your eyes
Are all I can see.

chapter 6

Six takes later and we've managed to record a very good version of 'Your Eyes'. We made various adjustments for when I would come in and when I would sing back up and when I would take the part for myself. I got more than a lot of applause for my abilities. It was nerve wracking because I didn't want to screw up, or make an ass out of myself, but I do have to say, it boosted my confidence just a little.

"You're amazing." Travis gives me praise as we wrap up.

I blush. "Thanks. That means a lot coming from you."

"Ah, yeah, I guess it could. You do a pretty good job of hiding what you do or don't know about someone."

I laugh. "I've been working in the industry for a while. But thank you just the same. I learned a long time ago that celebrities are people too."

"That's a great attitude, wanna teach that to all the crazies out there?"

I laugh. "Sure, but it won't help. I won't say that meeting someone new doesn't send my heart racing and my palms sweating, but I do a pretty good job of hiding it."

"Yes, you do. Thank you for tonight," he says.

I cock my head at him. "The private show. I wish we'd been able to attend the concert."

"We'll be in LA in June for the final shows of the tour. You should come. Cami has the dates, check with her and have her let me know if you're coming, I'll make sure you get VIP access."

"That would be great," Travis says as his eyes light up.

Just then I can hear a guitar being played. I turn around and see Talon sitting alone on the stage. He's looking at me. The tone is soft, but very typical of Talon and 69 Bottles.

Then he starts to sing...

Today you walked into my life
Tomorrow you'll walk away
But I can't let you
I won't be the one to
Watch you turn your back
I need you here, I need you now

I can't walk away from you
You mean the world to me
You're my everything,
You're all I need
All I need to be free

Chorus:
To be Free means loving you
To be Free means holding you
To be Free means needing you

To be me means loving you

One day soon, I'll make a mistake
One day soon you'll run away
The risk is so high, I cannot take
I need you to be free.
I need you to be me.

Chorus:
To be Free means loving you
To be Free means holding you
To be Free means needing you
To be me means loving you

When you're in my arms
You're everything I need
You're everything to me
You're all I need to be free

I sit down slowly into a chair, tears streaming down my cheeks. That's it, that's the song, the one he wrote last night. Everyone in the room is standing, clapping, whistling and hollering. I watch Talon carefully, his eyes are on me, watching me. His eyes are glassy with emotion. I blow him a kiss. "Play it again," I say. He smiles and begins playing the song again. Strumming on his guitar. Talon playing is truly something to watch. He's so confident, fluid and more than skilled at what he does. Though the melody isn't complicated, his fingers are deft and quick on the strings.

One of the things I've always been able to do is memorize songs very quickly. It's either a curse or a gift, and right now, it's a gift. I start to sing along with him, more to myself than anything, but I quickly find eyes and heads turning in my direction.

Cami snaps into action, putting Adam and his crew back on their jobs, though I don't think they stopped. Then she points at me and then at the microphone. I shake my head. She gets up and comes over to me, crouching down before me. "Is this the song?"

"I think so, I've never heard it before." Though I'm talking to her, I can't take my eyes off of Talon as he finishes the second go round of the song.

"Do it. Let's drop the recording on the label." I smile at her and her enthusiasm is infectious and I get up, walking toward Talon.

"Do you have the lyrics?" I ask him. He smiles and hands me his notebook. It's open to a page with 'To Be Free' written in bold, been scribbled on too many times, pencil. The lyrics are written rather nicely, and I'm impressed by his handwriting, but surprised by the fact that the song has it outlined which part I'm supposed to sing. "Sing it with me? I need the whole thing, I need to feel the pace. Then we can give it a go."

His eyes are happy and impressed. I kick off my heels and adjust the microphone to match my new height and Talon starts up with the melody.

He nods and starts to sing. I sing softly along with him, following along with the lyrics. When my part comes up, I try and sing it louder, but my confidence with the song isn't there. Talon pulls his voice back to let me sing it.

We play through the rest of the song, by the second time through the chorus, my confidence is boosted and I'm singing louder. And then I back off completely for him to finish out the song, as it should be.

By the time he's done, his eyes are glassy with unshed tears and I fight my own. I look over at Kyle who is leaning against the wall. I don't have a clear shot of his face, but I can tell he too is emotional over the performance.

"Let's do this, for real this time," I say confidently, and like when the lights dim in a theater, everyone in the room takes a seat. I turn my mic, bringing it with me as I step down off of the raised platform so that I can look at him. So that I can channel his emotion.

Amazingly enough, 'Your Eyes' took us six takes. 'To Be Free' takes us one. I know we have it when there isn't any immediate applause from our friends until Adam gives the all clear. Talon sets down his guitar and stands up, hopping down and wrapping his arms around me and picking me up. I screech in pain but I don't care.

I take his head in my hands. "Message received. Loud and clear." I crush his lips to mine and he kisses me back with fervor and the same desperation I feel. Guilt slides through my veins. Kyle has been neglected nearly all night and I feel awful for it. "Now, big man, put me down," I whisper.

He has a wicked smile on his face as my feet touch the floor. "You're so beautiful. Now go get our boy." He lets me go and I walk over to Kyle.

"Hi, panda girl."

"I want to kiss you so bad right now."

"So do it." I throw my arms around his neck and bring his lips to mine. There are more than a few whistles.

"About fucking time you guys admitted it." I hear Dex shout. I smile against Kyle's lips.

"You're amazing," he says as he pulls back from my kiss and I drop my arms, turning around.

"You lucky bitch." I hear Beau say with a laugh and I blush beet red. "Oh sweetheart, you're in the right company for that. Trust me," she says with a sweet smile on her lips.

Talon comes over to Kyle and I. "That was fucking hot," he breathes.

I laugh, of course it was. He's a fucking animal.

Shortly after that our new friends start to leave. Mick and Beau are the first to go. "Take care of that baby," I tell her when she hugs me.

She rubs her belly. "Oh, I plan too. I'll get your email from Cami, if that's okay. Keep you posted?"

"Absolutely. She's got my number too."

Mick hugs me too and shakes the guys' hands.

Cami is cleaning up beer bottles. I go to help her. She has her phone in one hand and like four bottles in the other. I grab a handful of bottles and follow her. "It's nearly midnight and you're glued to your phone."

She laughs. "A businesswoman's job never ends."

"Right?" I say with a laugh as we dump the empty bottles into the recycling can at the end of the bar.

"You're a damn minx, you know that? Both of them?"

I smile and nod with enthusiasm.

"Now I really don't know how you do it. They are both so much, but just keep this in mind, that connection with you and Talon is golden. I don't recommend losing it."

"I don't plan on it. But it's all so new and intense and overwhelming."

"Oh darlin, I know. Especially the celebrity aspect of it. Just remember to keep time for yourself. If you don't, it will overwhelm you beyond repair. I know that's the only thing that kept me sane. Separate from time to time. Especially if you're dealing with both of them." She winks.

We finish cleaning up and say our final good-byes to everyone. Travis and Naomi are going to ride back with Cami and those guys so that we can go straight to the hotel.

"We have a six hour drive to Albuquerque tomorrow and an eight o'clock start time. We have to be at the buses by five to beat traffic, so get back, get packed and be downstairs at five." Kyle tells everyone once we're in the car. "Do not be late."

It's after one when we arrive back at the hotel. We have four hours to pack and be back on the bus. Oh hell, who am I kidding? Packing is the last thing these two are going to be doing tonight. I smile to myself.

"Penny for your thoughts?" Kyle asks me. I look at him through my lashes. "Oh." He takes my hand and places it on his erection. My pussy pulses with excitement and undeniable anticipation.

chapter 7

The ride up in the elevator to our room is excruciating in so many ways. Talon has been quiet, but I can see it in his eyes that he's desperate to be alone with me and Kyle.

We say good night to the band quickly and before we even make it to the bedroom, Kyle is pulling my shirt over my head. I moan the moment his hands make contact with my breasts and throw my head back. His mouth is next, pulling a nipple in and causing my legs to tremble. Talon comes to stand behind me, giving me the support I need so I don't fall over.

With a gentle hand Talon moves my hair off of my neck and over my shoulder as his lips find my neck with passionate kisses. Talon's hands begin roaming over my entire body, from my shoulders, down my arms, across to my stomach and into the waistband of my jeans.

Kyle doesn't stop, licking and sucking his way from one hard nipple to the next and back again. The pleasure is so intense I feel like I could explode right now.

Talon unbuttons my jeans and Kyle helps him slide them down my legs as he begins kissing down my stomach. Kyle's kisses are soft, causing my belly to jump and the fire within to spread far and wide. Kyle continues kissing down to my hips, where he first kisses one and then licking, kissing and sucking his way to the other. Talon too, is making his way south along my back with similar yet profoundly different open mouth kisses. His mustache tickles my skin and goosebumps radiate everywhere, making my nipples hard and my pussy ignites in a flood of desire.

Both men continue their kisses until Talon has reached my ass and he bites into the soft flesh. Kyle is moving closer to my clit and Talon's kisses are moving toward the tight pucker of my ass . "Ahh," I moan as soon as Kyle takes a long languid lap at my sex. Talon doesn't hesitate in spreading my butt cheeks and the next thing I know, Talon's tongue is licking the tight rosette. The dual assault is overwhelming, forcing my body to tremble uncontrollably with my need to come.

As if anticipating everything, both their hands clamp down on my legs, holding me still, their silent plea for me to come. Lick, lick..."Fuck!" I push my hand into Kyle's hair, reaching around to grab Talon's, holding both of them to me as my release consumes me, shattering me into millions of tiny pieces. Through the haze of my orgasm neither have stopped their licking and sucking, my body vibrates with the pleasure they provide for me.

Slowly they both back off of me, but neither takes their hands away. I am weak and shattered. "Take her," Talon says, "into the bedroom, I'll be right there." A whimper of disappointment escapes my lips. "I'll be right there," he breathes against my ear.

Kyle stands, wrapping one arm around my back then he leans down, hooking my knees on the other. He lifts me, carrying me into the bedroom where he sets me down gently on the bed. Kyle wastes no time in removing my flip flops, then my pants which are gathered around my calves.

Still reeling from my orgasm it takes me a minute more to compose myself enough to watch Kyle unwrap himself like candy from his clothes.

I lick my lips. "What do you want, baby girl?" His voice is sultry, needy.

I bite my bottom lip. "You, in my mouth," I breathe and he picks up his stripping pace. I smile because he quickly becomes all thumbs. I sit up. "Easy, cowboy." I take the waistband of his pants in my hands and pull him forward. Bringing his crotch level with my mouth. I begin rubbing my nose along the outline of his erection and he groans above me.

"You're killing me, baby girl."

I continue my little kitty routine on his cock as my hands work on the button and then finally his zipper. Achingly slow I pull his zipper down one tiny notch at a time. I bite the tip of his cock through his jeans and watch as the pleasure shimmers across his skin. Breathing hotly against his jeans, I can feel his dick twitch with my torture.

After what seems like forever, the zipper finally stops its descent and I pull back, grabbing his waistband, ready to free him from the confines of his jeans. I look up into his eyes and they're on fire with need and devotion.

The look sends a chill through me and I don't need to guess what's running through his mind.

I slowly slide his pants and boxers down, reach in and free his cock, wrapping my hand tightly around the base and he groans. I stroke his heavy length and then go back to removing his pants. As his pants reach his knees, my tongue flicks out, stroking the underside of his mushroomed head. My reward is his body quaking, a huff, and his salty sweet essence wreaking havoc on my taste buds. I moan in delight.

"You're making a meal out of me," he breathes, looking down at me. Eyes hooded and dangerous. I smile while I lick the head of his cock again.

"The best meal," I whisper back. I get the feeling I'm being watched, but I don't look, I don't need to. I know it's Talon. The idea that he's watching my torture of Kyle turns me on that much more. I've never been a voyeur but I just might start now.

I suck Kyle's cock deep into my mouth and watch as his eyes roll up into his head. The visual is heady. I know that with each little flick of my tongue against his shaft that I am pleasing him. He's taking pleasure from my mouth. I shiver and moan around his erection and he groans. I let his dick pop free of my mouth and I watch the sadness at the loss creep into his eyes. But I tease him a little more by sliding my middle finger into my mouth and sucking on it, licking it.

When I'm satisfied with its wetness I pop it free, swapping my finger for a lick on the head of his cock. I bring my now wet hand up to cup his balls. Sliding my hand gently along the underside, pushing it forward until my finger finds the tight ring of his ass and I press into it. He jerks in shock but lets a growl escape his lips. I let my finger roam around the outside, teasing him as my tongue dances across his erection. Feeling brave once again, I let my finger dip inside.

I am rewarded with a shot of pre-cum down my throat and the groan that hisses through his teeth is enough to make pleasure radiate from my core, causing a violent shiver of pleasure to rock through my body. Desperate to come, I start slowly sliding my finger in and out as he gently begins to pump into my mouth. "Don't stop," he breathes and I continue licking and sucking while gently finger fucking his ass.

His thrusts become more demanding in my mouth and I am given another salty taste on my tongue. I want him to come, but not yet. I slowly back off with my mouth and slow my ins and outs with my finger.

Looking up into his eyes, I can see the loss and realization that I'm not going to let him come radiating in his features. I let his cock fall from my mouth with an audible pop. "I'm not ready for you to come," I breathe against his erection as it twitches.

He smiles down at me. "Good."

I extract my hand from between his legs making sure to tease his balls just a little more before I slide back on the bed. I watch as he eagerly sheds his shoes and his pants disappear completely.

"Fuck, that was hot," Talon says from the doorway, bringing my attention from Kyle's nakedness to Talon. I see him standing in the doorway, the light from the sitting room behind him shining outward giving him slightly darkened features and I shiver with excitement and a thrill of fear. I notice now that one hand is around his cock, stroking slowly and in the other, a black bag.

"Enjoy the show?" I ask, he smirks.

"More than you know." I watch as he strokes his cock. It's by far the hottest thing I've ever seen in my entire life and my hand instantly dives down onto my clit and I begin rubbing it with slow gentle circles.

Talon stalks toward the bed, puts the bag down and motions for Kyle to come to him and I can hear Kyle's feet shuffling on the floor. I get an eyeful of Kyle's side profile and the hard-on protruding from between his legs and I moan.

Kyle moves next to Talon and I watch as Talon's hand takes a hold of Kyle's erection and my back arches, sending goosebumps across my flesh and my nipples harden. My other hand has a mind of its own when it begins to slide up my stomach in a feather light touch. I shiver.

Kyle, taking his cue from Talon, grips Talon's cock in his hand. With slow, gentle strokes they both begin pumping each other's erections at the same time as my hand brushes across my nipple. "Ahh," I moan as I watch them stroke each other. They both have devilish grins on their faces and I know they're doing this for me. Giving me a visual that is far better than any porn on the planet. "Kiss him," I command.

They both smile at me and turn, now both their side profiles are in view and I can watch them stroking each other as their lips come together. Their kissing is spotlighted from behind by the light of the sitting room. Their faces thrown into shadows. The silhouette of their profiles is mysterious and sexy.

Lost in their show, my hand stills against my pussy, completely entranced watching them kiss each other. A moan escapes Talon's mouth on an upstroke of his cock and I can see his legs tremble. Then he pulls back from the kiss, gently pulling Kyle's hand from his own erection, he drops to his knees in front of Kyle. "Ah fuck!" I cry out.

My hand immediately starts moving with ardor and the moment Talon's tongue meets Kyle's erection, I explode. My orgasm is like a raging fire in my veins.

chapter 8

Somehow, I don't know exactly how, I've ended up on the floor, on all fours, between the two men that mean the world to me. Talon is ferociously working Kyle's cock with his mouth and my mouth is sucking and swallowing down Talon's.

I feel Talon's hand slide along my back, working his way towards my ass and my dripping slit. I feel the flick and pressure against my tight entrance and I moan around his erection. His hand slips past my back entrance and I feel a finger slide into my pussy. My back arches, spurring me on, I start working his cock harder in my mouth. I wish I could see what's above me but the possession Talon has over my sex tells me that I won't be able to move.

His finger is sliding in and out with abandon as I work his cock with my mouth. He's so big around that it is hard to pull in more than a few inches without making my jaw burn, but I don't care.

His fingers don't let up; my orgasm simmers just below the surface. Anticipation builds. He moans as my tongue strokes along his cock and then he stops. Extracting his fingers from my pussy and cupping my face with his other hand. "Get on the bed. Just like this," Talon says with a commanding tone in his voice and I don't hesitate. Crawling my way up onto the bed, my arms and legs are shaky from the near orgasm I've been denied, but I do my best not to show it.

"Grab a pillow, get comfortable, but keep that sexy ass in the air," Talon tells me. I do as he asks, grabbing the closest pillow, wrapping my arms around it and arching my back. My action opens me up to them, inviting them into me. The bed dips as one of them climbs up behind me followed by the rustling of a plastic bag. Then the bed dips to my right and now I know they're both here with me.

I wait patiently through the rustling, the shifting on the bed and then without warning, two warm hands begin caressing along my lower back, along my hips. Grabbing onto my ass cheeks. I close my eyes, soaking in the pleasure brought on by the massaging strokes. I think it's Talon judging by the slightly callused fingertips.

The caresses continue until my cheeks are spread wide. Without a word, a warm, wet tongue is stroking along the tight ring and I moan. My back arches deeper and I push back into the mouth of whoever is licking my ass.

He keeps licking my hole and massaging my ass cheeks. Then out of nowhere I hear the click then the buzz of a vibrator. I shiver in anticipation but before I can dwell on what they plan to do with it, it is pressed against my clit. "Ahh! Fuck!" I moan.

Pleasure rocks through my body and I begin grinding against the mouth and the vibration against my clit. The tonguing stops. "Settle down, love. I know you want to come, but you need to relax," Talon says. I feel a hand caressing my back, calming me down and I know it's Kyle.

There is some more bag rustling and then I hear what sounds like a cap popping open. I try to turn, but I am held steady by their hands. The anticipation of the unknown sends a thrill of excitement through me while the vibrator continues to hum against my clit.

I hear what sounds like a ketchup bottle squirting and I try again to look but my attempts are thwarted. "Angel?"

"Hmm." My mind is blanking out complements of the vibration against my slit and the hands caressing my body.

"This is gonna be cold," he says as I hear the bottle squeeze.

"Ahh." I jump as a cool glob lands right on the tight pucker of my ass. "What are you doing?" My voice sounds more like a wanton whore than myself.

I feel something press against my ass. It's cool and hard. At the same time a finger slides inside my soaking pussy. "Argh," I moan out.

"Does it hurt?" Talon asks.

"No, fuck, it feels...ahhh."

"Just relax," he says as he pushes the object into my ass, and retracts. He repeats the process, pushing in a little further with each pass. The finger inside my pussy and the vibrator against my clit are too much and my muscles contract. "Breathe, angel," Talon says as my pussy is emptied and the vibrator comes away. But there is still something being pushed and pulled, sliding in and out gently.

With each thrust in, I stretch a little more and it burns, but the burn is quickly replaced by pleasure as he extracts it, then the in and out thrust continues as I grow more accustomed to the width. It feels like the size of a baseball bat, but the motions are sending sharp ripples of pain and pleasure throughout my body.

Finally on one last thrust, he stops and the plug gets smaller, I can feel myself tighten around it. The click of the vibrator comes back on and it is pressed against the plug.

The sensation is too much, too fast. Sending white hot sparks flashing behind my eyelids and I moan, loud and desperate. "It's alright." I feel hands along my back. "Let it go," Kyle says softly as the vibrator bounces against the toy in my ass which radiates deep inside. "Come on, baby girl." I moan, panting like a hooker. Desperate need pulses through my core. I need more. I need to be filled full.

"More," I moan.

As if reading my mind, things shift behind me. I writhe as I feel the head of an erection, Talon's; pressing against my entrance.

"Fuck!" I scream as he slowly slides himself inside. I am full, so full, so ready to explode. I rock back, sucking his cock into me as fast as I can manage.

"Easy," Talon warns. Then the vibrator disappears. Talon is still buried inside my pussy, the plug is pushed all the way in my ass. I feel a tugging on the pillow as it is slowly pulled out from under me. Kyle awkwardly shifts, maneuvering himself into position for me to take his cock into my mouth. I slowly lift myself up on shaky arms as he slides closer to me. His cock is a rock hard extension of his body.

Talon hasn't moved inside of me so that I can position myself. "Take it, Addison. Take his cock," Talon groans. "I want to watch you suck his cock while I fuck you. Take it, angel."

And I do. I suck Kyle's cock into my mouth with no inhibitions, desperate to be filled full, to be filled with the men I love.

I moan around Kyle's cock, too wrapped up to realize the thought that's passed through my head. Talon's cock begins its slow torturous thrusts into my pussy. With each inward thrust I can feel the plug turning inside me. It's a heady mixture of pleasure and pain. My pussy clamps down hard on Talon's erection, holding him there, then sucking him in as my orgasm builds to new heights.

Something I've never experienced before is happening. My orgasm is different, it's stronger, more powerful than anything I've ever known and I'm desperate to reach it. Desperate to feel it consume me.

I begin sliding back and forth, helping Talon fuck me faster and harder while I suck, lick and moan against Kyle's erection. I shift, bringing my hand up to Kyle's cock, needing the help to massage his cock in sync with my mouth. A silent plea to come is in my eyes as I look into Kyle's.

His hand comes to stroke my head as it bobs up and down his shaft. "So fucking beautiful," he breathes. I watch his eyes roll up and Talon's pace increases, thrusting faster, my pussy tightens down, holding him to me, and he thrusts harder. Turning the plug another turn and I explode into millions of pieces around my men. My orgasm is so intense I feel a rush of liquid spilling from my sex as Talon plows into me, taking me to a new height in my orgasm, once again turning the plug and drawing out the pleasure I feel.

My moans are cut off by Kyle's cock in my mouth as I pump him harder and faster, pleading for him to give me his orgasm.

In tandem, I hear their cries of pleasure and feel their seed pouring into me, reaching my soul and making me whole once again.

The pleasure is so intense that I think I pass out, because when I come to, the plug is gone and I am surrounded by these two gorgeous, sexy men who are mine. All mine.

chapter 9

The guys are so sweet. Laying with me, touching me, but it is not sexual in any way. It's almost as if they need to be touching me in order to survive, to breathe. I get little kisses on my shoulders and along my neck. But it is so sweet, I'm incapable of finding sexual pleasure in it. Besides, I think it would take an army to get me going again.

They stay like that for some time before Kyle groans, "We need to get packed up."

I groan too. "Alright, let's do this." I start to sit up.

"Oh no, we got this," Talon says. "You rest, angel."

I plop back on the pillow. "I'm not going to argue."

They both laugh and kiss me on my cheeks and set about getting us packed up and I doze off.

"Baby girl?"

"Go away," I mumble.

Kyle laughs. "I would, but we need to get some clothes on you. Can you sit up?"

"No," I pout.

"Come on, panda. We just need to throw a t-shirt, your jammie pants and your flip flops on."

"You're so cute," I tell him.

He laughs again and helps me sit up. He has a t-shirt ready for me to slip my arms into. He helps me because it is impossible for me to keep my eyes open. He slips the shirt over my head and I fall back to the bed.

Kyle is laughing the entire time. "You wear me out," I grumble.

He chuckles louder and I hear Talon join in. "You wear us out, angel."

"Hmph."

The next thing I know my feet are being moved around and I feel my soft flannel pajama bottoms being pulled up. "Lift those sexy hips, baby girl." I do as Kyle asks and he slides them up. "Now it's time to go," he says as he slips my flip flops on. "Can you walk or do I need to carry you?"

My eyes fly open and he laughs. "No, I can walk."

He smiles. "Then come on, panda girl. Let's go." I sit up and slide to the end of the bed. Both Talon and Kyle help me up and they escort me from the bedroom where I see Mills, Beck and Rusty grabbing our bags from the sitting room. There are several of them and I notice now the new purple luggage with decorative skulls on it that the guys bought for me. It's actually cute and I like it.

Talon and Kyle leave me to my own devices while they go help the guys with the bags. Making it only one trip down. Talon smiles at me when he comes over. He has his guitar case in his hands as he leans down and says, "This is my life," he slips the strap over my head, "and it's in your hands." Then he kisses me.

"I'll guard it with my life." I smile at him.

After the song last night and everything that's been happening, it's all starting to fall into place. These things are Talon's way of telling me he loves me. My heart swells.

"You ready, baby girl?" Kyle pulls me out of my revelation and I nod.

Following them out of the suite, I take one last look around. Soaking up the surroundings of where everything has changed and is changing in my life.

Twenty minutes later we arrive at the lot where the buses are parked and there is surprisingly no fans, no paparazzi, no reporters, nothing. Just the buses and it is refreshing to see. It's just after five and everyone is ready to go on time, which is great.

The Suburban pulls up next to the door of our bus and the other bus seems to be packed and ready to go. I can see movement through the front window, so I am assuming everyone is on board. A couple of the crew jump off of the bus to help the guys unload the luggage from the Suburban. They make quick work of it while I climb on board the bus and stumble my way back to mine and Kyle's room with my messenger bag. I toss it up on the bunk and slip off my flip flops. All I want to do is sleep.

I start to climb up. "What are you doing, angel?"

I turn to see Talon standing in the curtained doorway. "Going to bed."

He smiles, "You don't sleep here anymore." The tone of his voice doesn't match his smile, he's dead serious.

I scowl. "Wha..." I'm so confused and so tired. With the assistant job does this mean I have to sleep on the other bus? No, they said...

He enjoys my misery just a little too long, then takes the three steps into the room to wrap his arms around me. "You sleep in my bed," he says against my lips.

59

"What about Kyle?"

He smiles, his lips brushing against mine, my body melting into his. "We all sleep together."

I smile against his lips and kiss him sweetly. The touch certainly turns me on, but I am too tired to do anything about it. "Let's put you to bed," he says as he leads me out of my room and into his.

Once inside his room, he pulls back the covers of his bed and helps me climb under them. I slide to the center to make room for him, but he just tucks me in. "I have some things to do, but I'll be in soon." He puts a knee on the bed and leans over to kiss my forehead. "You have a big night tonight. Get some sleep," he says with one final kiss before leaving the room and closing the door behind him. I snuggle in as best as I can. I hate sleeping on my back, but with double ink, it's the best I can do for now. Soon I fall fast asleep.

talon

Kyle rounds the corner just as I close the door to my room. "Hey," he says with a smile.

"Hey yourself." He steps into the compartment he shared with Addison.

"Where'd she go?" He looks around.

"She's in my room," I tell him and he visibly slumps. "It's where she sleeps from now on." I watch as he puts his hands against her bunk, holding himself up.

"You can't, that's not...," he stutters through his words and I walk up behind him, wrapping my arms around his chest, holding him to me and he relaxes against me.

I kiss the back of his neck. "It's where you sleep now too," I say quietly.

"Talon." His voice is breathy and it turns me on more than I already am. "We need to talk." I smile against his neck and kiss him.

"Let's get everyone settled and get on the road. Then I'm all yours," I tell him, kissing him one last time then I loosen my hold on his chest. His hand comes up to stop me, holding me to him. "It's alright." I rest my forehead against his shoulder. "I feel it too." I close my eyes, wondering if what I'm feeling is the same. God, I hope it is.

He grabs my hand and brings it to his mouth where he kisses my knuckles. "It's too much," he says.

"Believe me, I know." He lets my hand go and I stand up a little straighter, releasing him from my grip. "Come on, let's get this over with so we can talk."

chapter10
talon

Twenty minutes later, the buses are loaded and we're ready to go. The guys have all fallen into their racks and the bodyguards have gone over to the other bus for their own rack time. We're a little ahead of schedule which is a good thing because that means we can all sleep more. Kyle is sitting at one of the tables in the galley area when I come up from checking on Addison, who's sound asleep in my room.

"She sleeping?" Kyle asks.

"She is. Do you want to talk here? Or..." This isn't the most private area for a conversation. We're feet away from the guys in their racks, who are no doubt sleeping, but they're still here.

"Your room?" He asks.

"I don't want to wake her," I tell him.

"Good point, we could go back to my room. It's not private but…" He hesitates.

"Let's do that." I grab a drink from the fridge. "Want one?"

"Yeah." I grab him one too and head back toward his room. Once we're inside he sits down against the wall that separates this room from mine. I leave the curtain cracked, just in case Addison gets up or someone comes looking for us. I take a seat on the opposite wall, handing him his sports drink as I sit.

"What's going on, Kyle? You seem…off," I tell him. I noticed last night he wasn't his usual self, but I didn't want to press. If I know Kyle, he'll usually talk when he's ready.

"Do you love her?" he asks, no beating around that bush then.

I take a drink and watch as his fingers play with the cap of his. "Yeah, I think I do."

"Me too," he says quietly. "So what now?"

"What do you mean?" I ask him.

"Between the three of us. Where do we go from here?" He doesn't look at me and that's strangely okay. I can tell he's worried about this conversation.

"Nothing changes, Kyle. Nothing about her, about us, the three of us, the way we are, nothing changes. Just because we love her doesn't mean we have to make her choose. What are you so afraid of?" I cock my head at him.

He starts talking and my eyes drift to the floor. "Loving her is easy. She makes it so easy because she is such an amazing woman." I nod in agreement. "But I'm afraid of loving you." My eyes shoot to his.

"Do you love me?" I ask him, trying to understand where he's going with all of this.

"That's just it, Talon. I don't know and that's what scares me." He gives me his sad smile. "Loving her is easy, it's natural. I'm...," he takes a deep breath, "I don't know if I can..."

"Kyle, this is so new for all of us. I think I'd be more afraid if you fell in love with me before her. Believe that or don't, it's up to you. But neither one of us has ever done anything like what we're doing. But I can tell you this." I shift my head to bring his eyes to mine again, "I won't change it. These last few days have been the best days of my life. When I'm around you, everything in me gets excited." Fuck, I sound like a damn sap. "And sometimes I just can't control it, like in here," I look around the room, "when we got on board. Kyle, I want to be with you, be with her, be the three of us. If that is something you don't want, then tell me because I need to know." God, I've never been so open about anything like this, but with Kyle it's easy, it's natural and it's unnerving.

He doesn't say anything. I go back to playing with my bottle, oblivious to him, until he is right there, in my face. "There is nothing more, besides Addison, that's more pleasurable than..." he kisses me, "this, or" he touches his hand to my cheek, "this." I lean into his touch.

"Your touch is electric," I tell him and he smiles.

"So is yours." He takes my hand and puts it to his cheek. I smile at him.

We sit there for a moment, just looking at each other. After all these years, I can't believe we've gone from friendship to this. Kyle and I have always been close. He knows more about me, and my history, than anyone. Even Addison. She knows about my childhood, I had to tell her about that, but we haven't talked about my history of drug abuse. She knows about Kyle's, but I wonder how she'd feel if she knew about mine. "She has two very broken men on her hands," I say softly.

Kyle gives me a half smile, "She does." He sits back down, but this time he leans against his bunk, closer to me. As he gets settled he says, "I talked to my mother yesterday." The comment is random, but I know this is the root cause of what's actually bothering him.

I raise an eyebrow at him. "How'd that go?"

"As fucking awful as I expected it to."

"Why do you even bother?" I ask him seriously.

"Because she's my mother. I guess I keep hoping she'll wake up one day and realize that Daniel wasn't her only son."

I give him a sad smile. "You must have had something important to talk to her about if you called her."

He nods and takes a drink. "I wanted her to meet Addison when we're in OKC."

I sit up a little straighter. "Did you tell her about Addison and who she is?"

He shakes his head. "No, she rejected me before I could even consider telling her anything else. Said that she was busy, before I even told her when. It was a waste of time." He begins picking at the carpet.

"Man, I'm sorry. I wish I could..."

"No, it's alright. I set myself up for it. I haven't talked to her in so long. I wanted to tell her about the tour and the band's success, but I highly doubt she remembers anything I've told her in the past about you guys. She just doesn't care."

"Then maybe you should find it in yourself to not care. I mean, look around you, brother. You got all this family, plus now you have me and Addison."

"Yeah, I know, like I said, I guess I just keep holding out hope that sometime before she dies, she'll remember who I am."

"And what good would that do you?" I ask. "Believe me, that's only going to make it worse for you, because while she may magically remember, you've got years of heartache and misery to deal with, you'll never be able to get over that. As much as you want her to remember, it will take years for things to right themselves between the two of you. Believe me, I know."

"Yeah, I know." He's very sad and for that I'm sorry. I don't know how to help him with this.

"Maybe you should talk to Addison about this. She knows your mom, or at least she did. Maybe she can lend some insight, but in the same vein, your mom did to her what she's doing to you. She pulled herself out of it, you've had to endure it."

"Fuck. I didn't even think about that."

"Don't stress it. Look, don't take it to heart. I know that's hard, but every time you talk to her, you get like this for a day or two, then you're fine, you go about your life. Maybe next time you don't need to call her, or drink a lot of alcohol, call her and stand up to her, maybe that will scare her straight."

He snorts a laugh. "I doubt that, but it's not a half bad idea."

I let him stew on what he's told me and what I've told him. Kyle isn't the type of guy that can turn off his emotions immediately. He has to work through them.

In an attempt to change the subject I say, "I need to know something."

"Anything." He smiles a little and I can see the stress of his mother washing out of him the longer he looks at me. I take pride in that. His eyes are full of so much emotion and he's so easy to read when he opens himself up to that kind of exposure. Which I've seen him do a lot since Addison came on this bus.

"What are your boundaries?" I ask.

"What are my boundaries? As in when it comes to you and I, in bed?" He raises an eyebrow at me.

"I need to know what I can and can't do to you."

"I will tell you, but you have to tell me too." I nod in agreement. "There is nothing you can't do to me." I look into his eyes. "There is no place that is off limits to you or Addison."

"Are you sure you're ready for that?" I ask.

"No, but it doesn't mean I'm not ready to try. Now, it's your turn." He smiles, there is a wicked little gleam in his eyes.

"I am all yours. I am dying to take it beyond kisses and dicks." I smirk and give him my wicked little sultry glare that works so well on Addie.

He laughs.

"Boundaries are set then?" I ask.

He nods and comes in closer, kissing me on the lips. Just like Addison's touch, Kyle's makes my body come alive with desperation. His lips are rough, the scruff of his mustache against my lips sends a shiver through me. Every time we kiss I can't help but feel the twinge of taboo, but it's quickly swept away by the fact that I don't care.

He pulls back, too soon in my opinion, but I don't stop him. He backs up toward his wall and takes a seat. My cock is hard as a rock and being pinched against my jeans. I shift.

Kyle blushes. "Sorry."

"You mean to tell me you're not hard?" I say with a raised eyebrow.

"Oh I'm hard, believe me."

There is that ever familiar tingle in my balls and I want nothing more than to stick it in his mouth, but I stomp down the thought, for now.

I smile. "Now, let's go get some sleep. I'm beat."

I stand up and take a step forward to help him up. His eyes, full of hunger and desire, fall to my cock. I watch him lick his lips. "You really like sucking it, don't you?"

He smiles, looking up at me, "Next to her pussy, it's the best thing on the planet." He reaches up, stroking his hand along my shaft, and I shiver.

"Don't start what you can't finish, cowboy," I tease him.

"Who said I wouldn't finish it?"

"Fuck!" I groan, tightening the cap on my bottle and tossing it onto the bunk. I reach for my fly and tear it open. I pull out my cock, hold it firmly in my fist. "Take it," I command him. I watch as his body goes into full submissive mode. I'm not a dominant, but there is something special about topping Kyle. He responds so greedily as he gets to his knees and grips my cock in his hand. He tugs, pulling it toward his mouth, licking the tip. I put my hand against the wall, bracing myself as he begins his assault.

Fist pumping, mouth fucking. "I want to see your cock," I breathe. He straightens, undoes his fly, slides his jeans down and pulls his cock free. I groan as he sucks me into his mouth hot and hard. "Stroke yourself."

He begins sucking my cock and fisting his own with gusto. I feel a trickle of pre-cum drop onto his tongue and he moans, the vibrations reaching into my nuts as he continues fucking me with his hand and mouth. "God, you're so fucking hot with my dick in your mouth. I wonder what you'll look like with it in your ass."

My words fall upon him and he moans, his eyes roll back and I see his legs tense. "Are you going to come?" He nods his head. "Does the idea of having my cock in your ass turn you on?" He hollows his cheeks, sucking me in so far I can feel the back of his throat; he hums around my cock and nods his head.

I place my hand in his hair, gripping it while he fucks my mouth. "I'm going to come in your mouth, Kyle. Do you want that?" His answering moan and pumping of his hand is enough of a response. "Are you ready to come for me?"

He hums again, nods his head and I can feel the burning need to come rising from my balls. My balls tighten, my cock pulses and hardens and just like that I explode into his mouth. He drinks it all. Swallowing and sucking every last drop. "Come for me, Kyle," I order and I watch his body convulse as thick streams of cum pour from his cock, his fist pumps ferociously, milking himself for every drop while his mouth sucks every drop from me.

chapter 11

addison

Waking up from what feels like a very long nap is probably the hardest thing I'm going to do today. But what I find sweeter than anything is the fact that both my guys are still sound asleep, but their sleeping involves touching me. Skin to skin. Both of them have their hands up my t-shirt laying on my stomach. The possession I feel is unreal and my heart swells. I don't want to move, but I have to. Thankfully Talon's covers are sandwiched between us so it will make my escape easier.

Extracting their hands is another story. I pull back the covers and very gently slide Talon's hand out first. It's heavy, but I manage to bring it up near my shoulder and he snuggles in, I do the same thing with Kyle and he doesn't even seem to move. I smile to myself as I sit up and slide out, down toward the foot of the bed.

I sit for a minute, catching my bearings and I look up at the clock on the wall, it's 12:30. I try to feel if the bus is still moving and I can't quite tell, but it's quiet so I'm assuming we're stopped.

I tiptoe from the room, desperate to keep them sleeping as long as possible. I, on the other hand, am wide awake and I need to get some work done. I leave the room, quietly closing the door behind me. I slip into mine and Kyle's room; I pull my messenger bag from the top bunk, grab my flip-flops and walk toward the front of the bus. The curtains of Dex, Mouse and Peacock are all closed, but I can see we're here. The front door to the bus is open.

I set my bag down, throw my shoes to the floor so I can put them on and duck into the bathroom.

When I emerge, all is still quiet on the bus. I walk toward the door and peek out. Rusty is standing next to the door so I step down. "Good morning," I say and he jumps.

"Jeez girl, give a guy a heart attack."

I laugh. "Sorry, didn't mean to. How are things out here?"

"They're good. Everyone still sleeping?" he asks.

"As far as I know. Do we have a timetable?"

"Set up should be done by four for sound check. We have no parties planned for tonight and the guys need to decide when they want to get to Galveston. Drivers are sleeping now in case they want to leave after the show. We will have to stop to change drivers along the way which could be a nice stop for tomorrow night. Mills usually handles all that with Talon or Kyle." He gives me a smile.

"That's fine. Thanks for letting me know."

"Anytime. Do you need anything?"

I smile. "Coffee and lots of it."

He laughs and I step back onto the bus and go for the coffee maker only to stop when I see Kyle standing in the hallway, looking confused. "Hey cowboy, what's wrong?"

He looks at me but the confusion doesn't clear. "I couldn't figure out where you were. I guess I'm not awake yet."

I go over and wrap my arms around him. "Go back to sleep, we're here and we have about three hours before sound check." He bends down and kisses me square on the lips.

"You good?"

"I'm great. I have some work to do, so I'm going to get started. I'll come wake you guys in what, an hour? Two?"

He gives me smirk. "An hour if you want some before the concert."

I roll my eyes. "Insatiable much?"

"Maybe." He kisses me again and stumbles back to bed.

I get my coffee started and pull out my laptop, plugging it in and firing it up.

Twenty minutes later, with coffee in hand, I have my emails filtered. After a brief glance at the alerts for the day, I decide that there is very little in the way of news. A couple of outlets are still speculating on Dex's night of drugs and women, but the story has died from the respectable outlets. Many are still discussing me, including headlines regarding tonight's show.

"Will she be back?" and "Who is she?" seem to be the number one headlines.

"Yes, I will be back. Tonight? That is the question," I mumble to myself as I switch to Trinity and Cami's folder.

I start with the oldest stuff. Mostly Bold related, little to do with me, until I get to four emails.

The first one:

From: Cameron Micheals

To: Addison Beltrand
Subject: Performance Contract.

Good Morning,
I hope you and the guys made it on the bus and out of town on time. I have been hard at work since very early this morning, but don't fret, Jaden had me up so I got some work done.

Vicious Records has agreed to the performance deal I sent them, which means, you're free to perform both songs with 69 Bottles during Albuquerque and the rest of the tour. The only thing I couldn't negotiate on was how many shows. At this point they're requiring all shows from now until the end of the tour, and due to recent events, the tour is under review for length and added shows. However, the contract at this point only covers through LA.

There is a hefty salary for you for each show of about $75,000. Which is damn good for eight minutes worth of work.

More to come on the recordings. They're being remastered as I type this and let me tell you, they sound AMAZING!

Have a GREAT Day!!
Cami

Cameron Michaels
CEO Bold International, Inc.

I slump back in the bench seat. God, that is a lot of money for two freaking songs. Makes me wonder what the guys are getting paid for a whole show.

I move onto the next one.

From: Cameron Michaels
To: Addison Beltrand
Subject: Recordings

Hello again,
I'm guessing by the lack of reply on my last email that you're more than likely sleeping or haven't gotten around to checking your email, or judging by the immediate voicemail I received, your phone is off or dead. :-)

For the recordings, Vicious approved the recording for 'Your Eyes', in fact they love it. We didn't even get to talking about 'To Be Free' and they agreed to record it in New York for album sales, provided the band agrees to make it a single or a preview to their upcoming album. That's between the band and Vicious so I'm assuming Kyle will be all over that.
Financials are still to be determined.

You're well on your way!

Break a leg tonight,
Cami

Cameron Michaels
CEO, Bold International, Inc

From: Cameron Michaels
To: Addison Beltrand
CC: Kyle Black
Subject: Recording Contracts

Hello Again!

Attached you will find for your review, the initial contracts for both the recordings completed last night. You will notice a significant increase in the dollar amount for 'To Be Free'.

Also you will find the contract for the New York recordings, this just covers what is being paid to complete the recordings.

The final contract, regarding single sales on 'Your Eyes' - Duet and 'To Be Free' is still under negotiations and I don't expect that to be completed until about a week before the recordings are scheduled.

Congrats! You should both be very proud!! 69 Bottles is at the top of their game right now! Keep it that way! :-)

Cami

Cameron Michaels
CEO Bold International, Inc

I spend the next twenty minutes reading over the contracts she attached. Holy crap! I knew musicians made a ton of money, even some of the lesser known musicians make bank, but fuck. I had no idea a little no name like myself could make so much money. The 'To Be Free' recording is budgeted in its entirety, with expenses, over ten million dollars. My percent still stands at fifteen after expenses, but with that kind of money, it's still a hell of a lot. The contract for 'To Be Free' really only outlines Talon and not the band.

I wonder idly if that has to do with the fact that we recorded it with just him and me.

My iMessage chimes. I click on it, it's Cami.

Cami: you're alive?

Me: If you want to call it that, lol. I just got through your emails. Are you for real?

Cami: LOL! Yes, welcome to the big times.

Me: I'm still not sure about all of this.

Cami: It's well deserved, you're amazing. Tristan always told me that I'd find a talent all my own. I think I've done that with you.

Me: No pressure or anything.

Cami: HAHA, no pressure. Listen, I forgot something in my last email with the recordings. If you guys perform To Be Free it should be performed the way it's recorded.

Me: So just me and Talon?

Cami: Yup.

Me: I don't think that will be a problem. I'll talk to him when he wakes up.

Cami: Wearing him out huh? LOL

Me: OMG I can't believe you said that. LOL!

Cami: Well, if there is one thing you will learn about me, I'm not subtle and more than that, I'm a very open minded person. Who you are is who you are and if you're keeping both those boys comfortable, all the power to you.

Me: OMG you're making me blush over here.

Cami: HAHA! Sorry. I'm nothing if not honest. Gotta run. I'll keep you posted, but I think we're all set for now. Knock em dead tonight and I look forward to the youtube videos tomorrow.

Cami: Crap, I almost forgot. Vicious is working on putting together a live recording of the concert. They want to discuss the possibilities of releasing a live album with the band, but shhh, okay fine tell Talon, but it's not set in stone. Earliest ETA is Chicago. Latest would probably be Denver.

Me: Live recording, jesus, they really are bigger than I thought they were.

Cami: LOL! They're getting there. Gotta jet. Have a great afternoon.

Me: Thanks, you're the best.

chapter 12

Riding high on adrenaline from the conversation and emails from Cami, I bound toward mine and Kyle's room, looking for my stuff. I'm gonna jump in the shower and start getting ready for tonight. When I get into the room, I notice a sports bottle on Kyle's bed and wonder where that came from, Kyle doesn't usually drink that stuff, but I shrug it off.

I find my suitcase along with the two new suitcases and matching travel bag tucked between the bunks and the closet. I have no idea where they put everything when they packed so I start with the bag. Opening it up I find the majority of my bathroom stuff inside. My curling iron, flat iron, and all my make-up.

I pull out the smaller of the two new suitcases and lay it out on the floor. "Oh," I squeak. Inside the smaller of the two are the sexier things they bought for me when they went shopping along with three black bags. I open up one of them and find some open packages and a black...Oh.

It's the butt plug Talon used on me this morning. It's really small. God, it felt ten times that size. I look further into the bag and find the lubricant and the vibrator which is just a little bullet looking thing. Also inside the bag are two additional butt plugs, each one larger than the other. Progression is all I can think when I see them. I tuck the bag back in the suitcase and while I am eager about what else they bought, I zip up the case and set it aside, finally going for the larger one.

I look around for my original suitcase. I don't see it at first and I know that it came down from the hotel. Finally looking up I see it's sitting on my bed. Phew. Okay, back to the big purple one. Unzipping it, I find all the new clothes they bought for me and I go digging for two things. The black and purple corset and the very full, super short, black skirt. The corset is option one, but if it's too painful, I think I'll go back to the top I wore last night with the black skirt.

For now, I grab my towel, a pair of shorts and a tank top and step through the curtain, nearly slamming into Kyle. "Shit," I say as I stumble backward. He catches me.

"Fancy meeting you here," he smirks. "Where's the fire?"

"Shower." I smile.

"Want some company?" He wiggles his eyebrows.

"On the bus, I barely fit in that thing." I laugh.

"Oh, we can make it work."

I smile at him and slide past him, wiggling my butt in his direction. "You comin' or what?"

"Right behind you," he smirks again and I shove off to the bathroom. I step inside and shut the door, but I don't lock it. I turn on the water and strip out of my clothes. I'm just barely stepping in when Kyle opens the door. The same Cheshire smirk is on his lips when he takes in my naked form.

"What?" I breathe.

"You're like a goddess, you know that?" He pulls off his t-shirt, locks the door, pushes his shorts down, freeing himself and I can see that he's already hard. "You're perfect in every way." He steps toward me, "So soft, with luscious curves and a beautiful rack."

I snort. "You almost had me turning into a puddle."

"Oh, I'm sure I can still turn you into a puddle," he breathes against my neck.

"I know you can," I say breathily.

He pushes me gently backwards and into the shower. "Turn around," he commands and I do.

The water rushes down my chest as he presses into my back. I can feel his erection pressing against my ass and I flick my hips. His hands come up to cup my breasts, his fingers taking my nipples and tugging on them. I moan. He continues tugging and twisting. I writhe against his erection and I hear his breath hitch in his throat.

One of his hands begins roaming south, across my stomach to cup my mound and I feel his finger sliding against my clit. "Kyle," I groan and he picks up his pace. The sensations are intense as he plays with my clit, while his other hand massages my nipple. His hips grind his erection against my backside. "Take me," I moan. "I need you inside me."

His hand falls away from my breast and I can feel him adjusting himself, preparing to enter me. I raise myself onto my toes, giving him a little more leverage to slide inside. He guides my hips back, forcing me to bend forward. Water is cascading down my back as I feel the head of his cock against my entrance. "Please," I beg him and I feel him push inside me. He keeps pushing until he's sheathed inside. "Fuck," I pant when I feel his sigh of contentment as he slides home. I'm trying to stay quiet but his hand on my clit and his cock buried inside of me has my legs trembling and my orgasm building.

"So beautiful," he breathes. "The way your skin blushes when you're aroused." He pounds into me. "So fucking beautiful." He starts sliding in and out of me faster and harder. Spurring my orgasm on. The fire in my veins flows hard and fast. My clit hardens under his touch; gentle strokes that match his pushing and pulling inside of me. "Arghh," he moans, slamming harder into me, sliding out again he almost falls out, I push my hips back into him, burying him again. "Damn it, baby girl," he growls. "I'm gonna fucking come if you keep that up."

Enriched by his declaration, I begin thrusting my hips against his, matching his pace and rhythm. I need him, I need his cum. I pound back harder and he pinches my clit between his fingers, sending a shock of pain and an explosion of pleasure. My pussy clenches and releases on his cock. He knows I'm there, I'm ready. "Give it to me, Addison," he growls and I come, coating his cock in my juices. He pumps into me hard and fast once, twice and stills on the third as he growls into my ear, "Fucking beautiful." He helps me stand up, and stretch my legs a little after being spread eagle.

He doesn't say anything. He just holds me in the shower, letting the water run over us. Eventually he grabs my body wash and starts washing me. I take so much comfort in his touch that nothing else matters. He continues until I'm clean from head to toe.

Taking his cue, I start washing him, soaping my hands up and rubbing slow, massaging circles across his chest. He doesn't say anything, just watches as I wash his body. When I get to his cock, which is still hard, I lather my hands really well and begin stroking with both hands. He lets out a moan of pleasure, so I continue. After a few more strokes, I move onto his scrotum and then along the crack of his ass.

He still doesn't say anything. I stand up, staring at him. "Say something."

His hand comes up to my cheek, pushing his fingers into my wet hair. He brings me forward to his lips. Our lips crash together and the sparks fly. His tongue licks at my lower lip, then I feel his teeth graze, coaxing me to open. His tongue slides inside, instantly finding mine. He steals my breath away and I wrap my arms around his neck, pulling him to me, his cock is pressed against my belly, but I don't care about that. His lips are soft and warm against my own. His mustache tickles.

"You're scaring me," I breathe against his lips.

"I don't have the right words," he whispers.

"Then show me," I say as I reach over and turn off the water." He pushes me against the opposite wall, cupping my cheeks in his hands, lifting my lips to his. He kisses me gently, but I can feel the urgency in his lips.

My breath comes in short bursts as he continues to assault my lips. He slowly pulls back. "I need a bed to really show you," he whispers and I shiver, both from his words and the chill in the air surrounding us. "Later." He kisses me chastely a couple more times and he steps out of the shower. Grabbing my towel first, he wraps it around me, then grabs his own. "I promise, I will show you, soon," he says and exits the bathroom. I lean against the closed door. I know what he's trying to tell me, but he needs to say it in his own time.

Am I honestly ready to admit that I'm falling in love with these two very overwhelming, sexy, god-like men? Yes, I think I am.

*chapter*13

After drying off, I throw on my clothes and step out of the bathroom. The air outside the bathroom is cooler and I shiver. Something catches my eye and I look over to see Kyle is sitting on the bench between the tables. He looks so sad.

I walk over to him and I straddle him, putting my knees on either side. I put my arms around his neck. "I know what you're trying to say." He looks at me, fear in his eyes. "I understand why you can't tell me, and that's okay."

He brings his forehead to mine. "I'm so scared," he whispers.

"So am I, Kyle. This is all so new to me and I'm doing it two-fold. But that doesn't mean that my feelings for you are any less than what you're feeling for me."

"Everyone I've ever cared about has left me," he admits quietly. "Dan, my mother, my father, they're all gone. I've walked through life alone for so long, I don't know how to do this."

My heart aches for him. "Neither do I. I've lost every man I've loved. My dad, Dan. This scares the living hell out of me, but I'm ready and willing to take that chance. I've never been more ready for anything like I am for this."

"I need you," he breathes, wrapping his arms around me. He holds me to him. "The last twenty-four hours have been really tough. I'm sorry to be so emotional."

I run my fingers through his still damp hair. "What happened?"

"The same thing that happens every time I talk to my mother."

"Do I even want to know?"

He laughs a little. "No, probably not. Let's just say you're not the only one she's blown off since Dan's death."

"Oh sweetheart." I can't help the tear that escapes my eye. "I had no idea."

"I called her to tell her I'd be in town, and I wanted to see her, I wanted to take you with me. But before I even got to the when, she said she was busy. It tears me up every time she does that. I just wish- just once- she'd remember Dan wasn't her only son." He lowers his head to my chest.

"Sweet, sweet Kyle, please listen to me. I know how you feel. I really do, I've been there."

"How'd you get over it?"

"I don't know that I have, but I threw myself into my job, I secluded myself from everyone and went about my life. It wasn't the brightest decision because here I am, scared of loving, scared of trying, scared of everything, because the only way I've ever been hurt by a man is through death. I'm afraid that if I fall in love, it becomes a death sentence." His arms wrap tighter around me. "But it won't stop me. It won't stop me anymore. I know the risk, I understand the reward, and I am desperately hoping that everything I'm feeling is real and not superficial, that it's not because it's here and it's now. Which is why I know what you're trying to say, what you're scared to say, because I'm scared to feel it, to understand it, and to say it too."

"You're too good, you know that? I meant what I said. You're a goddess, not just in looks but in the things you do, the way you do them, and how you handle them. It's genuine and pure and I admire you for that," he says softly.

"You flatter me and stroke my ego."

He smiles. "You deserve to have your ego stroked. You're an angel."

"I'm your panda girl."

"And I'm your cowboy."

"Yes, you are." We both smile. "Thank you for opening up to me. Do you feel better?"

He lifts his head, smiles the beautiful smile I love to see and nods. "Much better, thank you." He kisses me soft and gentle, but not without passion.

"You can't fix everything. I've learned that the hard way."

"I'm trying."

My phone chimes with an email. "We need to discuss business," I say.

He snorts a laugh. "Pleasure before business. I like it." I laugh and peak at my email. It's from Cami with the subject 'press release'. I open it up.

This is a copy of the press release that will go out at 8p.m. Pacific time announcing the venture between you and 69 Bottles. I hope it's favorable, but you have time to make some changes if you'd like.

"Everything okay?" Kyle asks anxiously.

I nod. "It's perfect. The label bought the 'Your Eyes' recording we did last night. I imagine sometime in the next few days, it will hit the airways."

"How do you feel about that?" he asks honest curiosity in his voice.

"Petrified." I smile sweetly. "They also bought 'To Be Free'."

"Jesus, talk about throwing you out there."

"Well, you know Cami, she doesn't sit on anything she feels is extraordinary. Couple that with the fact that I now have a performance contract for the rest of the tour, a contract being finalized for the recordings in New York, in which they want both songs, provided 69 Bottles agrees to make 'To Be Free' their primary single on the new album."

"That's kind of a no brainer. I'll discuss it with Talon, but I doubt he will turn down a chance to get it recorded. What else?"

"The contract for sales following the recording will be finalized prior to recording in New York. If we sing 'To Be Free' during a concert, we're required to do it with Talon and I alone. The way we recorded it." I smile at the look on his face.

"That won't be hard because I'm pretty sure there are no other parts written to that song, though knowing him, if it's getting recorded, he'll have both an acoustic and a full band version. Anything else?"

"Oh my goodness, yeah. The label is working to set up a live recording of the concert, wanting to put together a live album."

He scowls, "Already? God, they're moving fast, they usually wait a few years for that. Then they can put together a 'best of'."

"I don't know what their intentions are, just that the earliest is Chicago and the latest is Denver for when they'll do it."

"Hmm, weird, but I'm not going to complain. We knew before we set off that there was a chance of that, depending on the tour." I can see the worry lifting from his face as he sets into business mode.

"Lastly, I think, is that we need to prepare the band for an extension on the tour."

"That's going to be a lot harder to handle. I think that is something we'll have to deal with when and if it arises. They were okay with the shows being added, but I don't know how they'll feel extending it. Plus there is one hell of a party planned for LA." He smiles. "Not to mention a chance to go home."

I laugh. "Oh, and Cami forwarded me a press release that will go out tonight regarding the band and me."

"Well that's good, at least they're waiting for show time. Though the show is sold out. I think that video would have sold out the shows if they weren't already, which scares me as to why they'd extend the tour. But if they get us back into the studio, they'd be better to keep it as is, then schedule a new tour for later in the year..." He keeps rambling and I just let him go. It's really cute listening to him ramble.

"You're rambling."

He laughs. "I know, I'm sorry. I do that a lot."

"Don't be sorry. I like it." I kiss him. "It's time to go wake up a rock star," I say and he nods. "Come with me?" He nods again and I climb off his lap and help him stand up. "Do you know where the bottle on your bed came from?" I ask and he blushes.

He runs his hand through his hair. "It was Talon's."

"You animal, and here I thought I was insatiable."

He laughs. "It just kind of happened. We were talking about my mom and you."

"You didn't..." I let the question fall off.

He blushes again. "No, but I think we're both breaking down our walls and our hesitations."

I smile wide. "Really?"

He laughs. "Yes, really. It just takes time and I think we both needed some reassurance and we were able to give that to each other."

"Do I get to be in on the secret?" I ask him sweetly.

"Always." He rubs his hand along my shoulder. "We set our boundaries on what we will or won't do."

"And what are those?"

He leans down and whispers, "We have none."

"Okay, that is so fucking hot," I breathe as he backs away from me, grabbing my hand and pulling me toward our bedroom.

chapter 14
kyle

Well, that was not what I was expecting to happen this morning, err, today. Strong and silent has always been my motto, at least when it comes to girls, but Addison shattered that. She wasn't going to let me get away with my mood and I adore her all the more for it. The way she took control, telling me that she knows and it's okay, damn it, it's too...too--god, I don't even know what I want to say, I can't even think straight.

After talking to Talon this morning, knowing and realizing that I'm not alone in my feelings made me brave. I wanted to say it, but I couldn't, so I said nothing. Building that wall, but she knocked it down.

"I have an idea," she whispers behind me as I reach for Talon's door knob. "Do we have time?" I look at her and she has her sexy look on. I look at my watch.

"It's 2:15."

"Perfect. Open the door."

I smile and open the door quietly, then usher her inside. She gets a little giddy when she sees that Talon is on his back with his head facing the wall. Then she strips out of her tank top exposing her beautiful tits. Fuck, they're perfect. She has these beautiful puffy nipples that make you instantly want to suck on them. My mouth is watering just thinking about it.

I watch as she goes to where Talon's head is resting. His mouth is slightly open and I can hear him breathing. Though he isn't snoring, he's not the quietest sleeper ever. But he looks so peaceful.

What happens next is a testament to both Talon and how in tune to Addison he is. In one hand she takes her left breast, flinching slightly when her hand grazes her fresh ink, and she grabs hold and gently guides her nipple over his lips. I watch as she shutters with the contact.

"Now I have an idea," I whisper. Talon is a boxer sleeper and he's out from under the covers. His one leg is bent, with his foot under his other knee. I can tell that he's semi-hard because of the outline. "Keep going," I whisper as I come up alongside her. Gently undoing the button on the fly of his boxers, I watch as she repeats her nipple tease on his lips.

Talon's tongue shoots out of his mouth licking his lips and catching a taste of her nipple. Her breath hitches. So she does it again, coaxing his mouth open a little wider. This time she pushes her nipple into his mouth, holding it there, gently touching his lips with it, then his mouth closes, pulling her nipple in and sucking on it.

I work slowly, gingerly, to pull his cock from his boxers. I free it just in time to set it back against his hip. I tap Addison, pointing at his dick and she watches, mouth wide as his dick instantly lengthens and hardens. He continues sucking on Addison's left nipple. I take her right one in between my fingers and begin massaging it gently. I wrap my other hand around Talon's erection, holding it softly before leaning in and licking the tip.

He jerks, then goes back to sucking sweetly on Addison's nipple. I lick the tip of his cock again, watching him as he suckles. I begin sucking with abandon and he moans around the nipple in his mouth. My hand on her nipple travels south, I want to feel her pussy milking my fingers, but she is too far away to get a good hold on it so I go back to licking and sucking Talon's cock.

His dick jumps and he moans- coming alive, his hips flick in my direction, pushing his cock further down my throat and his hand comes up to cup the breast he is so lovingly sucking on.

"Good morning," she breathes. Her left hand comes up to stroke his hair as he continues to lick and suck. He moves his hand away from her breast and brings it to rest in my hair. His touch is soft and it makes me moan around his cock.

She pulls back, forcing her nipple from his mouth then stands up to shove her shorts to the floor. Both Talon and I moan. I watch as she pulls the pillow out from under Talon's head. "Scoot over, big man," she says with such reverence it reminds me of the look she had in her eyes when she was telling me she knew what I was trying to say.

I release Talon's cock and he slides toward the middle of the bed. Then Addison climbs on the bed, straddling his face. I shiver. Fuck, she's so fucking beautiful. Her tattoos are amazing and every bit is a part of who she is and where she's been. When she is naked, she is the picture of perfection.

"This is one hell of a way to wake up," he says as she positions her slit for his taking. She is facing me and gestures for me to join them.

"Take off your clothes, cowboy." For some strange reason, her nickname for me sends shivers up my spine. I do as she's asked me to do, stripping out of the jeans and t-shirt I put on after our shower. "Now, help me," she says as she leans forward so that Talon's cock is right in her face. Talon spreads his legs to make room for me and I climb up between them.

She sticks her tongue out like she is going to lick the popsicle in front of her and I follow suit. Talon shutters as both of our tongues land on his cock at the same time, from the top and the bottom. "Bend your knees," she orders Talon. As he shifts to obey, he laps faster at her sex, causing her to moan. She reaches for one of my hands. I'm puzzled, but curiosity is winning this battle so I give it to her. She puts a finger in her mouth. I hesitate momentarily and she gives me a look, one that says this is it, your next step. I don't know how that was possible but the silent message was received.

She continues letting me finger fuck her mouth, soaking it, getting it ready for what's supposed to happen next. She moans again in delight as Talon's strokes on her pussy and I can see the pleasure radiating on her face. All tension is gone and she is loving the finger in her mouth and the tongue on her slit. I watch Talon make some adjustments so that he's able to get a hand behind her. I know the moment he enters her because she shudders and whimpers. I smile, taking unbelievable pleasure in watching her come undone. She hasn't come, but I can tell she's close.

I nod to her, letting her know I'm ready. She licks and sucks one more time, then releases my hand. She takes

Talon's cock from me and pulls it into her mouth. His hips jerk at the sudden contact then he melts back into the mattress. I take my tongue and lick along his balls. Right along the seam and both Talon and Addison moan.

I don't stop, dipping my tongue lower and am pushed on by the fact that Talon lifts his hips so that I have easier access. I continue licking along his balls and that sweet spot just below. His legs tremble. I run my tongue, fat and wet along the tight bud of his ass. The taste is intense, but it's not unpleasant as I continue to lick.

I pull back, pop my finger in my mouth one more time and I set out rubbing it around Talon's tight hole. "Fuck!" I hear him moan into Addison's pussy. She stops sucking his cock, letting me have the fun. I add pressure, pushing against the tight ring and he shakes, falling back to the bed, but I still have room, I can still finish this.

Addison sits up completely for a better view. Now I can see Talon's tongue on her slit, assaulting her pussy and I push harder, popping that barrier. "Ahh fuck," he moans. "Don't stop," he groans and I slip in further, past the first knuckle. I can feel him constrict against my hand.

"It's okay, just relax," I tell him and I use my free hand to rub along his leg, comforting him and he relaxes, letting me slip in further. I am in to the second knuckle but the angle is bad and I can't push much further so I begin to move my tip.

"Fuck Fuck Fuck!" he shouts as he writhes under my touch and I watch as the pre-cum slides down his erection. I want it in my mouth so I lick his cock from base to tip, moving my finger in and out of him "Fuck, Kyle. Take it, suck it. I'm gonna…Fuck." I wrap my mouth around his cock, sucking him hard and fast. Using my other hand to grip him while my finger continues its stroking inside against his prostate.

He explodes in my mouth. His arms wrap around Addison's legs and he buries his face in her slit. Absorbing his cries of pleasure.

chapter 15

talon

Fuck! Fuck! Fuck! That was fucking intense. I can't even begin to open my eyes right now. For the first time, though my cock is still hard as a rock, I'm fucking shattered. I never knew that playing with my ass could elicit such an intense orgasm. Fuck, I would have been doing it for years. Then again, maybe it's because it's Kyle and Addison.

Fuck, that's way too much shit to think about right now.

"Come here, baby girl," I hear Kyle and feel Addison shift from on top of me. The bed bounces and dips and I can tell that they're coming together. But I can't open my eyes.

The shifting stops momentarily and I jump when a hand lands on my cock. It's hers, I can tell because it is softer, more delicate. Then I feel the bed jump and she moans.

"You're so fucking tight," Kyle growls and I know the moment the bed starts bouncing he's pounding into her. Open your eyes, damn it. Watch them. I will my eyes to open. Finally they do.

Addison is on her back, hand on my cock, stroking me as Kyle pounds into her. "Fuck!" She moans again as Kyle spreads her legs wide so that he can watch himself disappear inside her. I sit up and run my hand along Kyle's arm and he looks at me.

His eyes roll up in his head. I let my arm fall to Addison and I begin rolling her beautiful puffy nipple between my fingers. She moans and Kyle takes the other one in his hand, but it doesn't last. He gets himself positioned and held up, then dips his head to lick and suck. I follow him, bringing my mouth to her other nipple, sucking it hard into my mouth.

"Ahh! Damn it, you're..." She can't finish her sentence as we continue licking and sucking her breasts and Kyle pounds into her pussy. I can hear the sound of their skin slapping together and it is the most beautiful sound in the world. I look toward where they come together and watch Kyle's cock, slick with her juices, slide in and out.

I let Addison's nipple pop from my mouth and I sit up. Sliding off of the side of the bed, I stand. Addison's lips form the cutest pout. I smile at her and walk around the foot of the bed and I climb up between Kyle's legs. Rubbing my hands along his back, he arches, pushing himself deeper inside of her.

Before you go getting all antsy, I'm not going to fuck him, not yet. But I want to show him what I have in mind for us very soon. I wrap my arms around his shoulders, hovering slightly above his ass. Moving with him as he pounds into her. She's moaning and I can see her muscles tightening. She's close, very close. I bring my cock to rest along his back, holding him to me, I feel the muscles of his back constrict and relax.

"This is what I want to do to you," I breathe into his neck; he groans. "I want to fuck you while you fuck her."

"Yes," he moans like a porn star.

I feel her legs along my hips and her heels digging into my ass, pushing us both forward and backward as Kyle fucks her.

"Tell me, Kyle, how does she feel squeezing your dick?"

"Fucking amazing," he breathes and I look down at Addison who is watching us. I lick and kiss Kyle's neck and her eyes roll up. Her hands go to her nipples and she begins playing with them. I let my hand slide down his chest, brushing his nipple with my fingers and he shivers. I continue downward. My goal is her clit. I want him to make our girl come.

"What about you, angel? You want me to fuck your boy?"

"Yes, oh god yes!" she mewls, her back arching and Kyle's assault on her pussy increases, I start strumming her clit.

"Oh fuck! I'm..."

"Come for her," I growl in Kyle's ear and both of them explode. Addison convulses with her orgasm and Kyle empties himself into her. I let them rest only briefly. "Now, it's my turn," I say and Addison shudders.

Slowly Kyle extracts himself from her and I watch as their combined juices pour from her pussy. "Fuck me, that's hot," I groan, backing off so that Kyle has room to move. He extracts himself from between us and I slide hard and fast into Addison's dripping cunt. My balls tighten immediately.

Kyle helps me by sucking her nipple, I lean down and take the other one into my mouth and I feel Kyle's hand slide to her clit. I feel her pussy tighten around my cock and I know neither one of us will last long. "Harder," she moans and I pull back and slam into her, hard and fast and she cries out.

Kyle continues to lick at her nipple, fingering her clit and I can tell she's close. Her muscles around my dick contract. "Are you ready to come?" I ask her.

"Yes, god, please." She arches her back and I slam into her.

"Then come for me, angel, and come hard."

Her pussy contracts, sucking me in deeper as I slip in and out of her wet slit. She's milking my cock as she shatters, her body pulsing with each flick of Kyle's finger. My balls tighten and my orgasm burns as it explodes, emptying into her.

We all collapse, panting and sated.

chapter 16
addison

"We have sound check in forty-five minutes." I hear Kyle say, but I don't want to move. So I groan instead.

"Come on, angel. Gotta get movin'."

"I don't wanna, you guys wear me out," I grumble.

They both laugh and climb off of the bed, pulling me with them. I play the dramatic card and slump back onto the bed. "Baby girl, you have your first show tonight."

Panic takes over and I really don't want to move. "Angel? Are you alright?"

"No," I moan. "I don't know if I can do this."

"Angel, look at me," Talon says and I open my eyes, he's leaning over me. "You can do this, you're brave, you're strong and I will be right there with you. So will Kyle."

Knowing that I need to talk to Talon about all that's transpired since I woke up a few hours ago, spurs me into action. I sit up and Talon helps me. "I need to take another shower."

They both laugh again. "Let's do sound, then you will have plenty of time to get yourself ready. Though, you naked is just fine for me," Talon teases me.

"For you, yes, but in front of twenty-thousand people?"

"Oh hell no!" he laughs. "You'll have plenty of time to get ready after sound."

"I've got to at least wash up." No need to mention that I can feel everything they've both left in me because it's starting to slide out.

"Alright, you go wash up, find some clothes and get ready to go to work. We need to run sound on you too, you know."

"Yeah, I know. Did you know that we have clearance from the label for 'Your Eyes'?"

He shrugs. "I'd do it with or without their approval. It's my band, my song."

"I know, but did you know that they also bought the recording of 'To Be Free', for quite a bit more money mind you, and that they want it added to the show."

I watch as his nerves visually take over. "It's not ready yet. I haven't even written the other parts."

I cup his cheek in my hand. "They want it acoustic, just you and me."

"Seriously?" Real shock crosses his face.

I nod. "If you put it in the middle of the set, it will give the guys a chance to take a break. But I'm wondering something."

"What, angel?"

"Since I have a solid part in that song, and it's kind of our song, can we wait 'til Kansas City to unleash it?" I ask quietly.

"What's so special about KC, panda girl?" Kyle asks.

"My mom will be there."

I watch as both men's faces light up. Talon kisses me on the forehead. "I think that's an amazing idea, plus it will give us some more time to practice it." He kisses me again. "Now go get cleaned up."

I slip my tank top back on and my shorts, just enough to make it to the bathroom. Thank god, because rounding the corner, Peacock is standing at his bunk.

"Hey Red," he says.

"Hey Eric." He smiles at his real name. "How you holding up?"

He shrugs. "Pretty good, I think. You?"

I slump in exhaustion. He laughs. "I'm doing my best, I need some more coffee."

"You jumping in the shower?" I nod. "I'll make you some."

I put my hand on his bicep, "Thank you."

"Anytime. Listen, when we get a chance, I'd like to talk to you."

I cock my head. "About?"

"Jess."

"Oh, that…"

"I didn't sleep with her."

"Wha…I'm sorry, it's none of my business." I clam up.

"No, its okay, I'd like a chance to explain. She's becoming a really good friend and I trust her. She says that I can trust you too, but I don't really know you. So…"

I squeeze his arm. "We will definitely talk. I think those two animals can deal without me for a while."

He laughs. "They're quite the pair, aren't they?"

I roll my eyes. "You have no idea."

"Oh, I think I do." He winks and heads toward the galley. I slip into the bathroom, dump my shorts and tank top and climb back into the shower. I just need to clean up the mess they made.

I come out about ten minutes later and Eric, Talon, Kyle, and Mouse are sitting around the tables in the galley. "Where's Dex?"

"I'm right here, love," he says from above my head.

I look up and smile. He looks to be in a better mood today, that's a good thing. "You alright?"

"Never better." He smiles and tucks his ear buds back into his ears.

"Yo Dex, when she's done, we need to have a meeting."

"Right," he says and goes back to whatever he's doing in his bunk, and judging by the curtain, I don't think I want to know. I go back to the curtained room and start digging for something comfortable to wear. Jeans would be great and a t-shirt even better.

"Addie?" I turn to see Kyle standing in the doorway.

"Hey, cowboy. What's up?"

"I got an email from the label."

"Oh, and?"

"They are going to be releasing 'Your Eyes' onto the radio sometime Monday or Tuesday next week. They want to release 'To Be Free' the week of Philly. They also said that the 'To Be Free' recording, thanks to the lack of band noise is of perfect quality to release before we get to New York. They'll still record it, and update the version on the digital sites with the new stuff."

"That's good, isn't it?"

"It's great. I don't know how Talon will feel about it. You want to talk to him about it?"

I shake my head. "That is your area of expertise. I didn't agree to do this because of the money. I'm doing it because Talon has asked me to, that's all. Everything that happens from here on out is on him."

Kyle smiles. "Okay, for the record, I think he does it because of you."

"Unfortunately, I don't doubt that. I think he wants me to do it because he doesn't know any other way to express himself to me. But in the same token, sometimes I wonder how he really feels about the fact that I've been suckered into this gig. It's all happened so fast, I'm worried how everyone feels. It's like I'm joining the band without asking everyone's permission and I don't want that. I don't want to force myself on them, and frankly I don't know about this whole singing career thing. Sometimes I just want to cry when I think about it because I don't know how to deal with it."

He comes in and wraps his arms around me. "The guys adore you."

"I just don't want it to cause any animosity down the road. Sure, they adore me now, but what...what if the band's fame going forward is because of me? I almost feel like if I don't do this, 69 Bottles will cease to exist."

He laughs a little. "Panda girl, 69 Bottles was here before you. Just because they partner with you for a couple of songs doesn't mean you will make or break the band. Trust me. But if it makes you feel better, talk to the guys, either individually or separate them from Talon and I to discuss it openly with them. They'll be honest with you, trust me. They didn't like me much in the beginning, but once they realized what an asset I was to them, they came around. It's the same thing with you. Whether you're singing with Talon or not." He strokes his hands along my back, calming me.

"God, I can talk to you about anything, can't I?"

He kisses the top of my head. "Always. Now get a move on, we need to talk to the band before sound."

"Alright, get out," I tease and he puts a fist over his chest and bows.

"As the lady wishes," he smirks and closes the curtain.

chapter 17

The meeting goes over better than I planned. My worries with Kyle seem to be forgotten and the concern is unnecessary. The guys are all pumped about me singing with Talon on 'Your Eyes' and they agree with waiting a little while for 'To Be Free'. Give the audience a chance to anticipate and then expect 'Your Eyes' after it hits the radio waves, then hit them with 'To Be Free' a few shows before that will start hitting the air.

On the way into the venue, I walk between Talon and Kyle.

"So how much did they buy 'To Be Free' for?" Talon asks.

"Budgeted at just over ten million," I say, serious.

"You're kidding me, right?"

"No, sweetheart, I'd never do that. Though they want it recorded in New York, they also want it as the single from the new album."

"Fuck me, I haven't even begun to think about the new album."

I laugh. "You mean you haven't written any songs?"

"No, I have plenty of those. In fact I have about three albums worth of songs written, I just haven't even begun to think about putting it together yet."

"Relax, you have time. And would 'To Be Free' be a bad single to release?"

He looks at me and smiles. "Absolutely not. I think it's perfect."

I smile. "I think you're biased."

I hear Kyle snort next to me. "No, he's right, it's perfect."

"You, sir, are biased too."

They both laugh. "Maybe a little, but it just may be a big ticket song, you never know," Talon says as he wraps his arm around my shoulders and kisses me on my forehead.

"Talon?" I slow my walk, we're about ten feet from the door and both he and Kyle slow with me.

"Yes, angel?"

"I'm worried about something."

"What?" he says sweetly.

"I'm worried that... that you think I'm... oh, how the hell do I put this?" I step out of his hold. "I don't want you to think that I'm trying to take over the band."

He scowls at me. "Explain, please?"

"I'm afraid that with all this hype surrounding our little 'Your Eyes' stunt and then coming up with 'To Be Free' that you think I'm trying to join the band or take it over, or be a part of everything you guys do going forward. I'm afraid that...oh hell, I'm afraid that you think using me, or having me sing with you, is the reason for the sudden rush of fame and fortune or that I'm using you to make a career and a name for myself."

He doesn't say anything for a heartbeat and it scares me. "Sweet heavens, no. Addison, I, shit, I would never use you for my career. If my career died tomorrow, it would be okay. I would be okay. As far as you making a name for yourself, I brought you on that stage in Phoenix, you never asked, you never expressed any interest in singing with me. Your reluctance to sing publicly tells me that. I've never thought that and I pray to god I never gave you that impression because if I did, it was not meant that way." He steps closer to me, grabbing my upper arms in his hands, staring down at me. "I love singing with you. I love playing for you, and I love writing songs for you, but if you told me no, you wouldn't sing with me, I'd be sad because a gift as beautiful as yours needs to be shared with the world. But I wouldn't be mad or hold it against you. If you told me you wanted off of the tour completely, to go back to LA, to walk away from it, Jesus, you'd break my fucking heart, but I'd let you. Addison, everything you're doing is your choice. I never intended to hold you to that pre-orgasm promise I made you give me. Hell no, some people are not cut out for this lifestyle, but you, they broke the mold with you, angel, because you're one of a kind."

Tears streak down my cheeks at his declaration. He didn't have to say the words, but the raw emotion is there in his voice. "You make me better. You make me believe in myself, you make me everything I've ever wanted to be and to feel." He continues and more tears flow. I feel Kyle come up behind me, wrapping his arms around my waist, pressing me to him. Talon's thumbs stroke my cheeks, wiping away my tears. "You and Kyle, you're my everything. If I have you two, then I don't need this," he breathes as his lips land on mine in a soft, heartfelt kiss that leaves me breathless.

I take his head in my hands, holding him to me, feeling his beard beneath my fingers, the softness of his skin and the depth of emotion in his eyes. He pulls back, kisses my forehead and then he releases one arm to take Kyle's face in his hand. "I mean it," he says to Kyle who squeezes his arms tighter around me.

"I know you do," Kyle says with a whisper.

The words are never exchanged. They don't have to be said. It's implied behind his words and emotion, I can feel it in Kyle's embrace and in the bond the three of us share together. It's been barely a week, and everything in my life has shifted and flipped and turned right side up. I never knew it was all so upside down until these two walked into my life.

When I think about all the times I was hit on, all the times I brushed them off like they were nothing, it makes me wonder now if it was because I knew that something bigger and better was coming for me. Though in my wildest dreams, I never imagined it would be in the form of these two men.

chapter 18

Over the course of the next few hours, everything falls back to normal. The sound check went awesome and being on stage was a comfort I wasn't expecting. I didn't realize how comfortable I'd gotten with the idea until I was back on stage, front and center. I know the next time I'm up there singing will rattle my nerves more than anything I thought possible but I find great comfort in Talon while singing with him.

Every time the number in attendance runs through my head I tense up. Fuck, I've never been in front of that many people other than to wave, but the lights were so bright the only thing I could do was hear their chants of delight.

As show time approaches, my nerves get more and more rattled. Talon says that he will wait until the second hour of the set to bring me out. Which doesn't make me feel any better at all. It just gives me more time to freak out.

While getting dressed I must have changed my outfit a hundred times. Clothes are strewn everywhere in the little room Kyle and I once shared. Though it was brief, it's no longer ours. It's empty. But Talon insists we keep it. It gives us each a private space to get away, something he knows we're all going to need, eventually.

Anyway, the corset didn't work, the ink is still too new and painful. I barely had it on before I pulled it off again, knowing full well that my ability to breathe would be cut off. That's kind of important when you're singing. Fuck, I'm singing. Gah, see what I mean? I can't even concentrate on getting dressed.

So I settle on a tank top, if you want to call it that, because it's only about half of one. Literally. There is a princess line that runs under my breasts, that is part of the strap that wraps around my shoulder and hooks to the top in the front. There is also a very thick strap that runs from one side to the other across my back. It flares out and lands just below the belt line on the skirt that I'm wearing. I'm still wearing the black, fluffy skirt I'd planned on wearing earlier, just with the new top, which is white by the way.

After the argument about the clothes, I realize now, when I was trying this all on, that most of the tops were purchased with my ink in mind. Showing off my arms at the very least, then of course my back whenever possible.

"If you're wearing that, you might want these." I turn to see Talon pulling out one of the white bags that was tucked into my new big suitcase. He pulls out two sticker looking things.

"Pasties?" Is he joking.

"Yeah, you know, since you can't wear a bra." He looks very pointedly at my chest and of course my nipples harden into tight peaks. My nipples are not small by any means and they are clearly visible through my top.

"Damn it," I mumble.

He laughs. "Oh believe me, they're perfect." He brushes the back of his hand along one of them, making it pebble once again. "I don't want to share them with the world."

"Should I change?" I ask.

"No, you look amazing. And because of the ink, you wearing a bra isn't possible, so no matter what you wear, you're going to have the same problem."

"Curse stupid big ass nipples," I grumble, more to myself.

"Can I ask you something personal?" He looks almost terrified.

"You want to know why the implants?" He blushes and nods slightly.

I smile at him. "Because I was all nipple. That's all I had for breasts, basically, was nipples. Here." I grab my phone where I keep the before and after pictures. I scroll through until I find the one of me before the surgery. "See." I turn the phone to show him. "It wasn't a very big confidence booster, trust me. It's hard to have anyone take you seriously when you're so flat chested. I did it about six years ago. I wanted something to help make me feel sexy and confident because what I had certainly didn't."

"I think you were gorgeous even then."

I smile. "Well, thank you."

"Why did you go so big?" he asks with honest curiosity.

"Because it fit me better. I wanted confidence and sexiness all in one package. Though I can't say the boob job gave me that, but it made me feel better about myself and my body. After careful consideration I decided the D's were more proportional to my body size and type. I'd hoped the nipples would have settled down but I think they actually got bigger."

His hand brushes against them again. "They're perfect. Just like you."

I smile and blush at his compliment. "If I could do it all over again, I wouldn't hesitate. All the pain, swelling, and everything I went through with adjusting to them, I'd do it all again just to hear that compliment." I cup his cheek. "Thank you for that."

"Pshhh." He blows it off. "You deserved it."

I blush a little bit more and he finally pulls back. Thank god, because if he kept going, I'd have to strip him down and we don't have time.

"Want some help?" he asks.

"You just want to see 'em," I chide.

"Maybe. Can you blame me?"

"No I can't, but you have a show to do. Now leave me be so I can make it less distracting for you to sing," I giggle.

chapter 19

Ugh, stupid pasties make my nipples itch. I know damn well each time my nipples try to harden because I can feel it pulling. But after a good solid look in the mirror, I agree with Talon. They will make a huge difference in not showing my nipples to the world. Though you can still see them slightly, it is nothing like it was when Talon was in here.

I'm surprised he asked the question, though not directly. I have no problem explaining to anyone who asks. Ironically, he's the first. When I'm clothed, it's harder to tell, but when you see me, like they have, it's obvious that I've had the work done. The scars faded away, but in just the right light, or in the right position, they pucker funny. All in all though, I've seen some pretty botched jobs, and mine look pretty fucking good. Lest we forget that I haven't had the unfortunate pleasure of losing sensation, as he so expertly pointed out. I don't care. I love my tits. What can I say?

Alright, enough about my boobs. I finish with my hair, going with a similar style to what I wore to Cami's last night. Up, but curly. I'm allowing myself to embrace Talon's request to show myself off a little more.

"Come on, Addie," Someone shouts from up front. "Time to roll." I look at my watch and it is five minutes to eight. The guys elected to skip the pre-show party, sending a message through Kyle that they would all be available after the show. I think the couple of days off has worn them down more than they thought, so getting pumped back up is taking a little longer. I can't say I blame them. Add to that the start of a very long and super busy couple of weeks.

We're here in Albuquerque tonight and by this time next week we will be in OKC, after Galveston, Dallas and New Orleans. Once we hit Kansas, we don't stop until Chicago, then things settle a little into Ohio, a long stay in Philly, then Boston and finally on to New York. At least at this point in time, if they choose to extend the tour, there isn't room. Not unless they're gonna start flying us everywhere and the guys get a second set of instruments.

"Come on, panda girl," Kyle shouts back. I fluff my hair, check my lipstick and oh fuck it, it is what it is.

When I come around the corner, the bus is empty except for my two men. Who of course are drooling all over themselves like idiots. "I'd expect this from Dex, or Mouse or even Peacock, but you both know damn well you get to unwrap this package at the end of the night, so why the drool?" I tease them.

"Because you don't understand just how fucking gorgeous you are," Kyle says with a smile.

Because of the skirt I have on tonight, I'm only wearing a pair of Docs, so I am much shorter to these two knuckleheads and they of course take full advantage by kissing my forehead and the top of my head when I wrap my arms around them. "Come on, let's go."

I lead them off of the bus to find Mills and Beck standing guard. "Hi boys," I say as we exit.

"Good evening, Addison," they say in unison. Aw hell, they can be so cute sometimes.

We walk toward the back of the venue with my arms linked in both of theirs. Kyle, ever the gentleman, opens the door for us and I usher Talon inside first. Those backstage are not here to see me.

Empty Chamber is already on stage, playing their last concert with us. After tonight we pick up a new band for our opening act. Like EC, I've never heard of them, but I'm assuming they're good or they wouldn't be joining us.

Talon turns to me. "I need to go talk with the guys. You'll be in your spot, right?"

"Ugh, I still have to kiss them all?" I tease.

"Yes, you do. Besides, I doubt they'd let you slip away that easily."

I laugh and Talon takes off. I turn to Kyle. "What can I do to help?"

He chuckles. "Go be their good luck charm, I got it." He leans down to kiss me on the forehead and I grab his neck, pulling him to my lips.

"So not fair," he murmurs against my lips. I tease him with my tongue. He shaved up his scruffiness and is back to having his very well trimmed chin beard and goatee. It's fucking sexy as hell and I want to lick his jaw, but he pulls away. "Later," he moans in disappointment and I smile wide.

The grin doesn't leave my lips as I walk to take my place along the stage, waiting patiently for my guys.

I begin dancing to Empty Chamber as they finish up their set. The adrenaline of the evening is kicking in and taking over, and for that, I'm thankful. I can't sit here turning myself into a nervous wreck waiting for my time on the stage.

Jesus, I can't believe I'm actually going to do this intentionally. The last time was a fluke. He wanted me on stage to sing to me, to thank me for whatever hard work I'd done to that point, and that was all, now I've turned into an overnight Youtube sensation. Oh by the way, the last I checked the video had jumped to more than twelve million views. After I saw that I decided not to look anymore and told myself it had to do with Talon and not with me.

Empty Chamber wraps up their set and the equipment dance begins.

The crowd starts chanting for 69 Bottles just a few minutes into the changeover. I smile knowing that my boys are about to take the stage.

I look down the hallway and here they come. Dex in the lead, Peacock, then Mouse, though I can't actually see him, and finally Talon. He has a smile on his face as he looks at me. I can't help but smile back.

"You sexy little minx," Dex says as he comes up to me, wrapping his arms around me and planting one hell of a wet sloppy kiss on my lips. I think dogs use less slobber than this one does. He pulls back.

"Ugh, seriously."

"One day you'll start to love my kisses." And with one phrase the old Dex has returned with a vengeance.

"Not in a million years." He pulls away with a satisfied smirk on his face and saddles up to his drums.

Mouse and Peacock embrace me, planting their kisses and pulling away. "Break a leg, boys." Though the tradition of the kisses formed immediately, it's only now that I realize my lines to the boys are always the same.

The boys smile and walk to their spots on stage.

Kyle comes up behind me, wrapping his arms around my belly, holding me to him and a thought passes through my mind, but before I can grab hold of it, it's gone. Talon saunters up to me, taking my cheeks in his hands, he brings his lips to mine. I melt into the arms of my men. Loving every touch, every shiver and goosebump that forms across my skin.

One of Talon's hands comes away from my cheek and I can tell just by the movement that he's holding Kyle in his hand too. I feel Kyle's hand move along my belly touching both Talon and myself.

He pulls back. "Kick some ass, big man," I say with a breathy voice and a smile. He kisses me again, quick.

"That's for good luck." Then he kisses me one more time before taking my hand and backing away until distance separates us.

Kyle starts kissing on my neck. "Keep that up and I'm going to take you in the dressing room."

He licks again and I shiver. "I don't like the pasties," he says.

"How'd..."

"Because I love how your nipples pucker when you're turned on. Now, short of sticking my hand up your skirt, I have no idea."

I laugh. "Believe me, I'm turned on."

"Hello New Mexico!" I hear Talon growl into the microphone. I look at him and he looks back at me, the lust in his eyes is amazing and I'm dying to get my boys back beneath me.

The band kicks up and the show is off to a fabulous start. The crowd is cheering, the band is rocking and nothing else matters but watching them play.

That is until about halfway through their set, between songs the crowd starts chanting "We want Addison!"

Talon's shocked eyes turn to mine. Mutual expressions reflected back. "Told you this wasn't about you or him. It's all about them," Kyle says softly in my ear.

The chanting continues, Talon says something to the guys. From what he told me, they were going to play one more, then it was my turn, but it seems now is the time. The crowd continues to chant and the sound guy comes over giving me my microphone which is actually one that hooks into my ear so I can hear the playback of the band, and a slim, clear microphone that sits in front of my mouth.

The chanting continues and my heart starts pounding in my chest.

"You want Addison?" Talon asks the crowd and they go crazy. My heart swells as he looks over to me. Kyle is helping the sound guy tuck the cable under the strap at my back. "Why on earth would you want Addison?" he asks the crowd in a very playful manner and a good portion of them shout back, "Your Eyes."

"Fuck me," I breathe in wonder.

Kyle laughs, wrapping his arms around me from behind. I turn and the sound guy hooks me up by putting the clip in the belt I'm wearing.

"So you think I should bring out my dearest angel so she can sing for you all?" The crowd cheers like crazy and the band kicks up the soft opening of the song, quiet, but still there.

Kyle kisses me, hard and fast on the lips. "Go get 'em, panda," he says to me and I want to cry. I touch his cheek.

"Thank you," I mouth and I turn back to Talon.

"I don't know guys. What do you think?" he says toward the band and they kick up the sound to a fever pitch, the playback is in my ear. The crowd goes crazy. "I'll take that as a yes." He turns back to the crowd. "Ladies and gentlemen, it is my honor and privilege to welcome the one and only Addison Beltrand to the stage."

I take a deep breath and step out from behind the curtain. Focusing hard on Talon's face, his features, the softness and the love I can see radiating from his body as I walk closer. Feeling the overwhelming excitement from the roaring crowd, I'm spurred on and I wave with enthusiasm; the crowd goes nuts. The lights are so bright I can't see them, but I can certainly hear them.

I snuggle up to Talon and he wraps his arm around me, the one without the microphone. A bunch of people in the crowd start yelling for him to kiss me. I blush and he doesn't hesitate in planting a soft, yet firm kiss against my lips. "Let's do this," he says softly, I nod and the band starts at the beginning.

Talon doesn't leave my side the entire time. Holding on to me, though I finally draw the courage to face the crowd.

chapter 20

When we finish singing, the crowd goes crazy. Those that are not down on the floor stand, clapping and cheering. "You did it," Talon whispers in my ear. I smile wide and the crowd cheers some more. I wave to them.

"Thank you," I say to the crowd and they're seriously pumped up. Talon kisses me one more time and then lets me go. I drift backwards slowly, waving to the crowd as they continue to cheer. As soon as I'm out of the line of sight, Kyle's arms are around me and I slump down into them.

"Jesus, you're amazing," he says as he grabs the pack off of my belt and untangles me from the mic. After it's gone he wraps his arms around me from the front. "Well done, panda girl. Well done."

Kyle and I spend the rest of the show dancing back stage, rocking out to Talon and the boys of 69 Bottles. They put on one hell of a show and even with all of these shows I'll be seeing; I don't think it will ever get old. The last show in Vegas killed me to miss but I was hurting too bad to get out of bed.

The guys wrap up their show to another encore, this time they play three songs, instead of two, and I was the focus of Talon's attention between the sets. He doted on me, kissed me, loved on me; it was amazing to have him back in my arms. His praise was unbelievable and he tried to convince me to come out for a final bow, but I told him that this was his show, not mine. He winked and then went back on stage.

After the show was over, the guys met in the greenroom and there was a very long line waiting to see them. Talon dragged me in there with him. What happened after they opened the door was nothing I could have ever imagined. While the guys got the majority of the attention, I received more than my fair share too. Autographs were asked for and pictures were taken, with me alone, with me and Talon and with me and the entire band. It was enough to make a girls head explode. I know I thought mine was going to.

There is definitely something to this whole celebrity thing and I decide that Tristan and I need to talk sooner rather than later. I can already tell just how overwhelming the whole 'you're cool' status can be. About an hour after the show wraps up, near eleven thirty, Kyle comes in and starts shooing away our guests, thank god. My cheeks are killing me from smiling so much.

Once the room is empty, Kyle stands before us. "Tonight was Empty Chamber's last show with us and they'd like to go out to celebrate the tour success, Addison's addition and their farewell. Cars are being arranged. This wasn't a planned event so anyone who wants to stay back is more than welcome."

Everyone agrees to go. The show kicked ass tonight and they're all pumped up, even me. "I need to change. I don't want to go out in this."

"Absolutely," Kyle tells me. "Go ahead, I need to talk to Talon anyway. We'll meet you at the bus in what, ten minutes?"

"Sure." I kiss them both and leave them to their discussion.

kyle

"Seriously, that was a fucking amazing show," I tell Talon as soon as Addie leaves the room.

"It was pretty fucking awesome, wasn't it? Did you hear the crowd? Fuck, that was intense," he tells me as he slumps back onto the couch.

"The videos are already starting to pop up online."

"Cell phones," We say together. "How do they look?" he asks.

I shrug. "I haven't looked yet. But I need to warn Addie. She's gonna be all over the news tomorrow."

I watch as he runs his hand through his hair. "Do you think this is really what she wants?" he asks me, his tone is somber and unsure.

"The fame?"

"Yeah. Man, you should have seen them in here tonight. After they were done swooning over me and the guys, they pounced on her like white on rice. It was insane. She took it in stride, answered their questions, signed some autographs and took a shit ton of pictures. I have never in my life seen a celebrity pop so fast as it has with her and I'm not talking about the guys. There were so many girls, fuck! It blew me away."

"Honestly, I think she's more worried about stealing your spotlight than the fame of it all."

"She really did mean that earlier, didn't she?"

I nod my head. "We'd talked about it before she brought it up with you. She never wanted this. She never even so much as hoped to have a singing career. She's always been content doing what she does for a living."

"I feel so bad, roping her into this."

"You didn't do it on purpose. She was out there, you planned to sing it to her. You didn't expect her to sing along. Add to that the fact that she sings as well as she does? How were you to know?" I shrug, "And I'm sure you weren't thinking about the potential consequences for having her sing into the mic. Hell, a lot of artists do it at their concerts and the best they get is a ton of YouTube hits on some random piss poor video. She's an amazing singer, and I'm surprised she hasn't been discovered before this. She sounds like a grittier version of Amy Lee and a rock chick in this day and age is very hard to come by. Which is why she's so popular right now. The girls will gravitate toward her, the guys will 'fall in love with her' and what she chooses to do from there is entirely up to her. But I will tell you one thing, she will never ask for anything. She won't ask for another song. If you want her to keep this up, you're going to have to keep writing songs."

He looks at me. "Too late."

I laugh. "Well, unless you're dumping the guys, you can't bring her in constantly on everything."

"No, but I can try and work out an acoustic album deal."

"Going solo?" I scowl at him. "Dude, you've barely been with the band, I highly doubt..."

"Kyle, relax, that's not what I'm talking about. Look, it's a great fun idea, but I will never ever ditch the guys like that. I think we need to get through this tour, nail down the new album and then figure things out. Besides, if she makes a name for herself, one of two things will happen." His voice drops to a whisper. "One, she does nothing with it, continues along with us or two, she decides to run away with what's being thrown at her and the likelihood of us being able to sing together again will disappear."

I slouch into the couch. "I hadn't thought about that," I tell him.

"See, we're dwelling on all the things we don't know. We need to stop. Now come on, she's probably waiting for us."

I snort a laugh. "Two and a half hours. It took her two and half hours to get ready for tonight. You think she's ready now?"

He laughs with me. "No, but let's go anyway, I miss her."

I sigh, "Yeah, me too."

chapter 21
addison

"I need to clean up this pigsty tomorrow. Jesus," I say aloud.

"We'll do it." I turn to see Talon and Kyle standing in the hallway.

"No, your packing has put me in this pickle. Besides, I'm capable of cleaning, cooking and many other things. Speaking of food, I'm starving."

I watch as they both smile. "Well, then let's go so you can eat," Kyle says with a smirk. "Unless of course you prefer a liquid diet."

I giggle. "Unless it's alcohol, forget it, mister, you can wait."

He pouts. "I bet we can change her mind," Talon says looking at Kyle, who looks back at Talon.

"Oh, for the love of my vagina, you two are too much sometimes," I tease, dropping my skirt and their jaws drop. "Ha! Three can play at this game." I pull my shirt over my head.

"Shit, we gotta get her a stripper pole," Talon teases.

"Hell yeah, she'd make one hell of a stripper."

"In your dreams, boys." I set about trying to remove a pasty. "Fuck, this hurts."

"Water might help," Talon says flicking his tongue at me.

I roll my eyes. "Anything to get my nipples in your mouth."

"Fucking straight. Your nipples are by far the most beautiful, tasty things on the planet. I could suck on them all day long," Talon says with a salacious smile and Kyle's own expression matches.

"You're like babies being weaned from the boob." I stick my tongue out at them.

"Now that's an idea." Talon's eyes light up.

"Oh for Pete's sake, I'm on birth control, you know."

He snorts a laugh. "Oh, but I'm sure we could find a way without putting a baby in there, though that's..." He lets the thought trail off. He doesn't need to finish it, I know where he's going with that thought.

"I'm not opposed, please don't think that, but it is way, way too soon to be talking about babies," I tell him and he nods his head in agreement and the thought I had earlier, that I couldn't get a hold of before, comes back into my mind. I shake it off. It's way too soon to even be thinking about babies and what not.

"Can you let me finish?" I ask and the playful atmosphere disappears and I regret it instantly. But I need to be alone for a minute.

"Yeah, we'll be up front," Kyle says, though Talon hasn't moved much since he said what he did. I wonder what's running through his mind.

talon

"Dude, what was that all about?" Kyle asks when we get back to the galley.

"Fuck, it just slipped out. I have no idea where it came from."

"Maybe we should go back to wrapping…"

I shake my head. "I can't go from wrapped, to unwrapped and back to wrapped again. With you, that's different, but not with her. Fuck…" I scrub my face with my hands and sit down. "She's fucking petrified."

"Stop, it's alright. I think the whole conversation got away from everyone. Give her a minute. You know her, she'll be over it in no time and we'll go right back to the way it was before. Believe me, I've had the same thoughts," he tells me.

He sits down next to me. "The scary part about all this, with her, is that I've never wanted anything. No relationship, no family, no nothing before. Now it seems like it's all I can think about. Fucking scares the hell out of me." I scratch my chin.

"That's the way it's supposed to be."

"How so?"

"Well, imagine if you walked through life, desperate for a woman on your arm, a baby in your lap, a ring on your finger, what would happen?" I shrug. "You'd be consumed with it, constantly dating, falling in and out of love, thinking you've found the one only to have her cheat on you and it's over. But if you walk through life as you, she and I have, just going from one day to the next and the next, it's easier. Though it hasn't made us any less promiscuous, it's been easier for us to ignore the long term idea when the short term solution is sucking our dicks." Fuck, he has a point. "The girl, the one for you is supposed to make you stop sleeping around, stop being a dick and settle down, that's what she's supposed to do when you meet her. That's what she does to both of us."

"Fuck, it's just all so fast," I groan.

"But what's wrong with that? Do you want to run off and marry her this instant?" I shake my head. "Do you want to knock her up right now?" I shake my head again. "Do you want to go sleep with another woman?" I shake my head again. "See, what you feel for her is taking over that impulse to want to be with someone else, that's where this starts, that's where it all begins. In time, the rest of the stuff will come. That's not to say that if she does get pregnant, because we're not exactly careful, we won't want it to happen, it's just we're not going to plan for it to happen."

"Fuck, when you least expect it is when it always happens."

"So be it. Just let this whole thing run its course, let her be her, let us fall in love with her, let us devour her every chance we get and leave the real deep heady stuff for a day when we really need to deal with it."

He doesn't say anymore and we both set our heads back against the top of the couch. He's fucking right of course and I knew it before he said it, it's just I still can't believe it slipped out of my mouth like that.

"I need a drink."

"Me too," She says and both our heads pop up. She's smiling and dressed in her Nirvana t-shirt, no bra, the pasties are gone, yummy, and ripped skinny jeans tucked into a pair of knee high, three inch heel patent leather boots.

I can't stop staring. "Fuck me," I breathe.

She smiles. "Later." She winks and comes to stand between us, grabbing our hands and pulling us up. "Let's go drink."

chapter 22

addison

The night out was exactly what I needed after what happened on the bus. Though what happened wasn't anything bad, just unexpected. Couple that with the fleeting thought I had when Kyle wrapped his arms around me before the show and I was a mess. The only thing that pulled me out was the fact that I knew Talon was beating himself up over the idea. Not only by what he'd said.

So I haven't told you everything, just like I haven't told them. I have polycystic ovarian syndrome, or more commonly known as PCOS. I've had it since I was a teenager and it has constantly given me a hard time when it comes to periods and menstrual cycles, they're almost non-existent. One of my ovaries is completely blocked by a cyst and the other only functions half the time, which is why I'm on birth control. The ring to be exact and why I am not worried about getting pregnant. Add up all of the facts and the odds are stacked way against me.

But the thought I had tonight still dances in my mind. The idea of Kyle cradling a growing belly while Talon kisses me before his performance. Fuck, stop thinking about it and drink some more.

We're at some hole in the wall dive bar not too far away from the venue the guys played at tonight. Though the crowd is heavy for a Wednesday night, it's not totally over run with the bimbos that normally surround 69 Bottles after parties. Though Mouse and Dex have had no trouble scoring chicks.

Dex is back to his old self. Which as much as I hate to admit, I'm happy to see. Right now he's only working on one, who was actually hitting on Talon earlier. I took a huge hit to my pride when she waltzed up to him, only to be lifted when he turned her down, telling her that he had someone already. Kyle, on the other hand, has been turning them down left and right. Probably because once again I find him some distance away from Talon and I.

When one of the chippies finally walks off dejected, I use my finger to call him to me. Like the cutest puppy dog on the planet, he comes willingly. "Stop sitting so far away."

"I like turning them down," he smiles.

"Bullshit," Talon says.

Kyle laughs. "It's just hard because when I'm near you, I want to touch you, and if I do that, and Talon is doing that, well... I don't know, I don't..."

"You shouldn't care. I don't," I say to him.

"Neither do I," Talon joins in. "I understand your reservations, but I don't care what people think of me. I've had and lived the reputation of a different woman every night. I don't care if people know that I like you."

Melt my fucking heart.

"I don't care either. The three of us are together, we're happy, who gives a fuck what other people think. Besides, I like having you close to me, touching me, showing me how much you want me. It turns me on," I whisper.

His smile could light up the room. "Have you had enough to drink?" he asks me and I nod. "Tal?"

"If I say yes, does that mean we can leave?"

"Yes," Kyle and I say together.

"Then abso-fucking-lutely!"

I giggle. "Does big man need a bed time snack?" I give him a bad pouty face impression and he laughs.

"So long as it involves you and him, yes."

"Then let's go." I stand up way too fast and all the alcohol goes rushing to my head and I sway.

"Easy, panda. We got you," Kyle says as he links my arm in his. Talon stands, taking my hand and leading us toward the back of the bar where we came in.

Rusty is standing carside, opening the door as soon as we come out. Talon slides in first, then me and then Kyle, while Rusty slides in front. I don't question the arrangement and we take off back toward the bus.

After we're on the road for a couple of minutes, I lean into Talon's ear and whisper, "I want to watch you use that plug on Kyle." Talon's breathing hitches and his mouth falls open in shock. I continue whispering, "I can't wait to watch you fuck him."

"Angel," he growls, sending a shiver of anticipation up my spine. He leans in and whispers in my ear, "I have a better idea. How about I watch you fuck him?"

I let out a breathy moan because I can't control the radiating excitement that pulses through me. "How?" I breathe.

"We have a present for you," he says and then sits up straight, ending our conversation completely.

I look at Kyle who is curious but isn't going to press for information, besides, just a minute or two later we're pulling into the lot, going through the security gate and pulling up alongside the bus. Kyle slides out first, taking my hand and I slide across the seat, as Talon follows. Once we're both free of the door, Rusty closes it and we bound onto the bus. Headed straight for the bedroom.

"I'll be right back," Talon says and he leaves me and Kyle alone.

"What did you say to him?" he asks, his eyes alight with curiosity.

I smirk. "I told him that I wanted to watch him stick that butt plug in your ass. That I am dying to watch him fuck you." Kyle sinks onto the bed. "Then he said he had a better idea and that was him watching me fuck you." I smile but he looks dazed. "Kyle?"

He shivers himself out of his daze. "Fuck me? How would you fuck me?"

I smile, but I'm worried about what was in his head. "Forget that for a second, what's wrong?"

"Nervous, I guess. Though you haven't hurt me, the idea of something bigger than a finger is a little..." He shivers again and then swallows hard. "Well, it's fucking hot. I think I nearly came just thinking about it."

"So we're alright. This isn't a bad thing?"

"Oh my god, no, baby girl. I'm nervous, yes, but in the case of something like this, I'd rather know in advance before it gets sprung on me."

I smile. "Good," I say as I pull my top over my head and I watch as his mouth falls slack. My nipples are hard already, a little red from the pasties earlier, but I was able to wash them up before we left.

"Now that's a beautiful sight to see," Talon says as he walks into the room. I'm standing near the side of the bed, while Kyle is at the foot, all but drooling all over himself. Talon puts a bag of stuff on the bed.

"What's in there?" I ask.

Talon smirks, "A present for you and a little something for everyone." I raise an eyebrow at him and he digs into the bag. He pulls out a box and lays it on the bed.

I look at the package. "Feeldoe?" There is no picture of what's inside on the box.

"Open it," Talon tells me so I pick up the box, opening one end I am met with a plastic holder. I grab it and slide it out.

It's an odd shape, kind of like a J. One end has a large bulb on it, the other is shaped like a penis. It's not very big around and nowhere near as big as either one of my guys. I pop it free and hold it up. Then it hits me. "Oh my god, is this…is it like a strap on?" I ask.

Talon smiles, "It's a strapless strap-on. See this," he points to the bulb, "slides up inside your pussy. The ridges are for your stimulation and then the rest is well, self-explanatory."

I look at Kyle who is staring at it. He swallows hard. "It looks huge," he breathes.

Talon caresses his cheek and holds up the small butt plug, the one he used on me and takes the Feeldoe from my hand. "It's actually smaller, just a lot longer. If it's too much we can…"

"No, I want her to," he cuts him off, his voice laced with desire. "But, I have got to get off first. I'm already to the point of explosion."

I smile and turn to Talon and shrug. Talon gets a big wolfish grin on his face as he turns back to Kyle and commands, "Stand up." Kyle does and Talon kneels before him, unbuckling his pants and sliding them down his thighs. Kyle's cock pops free and Talon takes it into his mouth.

"Fuck, Talon," Kyle groans. "Fuck, I'm not gonna last long," he breathes as he wraps his fingers through Talon's hair, holding him in place briefly then letting him go, guiding Talon along his erection. "Fuck, don't stop. You're fucking mouth feels amazing," Kyle moans.

I'm frozen in place with my pussy dripping into my panties already. I slowly undo my button fly, ready to begin finger fucking my slit as I watch Talon's beautiful mouth sucking on Kyle's glorious cock.

chapter 23

As soon as my pants are down far enough, my hand is in my slit. I can't take it anymore, fuck me.

"Enjoying the show, baby girl?" I lean forward onto the bed, looking up at him, pleasure soaring in my veins.

"Fuck yes."

Talon's mouth lets Kyle's cock go audibly. "Don't you dare fucking come," he says in his commanding voice and I whimper my displeasure.

"Fuck, it's too good. I can't, argh, fuck, I can't stop."

Talon gives me a look that sends shivers across my skin and I stop immediately. "Take your boots and pants off. Get on the bed on all fours," he commands. I pout but I obey his word. Fuck, I love it when he's like this. He doesn't do anything physical, it's all in his words and it's the biggest turn on in the world.

I watch as he goes back to sucking on Kyle's erection and playing with his balls. Kyle is about to lose his load, I can tell because he's getting twitchy. He's fighting it, not ready to come yet. But Talon has other ideas.

I untie my boots and begin working them from my feet, desperate not to get distracted by what is happening a few inches away from me. I manage to shed the boots and my pants. I climb up on the bed on all fours, putting my face at the foot of the bed so that I am close to my lovers.

Watching up close is even hotter than watching far away. Talon continues stroking Kyle's cock and playing with his balls. He pulls his mouth back and looks at me. "You want this in your mouth?" I moan. "No, I think I'll take it." I watch as he looks up to Kyle. "Come for me, Kyle." Then he wraps his mouth around Kyle, ferociously sucking and pumping. Kyle tenses and then lets out a growl as he shoots his load into Talon's waiting mouth. Talon continues sucking and licking while swallowing down Kyle's salty cum. Jealousy rocks through me.

Talon knows this. He gradually lets up on Kyle's still hard erection and turns to me. "Kiss me," he commands and I lean forward. The salty taste of Kyle and the sweet, yummy morsel that is Talon assaults my taste buds and I moan, kissing him with ardor.

All too soon he pulls back from the kiss. His eyes are filled with need and lust. My pussy is dripping wet, ready for anything these two can throw at me. Talon stands up and pulls Kyle in for a kiss. It doesn't last that long, but tongues are definitely stroked. Then he comes around the bed where I've been standing and Kyle goes to the other side.

I look at Kyle. "How you doing, cowboy?"

His lips spread into a wide smile of satisfaction, but he's not done yet. His cock is still hard and I want to lick it. I lick my lips. "You're a fucking animal you know that, baby girl? Insatiable much?"

I smile a wide Cheshire grin and he chuckles. I hear Talon's zipper and some rustling bring my attention to the other side of the bed. Mind you, I am still on all fours. My ass in the air. I wiggle it as Talon looks me over. Then goes for the bag. He grabs the butt plug. "Wait a second," I protest.

"Hush, this is actually going to help, plus it gives you some added stretch time because I am dying to take your ass. I don't know how much longer I can hold out." I shiver in anticipation and my nipples harden. "Kyle, why don't you give those delicious nipples some attention while I get her ready to take you?"

"Oh fuck," I groan and Kyle slides onto the bed, flipping over onto his back. I raise up, straightening my arms so that he has some room. He gets his head underneath me and I feel the teasing licks of his tongue brush one nipple, while he rolls the other in his fingers. Tugging and twisting it while his tongue works me over. I writhe in need as Talon slides behind me, between my legs.

His hands come to my ass, spreading it wide, and I feel a glob of slick spit land right in the middle of it. Then his fingers gently go to work massaging the tight rim. Then he begins pressing inside of me with his finger. Slow gentle strokes, allowing me a chance to grow accustomed to his pace.

Kyle has switched nipples now, licking and sucking, twisting and pulling as I flick my hips against Talon's finger. I feel more wetness hit me right where his finger is inside of me. Then I feel the probing pressure of a second finger trying to dip inside. I tense as the pleasure of Kyle at my breast forces me to clamp down on my orgasm, savoring it and saving it for later.

Talon's hand comes to rub along my back, coaxing me to relax and I do almost instantly. He pushes that second finger past the tight ring, then I feel a cool glob of lube against my hole. He starts working it in and out of me with two fingers gently massaging inside, his pace is a little faster. My sex is dripping, my orgasm building.

I feel my body relax completely as the orgasm I was fighting begins to bubble to the surface. Kyle hasn't stopped sucking and I look down at him. His eyes are closed, savoring every second my nipple is in his mouth. I shift and reach over for his cock, wrapping my fingers around it.

"Leave him be, angel. He'll get his." I pout, looking at Kyle and he nods with a smile on his face as he licks his way back to my other nipple. There is new pressure against my ass, but Talon's fingers are still working inside of me. I know almost instantly that he is going for a third finger.

My hole stretches further, this time it burns, but his hand pulls back and slides in, turning pain to pleasure in an instant. "Good girl. You're doing amazing," he says softly. Kyle lets up on my nipple for a moment, then I feel him shift. His hand comes to my clit and I moan. "So eager," Talon teases. "Fine, if you must finger her pussy because you can't help yourself, just don't make her come."

"What?" I whimper. "Not fair."

"Trust me, angel," he murmurs with a soothing rub of my back. I melt into his touch and Kyle's finger slows to a gentle caress while Talon continues to move his three fingers in and out. My orgasm bubbles back to the surface and I moan again. "We're almost there," Talon says gently behind me and I feel another glob of cold hit my ass.

His fingers continue to work my hole, Kyle works my clit and my nipples and all the sensations are just too much. Slowly Talon begins to retreat, pulling himself free of me, only to press a cool hard object against my ass. "Do you want to come?" Talon asks and I moan out a semi-coherent yes.

Then Kyle begins stroking my clit harder, Talon pushes the butt plug deeper inside. It's bigger than the last one, but thanks to his fingers, it's a lot easier to take. He continues fucking my ass slowly while Kyle feverishly rubs my clit and my orgasm reaches an uncontrollable boil. "I'm gonna, fuck, I'm...argh!" I scream and explode. The orgasm sends juices sliding from my pussy and my body shakes as I reach my peak. At the same time, Talon comes to a halt with the plug and I can feel it's all the way inside. He turns it once, then again and my orgasm quickly begins to melt into another oncoming eruption. I feel all hands and mouths come away and I whimper at the loss.

Then I feel something pressing against the entrance of my pussy. It's wide, but hard and a little cold. I shiver. Talon continues pressing it into me. "You can't just use this out of the gate and expect perfect results," he says with a calm voice. Too calm almost. "But the plug should help, until you can build up the muscles required to use the Feeldoe on your own."

"Mmhmmm," I moan.

Kyle slides out from underneath me and I shiver. I want him back there, his breath caressing me is hot and comforting. I feel full. Not as full as I was with Talon inside of me, but full enough to be almost uncomfortable.

"Now, come up to your knees," Talon directs and I do. I want to see. I want to feel. "Slowly, angel, you're pretty full." I feel my walls tighten around the toy in my pussy. I know it's there, I'm glad it's there, but I don't want it to fall out either.

As I come back to rest my ass on my heels I get my first glimpse downward. "Ahh!" I moan as I take in the sight of the purple cock protruding from my body. "That's the sexiest thing I've ever seen."

Before you go getting weird on me, it's not like this has been a fantasy of mine in the past, but I think that at one point every woman wonders what it would be like to have a cock, if only for a day, and they fantasize about what they'd get to do with it. Well, my fantasy is coming true.

I feel Talon's hand on me. He kisses my neck. "Until I saw this, I thought Kyle was the sexiest thing with a cock, but Jesus, you're gorgeous."

I'm so stunned by what I'm seeing that I don't move. I can't. I'm afraid of it falling out, but I feel my walls automatically contracting and releasing to ensure it's in place.

"I need to go wash up," Talon says, kissing me on the cheek, then standing and leaving the room. I look over to Kyle whose cock is twitching with anticipation as his eyes roam over my body.

He doesn't say anything, he just slides over to me. His head between my legs. Without prompting he sucks the toy into his mouth, letting it slip in as far as it will go. While I can't actually feel the sensation there, the toy rubs my clit and moves inside of me, giving me a whole new sensation to work with.

I bring my hand to his hair. "How you doing, cowboy?" He moans around my purple cock and it vibrates against my sex. "Fuck. I can feel that."

"Mmmmmm." He does it again, longer and more drawn out and I nearly fall over from the sensations against my clit, in my pussy and the fact that my ass is filled. Helping to keep me on edge, keeping my walls tightening and loosening.

"Hold still," I tell him and he does. I gently start sliding in and out of his mouth in slow short strokes. The tugging and pulling are enough to make me weak in the knees.

With each thrust forward, my pussy loosens and with each pull backward it tightens.

"Fuck me," Talon says as he comes back into the room.

chapter 24
talon

I never had any desire to watch another man suck cock, at least other than Kyle sucking mine. But watching Addison slide her toy in and out of his waiting mouth, her breasts bouncing slightly with her little bursts, Jesus Christ, I want to come right now.

I walk over to the foot of the bed where Kyle's feet are. "Get on your knees for me, Kyle." He doesn't hesitate in lifting himself up, putting his ass in the air. His cheeks spread wide and his cock hangs down, hard as a rock. Without hesitation, mainly because I am so desperate to watch Addison fuck him, I climb up behind him, using both hands to spread his cheeks wider.

I run my tongue from just under his balls, all the way up to his hole. He trembles beneath me. I lick and lap at his tight ring. The taste is similar to Addison's and I soak it up. Licking and dipping my tongue just inside the rim. Kyle moans around Addison's cock and she shivers, letting a moan out.

Looking at her over Kyle's backside is beautiful. Her full tits and hard nipples bouncing with her thrusts into Kyle's waiting mouth is enough for me to come.

I continue lapping at Kyle's ass, readying him to take Addison's new addition. I smile at her as she looks at me with lust filled eyes. I nod and reach for the bottle of lube.

I pull back from my licking and Kyle moans in disappointment and Addison shivers with pleasure. I knew that toy would be amazing for her, the dual stimulation combined with the butt plug has her no doubt ready to explode. I drop a big glob of lube on Kyle's hole and he jumps. "Easy, cowboy," I tell him rubbing my hand along his ass and up his back. "It's just lube." He nods around Addison's cock. I begin rubbing the lube in small circles, both to coat him and my finger. I'm going to do what I did to Addison a few minutes ago. Helping him stretch, to be able to accommodate the toy. I got the slimmest model because I knew that this wasn't about size, it's about getting used to the idea. We can go bigger, later.

Addison continues to fuck his mouth while I press one finger, then another into his ass. With each insertion he tightens up so I use my other hand to gently stroke his back, helping him to stay calm and relaxed. By the time I make it to the third finger, Kyle is moaning regularly and I can see that she is about to come unglued with his humming against her toy cock.

"Okay, Kyle." His head pops up marginally. "I'm afraid to make Addison walk, I need you to turn yourself around. Can you do that, cowboy?" He nods and Addison moans. I watch as she pulls the cock from Kyle's mouth at the same time as I retract my fingers. I hand the lube to Addison. "Be generous on that thing. Remember, it's rubber." She looks at me with a lust filled smile. Then down at her new, though temporary, appendage and squirts some lube on the tip. "More, angel," I tell her and she puts on some more.

Then I watch as pleasure rocks her body as she begins stroking her cock. I feel my cock spurt a shot of pre-cum onto my leg. "Kyle, look at this," I tell him and he turns to look at her.

We both stare at her as she pleasures herself with expert strokes. Her body is rocking and vibrating with her own need to come. "Make yourself come, angel. Fuck your hand."

She doesn't stop, her strokes increase as she pushes and pulls her cock. "Fuck! Fuck! Fuck!" she growls and she shatters. I love watching her come unglued. Her skin flushes bright red right as she explodes. She slowly milks the orgasm through the protruding part of her toy.

"Maybe now I should tell her that there is a vibrator attachment to that thing?" Kyle laughs as Addison's eyes pop open and the slyest smile spreads on her lips.

"Oh really?" she says. "Do tell?"

"Later, baby. You can barely last as it is, imagine it vibrating too." She trembles. "Exactly."

"I can't help it. It's just so fucking hot," she says with a moan while she looks at her purple cock and Kyle finally settles into place. I watch as she adds a little more lube to her appendage and I look down at Kyle who's staring at my cock.

With my clean hand I cup his chin. "Do you want my cock in your mouth?"

"Yes, please."

I smile. "Soon," I say and he gives me a happy satisfied smile. If I didn't know better, I would think that Kyle was high, but I know it's the sexual endorphins his body is releasing, preparing himself for what's about to happen to him. I look at Addie, "You ready?" She nods and she moves into position behind Kyle. I can tell she's a little nervous and I would be too if it were me. "Okay, angel. Nice and easy. Kyle, slide down lower." They both adjust to the new height and I watch as Addison's gentle fingers begin working Kyle's hole and I hear him moan with pleasure.

She pulls back, stroking her cock again, making sure it's good and wet. Then she gently presses it against his ass. She's using her hand to guide, not her hips and I admire her for that. She pushes in a little further.

Kyle hisses through his teeth. I slide off of the bed to get eye level with him. She stops what she's doing and rubs his back. He relaxes again. "Are you hurt?" I ask and he shakes his head. "Are you uncomfortable?" He nods. "Do you want her to stop?" He shakes his head again and she goes back to sliding deeper inside of him. I know the moment she breaches that barrier because Kyle moans and she slides in just a little easier now.

She pulls back and then slides in, this time a little deeper. With each thrust in she goes in more, and with each pull he moans. I watch as they continue getting acquainted with each other. I look at Kyle. Bliss is on his face. He loves what she is doing to him. "Do you like the fact that our girl is fucking your ass?"

"Yes," he cries out as Addison slides in. She too moans. I stand up and walk from the room once again.

chapter 25
addison

Push in, pull out, rub clit, push against the plug. "Argh," I groan out as I continue sliding my beautiful purple cock in and out of Kyle's ass. He is beginning to move with me, sliding down on me as I slide in, increasing the pushing and pulling of the toy inside my core.

With each pull out, I can feel the toy slipping slightly, but with each push in, it slips back into place. I keep up my slow rhythm, not wanting to go too hard or too fast for Kyle but seeing him sprawled out on the bed, writhing and moaning to my actions is going to make me come again.

Talon comes back into the room. He's watching me as I continue to fuck Kyle. He takes his cock in his hand and begins stroking it in long languid strokes. My mouth waters and Kyle groans. "I want your cock," Kyle says as I thrust inside. His voice sounds full of lust and desire and Talon won't deny him anything like that. I nod at Talon and he slides over in front of Kyle who adjusts so that he is a little more on all fours.

"Fuck me," I groan as his motions send a new wave of pleasure across my clit and into my pussy. Kyle pulls Talon's cock into his mouth and he begins sucking it. I come up more on my knees, bringing Kyle's ass higher and allowing me more freedom. I squeeze my thighs together, increasing the sensation and tightening my hold on the cock between my legs. I can see clearly from here that Kyle's mouth is working feverishly over Talon's cock. Talon leans forward toward me and I do the same as I slide inside of Kyle once again.

Talon's mouth lands on mine and his hand comes to one of my nipples. He rubs it and pulls it between his fingers. I thrust into Kyle again and he cries out. But not in pain. "More?" I ask and Kyle's head nods.

I begin to gradually increase my pace. I notice that the faster I go, the better it feels and the more my pussy contracts around the bulb inside. Keeping it in place. "Fuck!" Kyle cries out.

I rub my hands along his back, taking hold of his hips to help guide me in and out. My eyes roll up into my head and Talon now has both hands playing with my nipples. Tugging and pulling, pushing and fucking. "Fuck. I'm gonna...."

I can barely finish the thought. I let my hand slip down around Kyle's hip and I take his cock in my hand. "You ready to come for your woman, cowboy?"

I watch as Kyle nods furiously around Talon's cock. I look at Talon, seeing an answer to my question and he nods.

I begin stroking Kyle's cock, but the position is awkward. Talon senses it. "Fuck your hand, Kyle." He commands and Kyle's hand immediately goes to his cock. I can feel his balls shifting against my legs as he strokes.

I move faster, sliding in and out of Kyle, fucking him. "Come on cowboy, give it to me. Give me that fucking orgasm," I cry out as I explode. The pressure in my pussy and my ass is so intense, it's nearly painful. Kyle throws his head back with his own lusty cry and Talon pumps his cock into Kyle's mouth.

We all continue riding our orgasms, but Kyle's hand is the first to stop moving as he slumps onto the bed. I shiver at the movement around my purple cock and slowly begin to pull it out of him. "Ah!" he says with a twinge of pain in his voice.

"I'm sorry, cowboy."

"'S'okay," he says into the mattress. I keep pulling back slowly. When I reach the thickest part, I rub my hand along his back, encouraging him to relax and he does. I pull free of him and he collapses onto the bed.

"Don't move, angel," Talon tells me and I stay still. "Let me help you." He stands and I'm relieved to see that he's still hard. I'm going to need that cock after he pulls this plug out of me. "Kyle?"

"Hmph." Talon and I both laugh.

"Are you able to move at all?" We both watch as he shakes his head no. So Talon lifts up his leg. "I need to get this stuff out of our baby." I help Talon lift his leg and Kyle rolls over onto his back, leaving half of the bed for me.

I notice, for the first time since we've been together that Kyle is limp and I swell with pride. I had something to do with that.

"Bend over, angel. Like before." I do as he tells me to and I feel him tugging on the purple cock and it flops free, immediately following its extraction there is a mess of liquid that spills out. "Shit," Talon says. "That's fucking unbelievably hot. Just when I thought you couldn't get any hotter." I snort a laugh. Then I feel his finger dip into my waiting slit and I moan. "I need to be inside you," he breathes and I wiggle my hips, inviting him in.

He saddles up behind me and I can feel the head of his cock pressing into me. It's too much, it actually hurts. "Ahh, please, take the plug out. Too sensitive."

"Okay, angel." I feel him going to work on the plug as he slowly slides in and out of me in small little spurts. The pulling of the plug has me near orgasm again and he can sense it, but he's trying to be gentle. As soon as the plug is free he slams into me, slamming home and forcing another orgasm to rock through my body. I come alive one more time for my big man while Kyle slumbers quietly on the other side of the bed.

Sometime while we slept soundly, the bus took off for Galveston. Everyone was on board who was supposed to be there and no one who wasn't. I actually feel kind of bad wrapping myself up with Talon and Kyle so much that I'm ignoring so much of my work or at least the things that I'm supposed to be doing from a PR stand point.

I wake up to another mountain of email notifications with story alerts, all of which involve me and my 'unbelievable', 'amazing' and 'surprising' performance with the band. There is also some speculation about a recorded duet with Talon and myself. I'm assuming the label had something to do with that news flash.

chapter 26

When we arrive in Galveston around eight on Thursday night, Kyle disappears pretty quickly. Taking off for the store he said with a kiss to my forehead. I continue working, reviewing some social media comments, especially on Twitter, tweeting and re-tweeting various comments about the band. Then finally end with a tweet about our arrival in Galveston. Tomorrow night is the show, which gives us tonight for ourselves. It doesn't take long before Dex, Peacock and Mouse are dressed to go out.

"You comin', Red?" Dex asks. I smile sweetly and shake my head. "Your loss." He gives me an evil smirk. Again, I'm strangely comforted by the fact that Dex has returned to himself. Though I suspect it is more of a show than a real desire.

A little while later, Kyle finally returns. "Hey panda."

"Hey, where'd you run off to?"

"Just needed to run to the store. Listen, are you about done?"

I look at my computer then back to Kyle, "I can be done whenever, what's up?"

"Why don't you go grab your hoodie and meet me outside?"

I reply with a confused smile, "Uh, sure." I close up my laptop, unplug it and set off toward the back of the bus when Kyle descends the stairs. When I enter our room, Talon is sitting on the bed looking at his phone. "Hey," I say and he looks up at me.

"Oh hey, what's up?"

I shrug, "Kyle wants me outside. Do you...?

He stands, comes over to me and wraps his arm around my waist, kissing my forehead. "Then you better go." He smiles sweetly.

"What's going on?"

He smiles, "He wants to talk to you."

"What about you?" I ask.

He shrugs and the smile doesn't leave his lips. "This is between the two of you. I'll join you in a little while," he says with conviction.

"Alright." I lift up on my toes and kiss his chin, feeling the scruff as his beard scrape against my lips. I shiver, remembering what that mouth feels like on me.

His silent chuckle tells me he knows exactly what I'm thinking. I extract myself; putting my laptop away and grabbing my hoodie. "Be gentle with him," Talon whispers as I reach for the knob.

"Always," I say with a small smile which he returns and goes back to whatever he was doing on his phone. I leave the room, and head toward the front of the bus. When I step down the steps I can see Kyle sitting on top of a picnic table. He has his elbows on his knees and his head hanging down. He looks so sad. There's a fire in the fire pit in front of him and the two busses and a camper owned by one of the roadies make a U-shaped area around the fire. Opposite the camper, though farther away, is the backside of the venue. There is little in the way of lights, which makes the fire a necessity.

"Kyle," I say softly and he lifts his head. "What's going on?" I can see his features are tight with worry. Something I haven't seen on his face since Phoenix, before we learned about his mom being a bitch. I walk over to him slowly.

He climbs down off of the picnic table, taking me in his arms, gently. He glides his hands from my hips along my back and his lips slant over mine. The kiss is full of passion, desperation and a need I've never felt before. I wrap my arms around his neck and hold him to me. I kiss him back with as much passion as he's throwing at me. Conveying everything I can't say to him, not yet anyway.

When our breathing becomes ragged and nearly impossible, he pulls back. I take a deep breath. "Wow, what was that for?" I breathe. He leads me to the picnic table and I climb up, just like he was, sitting on the table with my feet on the bench.

I watch as he bends down, picking something up off of the ground, he holds it up in front of me. "It's time we talked," he says quietly as he holds up a twelve pack of Sam Adams.

The air in my lungs leaves me in a rush. My heart pounds in my chest. Near panic. This is it, this is what we've put off. I look at him with unshed tears in my eyes. "Are you going to tell me good-bye?" I breathe. I wonder if he actually heard me.

He sets the twelve pack down, pulls a bottle free, popping the cap off, and hands it to me. He repeats the process for himself and takes a big swallow. He hasn't answered my question causing a tear to streak down my cheek. "That will only happen if you want it to happen."

I hiss through my teeth and take a big, big, nearly finishing the bottle swallow. "You think that because you're Dan's brother that I can't do this? That I can't be with you?"

He doesn't answer, he just looks away from me. I can see it in his eyes that he's petrified. Slowly, with shaky legs he climbs onto the bench next to me. He's backlit by the lights atop the building behind us, making it hard for me to see his face, read his eyes. "What was he like?" he asks.

I lean forward with my elbows on my knees, beer bottle rolling between my hands. "Until a few days ago, I had nothing to compare him to. I shut down when he died, Kyle. I breathed out of habit; I worked because I could forget about him. I forced myself to move out of our apartment within a month. I couldn't be there anymore. Everywhere I turned, I was reminded of him." I down the rest of my beer and reach for the bottle opener on the table and pop the top of another beer. I watch in my peripheral as Kyle drains his as well. I hand him the one I've just opened and grab another one.

"But when I think about it now," I continue, "I realize that Dan was like breathing, it was natural and habitual. There were no sparks, no fireworks, no doe eyes when I looked at him. It was convenient and natural." I look over at Kyle, "I loved your brother, but he doesn't hold a candle to what I feel when I'm with you or Talon. There's..." I pause, taking another swig of my beer. "Everything's different now. I see that now, I feel it."

"What about sex?" he breathes.

"Is that something you really want to know?" I ask and take another swig.

I watch him carefully as he drinks his own beer. Finishing it off. I do the same. If we're going to get through this, it's going to take the entire twelve pack. Setting my bottle on the table next to the other empties, I get him another beer, then myself. He finally answers me. "Yes."

I take a deep breath. "He took my virginity." I watch him cringe. "But I was so certain that I was a conquest to him. That he stuck around until he could take that and then he would bolt." I hear Kyle hiss through his teeth. "But he didn't. Things changed between us after that. Over time, I fell in love with him, or I thought I did."

"What do you mean?"

I smile at my beer bottle, "I understand differently now."

He doesn't say anything for some time. He just sits there, lost in thought, drinking his beer. He opened the door to the sex conversation, so I continue, "Sex with Dan was infrequent, I didn't know how to initiate anything. I was shy about my body, and the couple of times that I initiated anything usually led to me getting him off. He never worshipped me or my body the way you and Talon do and I very rarely got an orgasm from him. It always seemed rushed. Sometimes I wondered if he was getting some on the side for all the lack of sexual interest he had in me."

"Jesus, Addison, why were you going to marry him if it was like that?"

I take a big swig from my beer. I'm nearly done with my third bottle. "Because it seemed natural, normal. I didn't know any better. I mean, sure, my girlfriends talked about their sex lives and how great they were and sometimes how often, but..." I shrug, "how was I to know otherwise? Marriage was what everyone seemed to want, I wanted it too, but I think it's part of what led to the fight we had the afternoon before he died. I was stressing about the wedding and he just didn't give a shit." I finish off my beer before continuing, "I never got to apologize for our fight, I never got to tell him I loved him one last time. He was gone." Tears spill down my cheeks. "Everything changed after that."

"I'll never forgive myself for not being there."

"Stop it," I say turning toward him, "There is nothing for you to feel guilty about, Kyle. I didn't know you, you didn't know me. How could you have known what your mother and family would do after his death? You can't blame yourself for that."

"I was too caught up in the drugs and alcohol to even care," he breathes out. "I remember getting the call from my mom, telling me that he'd been killed. She told me to stay away, that she didn't want my problems anywhere near her."

I start to cry harder. "Jesus, Kyle, I... fuck, I had no idea."

"Shh, panda, it's alright. She had a point. I was in no condition to be around her, to see Dan buried, to... I was so fucked up, Addison, but my mother's words are what sent me to rehab. On the day you buried Dan, I was checking into rehab." He scrubs his face with his hand. "I knew I had to straighten out my life, that my mother would need me then more than she ever did. But when I got out, she didn't care." He finishes his beer, sets the empty with the rest and grabs another one. He pops the top and hands it to me. I swallow down the last little bit of my open one and add it to the growing pile. He pops his own and downs half of it. I finish the bottle.

"Addie?"

"Yes."

He doesn't say anything for a minute. Taking a couple more swigs of beer. "I need to know something."

"Anything, always," I say back, searching his features for some clue as to what he's thinking.

"Does it bother you that he was my brother?" he finally asks.

I grab another beer. He polishes his off, so I hand him his last one and I take mine. "Honestly?" He nods. "I don't think about it. You're not him, you've never been him in my mind. If I'd known you then, that might be different, but..." I take a sip. "I didn't. From the moment I saw you in LA, coming toward me, I was attracted to you. Once I knew who you were, it didn't change anything. I promised you that I wouldn't think of you as him and I've kept that promise, because you're not him. You are Kyle. You will always be Kyle and never be anyone else. I don't like to make comparisons, but you're a hundred and eighty degrees the opposite of Dan. If you did things the same way he did, it would be a problem, but you don't. Dan never complimented me, never got hard at my clothing choices, never showered with me, never took care of me the way you do. Dan was just there, a convenience. I know that now. If I knew then..." I don't need to finish the sentence. I finish off the last beer and my head is fuzzy from the alcohol. Only because we've drank so much so fast.

Kyle slides a little closer to me, wrapping his arm around my back, and I lay my head on his shoulder. He kisses me right between the ears of my panda hoodie. He doesn't say anything, he just holds me close. Letting me feel his warmth and his need to be close to me.

I've never imagined Kyle as Dan. I don't want to. My memory is tainted after so many years, but when you compare even the littlest of things that Kyle does, he is nothing like his brother. Though they share the same eyes and maybe even nose, that's as far as the similarities go. "I can't and won't compare you to Dan, there's no reason to. After all these years, I no longer love Dan the way I thought I once did. I also realize that I was being a prude and selfish by keeping to myself all these years. I was holding on to something I never really had in the first place. And if I'd let it all go sooner, I wouldn't be such a basket case now," I say aloud and his hand strokes along my back.

"You're not a basket case. Believe me, I understand. I spent a lot of time blaming and hating myself. Therapy helped me with that. Helped me to see that Dan's death was far from my fault. That my father's murder was something that no one could have been prepared for, and more than anything, I learned to let it all go. To accept it because I couldn't change it." He takes a deep breath. "I struggle so much with my mother because she is alive and breathing, it's something I can change, or at least I think I can." His hand strokes gently along my back, around the side and settling on my hip.

"I wish I could tell you how to fix things with your mom."

"No, it's okay. She's been through a lot," he states as he finishes off his beer.

"I think that she acts the way she does to protect herself." I finish off my beer and sit up.

"What do you mean?" he says with scrutinizing eyes.

"I mean that for her, mentally, pushing you away is easier for her to handle." I set my beer down and turn toward him. "Think about it, she's lost her husband and her oldest son. Pushing you away is easy to do because when you're gone, she won't feel the pain of loss again."

He leans forward, putting his elbows to his knees. "I never thought about it like that before."

I give him a small smile. "No, I didn't either until just now. It's kind of the same way I pushed everyone out after Dan died. I didn't want to be hurt again, I still don't. It was easier for me to push people away, ignore them and be on my own than it was to risk the idea of finding someone, befriending someone, only to lose them again. Your mother is doing the same thing by pushing you away, disconnecting herself so that when she gets the call that you're dead, she doesn't have to deal with the emotional fallout. Only it will actually be worse for her." I finish my beer.

"Why worse?"

My head is spinning with alcohol. "Because she will start to feel guilty over the lost years. It's inevitable. It will come back to bite her in the ass if you go before she does. Though I pray to God that doesn't happen." I shiver at the idea of losing Kyle, or Talon for that matter. It would shatter me into thousands of pieces that I would never bring back together again.

I survived Dan, but I will not survive losing these two.

chapter 27

Kyle and I didn't say much after that. The conversation between the two of us allowed Kyle's raw emotion to show, maybe even some of my own and I wonder idly if his holding back expressing his true feelings has anything to do with Dan. Did he just need to know what Dan and I were? That I'm not reliving my relationship with Dan through Kyle? In fact, it's the exact opposite. I've never felt freer than I do when I'm with these two.

Talon joins us and Kyle magically produces another twelve pack. I drink a seventh beer, but leave the two of them to polish off the rest. Me and beer are not always best friends and my head is fuzzy from the alcohol.

The conversation between the three of us flows effortlessly, from everything that's happening tomorrow, to Talon and Kyle telling stories about their college days. It's great to listen to them talk and tell their tales of women and bars. You'd think it would have made me jealous, but instead I found it intriguing to say the least.

We continue bantering back and forth for some time until my eyelids grow heavy and we all climb back onto the bus. Talon and Kyle waste no time in making love to me again before we all settle in to sleep.

I found out before tonight's show that the band opening for them tonight isn't staying with us for the next leg of the tour. Something happened that they can't continue on, so we are picking up another band in Dallas.

I didn't bother to learn their name because to be honest, I'm glad they're not moving on with us. Their performance was rather bland and they didn't do a very good job of working up the crowd. The crowd, through no help of the opening act, were pretty worked up for 69 Bottles. I didn't get the 'Addison' chant, but as soon as the guys started playing 'Your Eyes', the crowd went crazy.

Right after the Galveston show, we were right back on the bus because we have a show in Dallas tomorrow night, or tonight, I guess it depends on what time it is. Right now, who knows. The guys decided that we'd all go out after the show tonight and bring the new band with us to kick off the rest of the tour. Kyle put the guys under strict instructions that they are to be back on board by two thirty so we can leave by three because they all decided they wanted to head to New Orleans early. I mean, come on, it's New Orleans.

The time in New Orleans is a mini vacation for the guys. Giving them a chance to take a break from the tour.

When I fell asleep, I had both the guys' hands on my stomach. When I woke, it was the same.

Now I'm sitting in the galley of the bus with my laptop on the table working through another plethora of emails regarding news alerts under my name. More videos posted. A release from the label announcing the radio release of our duet next week and the purchasable release coming in early to late May.

Then an article catches my eye. I open it.

69 Bottles Addison Beltrand, ex-fiance of road manager's deceased brother....

I can't even bring myself to read the article. I don't want to see what they have to say, but my heart sinks for Kyle if his mother sees this. I put my head in my hands. I knew this was going to come up, but I didn't want to broach it with Kyle, but now it seems as though I'm going to have to. I decide I have no choice but to read the article.

Addison Beltrand, of Kansas City, Kansas is the mystery woman who's been tearing up YouTube with her performances with 69 Bottles lead singer Talon Carver. She has spent the last eight years working for Bold International, Inc. out of Los Angeles, where she's been a valuable public relations rep, earning her a coveted job of handling PR for the nation's hottest band. But she has more than a few skeletons in her closet.

She's the ex-fiance of 69 Bottles' road manager Kyle Black's deceased brother Daniel, who was killed in a car accident a little over seven years ago, just two weeks before their wedding was scheduled. So is Kyle the reason she's criss-crossing the country? Or did she land the job on her own?

The rumor mills are flying around that Addison and road manager Kyle are an item, but then there are other rumors that Addison and lead singer Talon are together. If you've seen the videos I'm sure you'd agree that Talon and Addison are the item of the moment. Maybe even the couple of the year. Guess only time will tell.

Our requests through Vicious and Bold have gone unanswered for comment.

Now the million dollar question. Do we comment back?

"What's the matter, panda?"

I look up to see Kyle leaning against the wall of the bathroom. "They've made a connection."

He scowls. "About what?"

"Me and Daniel, you and Daniel being brothers, the rumors spreading about me and you and me and Talon. Just the usual."

"Does it bother you that they've made the connection?"

I shake my head. "No, the first thing that came to mind was you, and your mom, and how she'd react to seeing this article."

"Oh baby girl, I don't care. I learned a lot with the last run in I had with her. I think it is best if I just don't care what she thinks. There is nothing I can do to fix it, I can't make it better, I can't make it right, so I'm just going to leave it alone. So regardless of what she thinks, I don't care."

"I don't know whether I should feel bad or be happy for you for that decision."

He smiles. "I'll let you know. So what are you going to do?"

"That's the million dollar question. We can argue it, put out a press release countering what they're saying. Which there isn't much to counter, other than to come out with our relationship; my relationship to one or both of you. They're already assuming, based on the videos going viral, that Talon and I are together. We can just let it roll with that. They're attacking my character more than anything. Assuming that my relationship with you is a product of me being engaged to your brother when he died and that I capitalized on that to get my job." I take a deep breath. "We could have Bold release a statement about why they chose me for the job. Or we can drop it. Right now, it's one paper. Tomorrow it could be fifty. Dan is the only skeleton in my closet, which isn't much of a skeleton, it's just a past."

He uncrosses then recrosses his arms. "I don't think we need to announce it as a three-way relationship. If we announce it, let's do it with Talon, maybe that would pull the pressure off of the Dan story, and our past ties, though truly non-existent. Then, with any luck, they won't attack my mother for more information."

"Is that honestly what you're worried about?"

"I don't want the press harassing her about Dan or our relationship, one that she doesn't know anything about, but Dan is a major trigger for her and god knows what she'd say. The can of worms she could open up scares the hell out of me."

"So what do we do?"

I hear him sigh. "You walk the red carpet with Talon's arms around you. Then you follow it up the next day with a full press release, confirming your relationship."

"We don't have any red carpet events until Chicago."

"Anonymous tip? In New Orleans. Have one of the bodyguards call in a tip about where you and Talon are at. Let them capture you being with Talon."

"What about you?" I plead with sadness.

"Oh, I know where my place is, and I know where I stand with you and Talon. I don't need the press to prove that to me. I know at the end of the night where I will be, where you will be, where he will be. We will all be together. Baby girl, it doesn't matter to me what people think about the three of us, who they think you're with, or what they think they know. I know the truth and that is more than enough for me." He smiles sweetly at me. "I mean it, Addison. I don't need the press involved for me to know that I have you, that I have Talon."

"You know I don't want that either, I don't need that. I'll do it to make things a little easier for your mom, to make things easier for you. I will always do anything to make things easier for everyone, that's who I am," I tell him.

"You've spent your life doing things for everyone else. You don't need to do it for me, or Talon, or even my mother. I just suggest it because you can never tell what kind of mood she's in. She could stand in front of those cameras and tell them all that you're responsible for Dan's death. Or that Dan never loved you, that the wedding was a hoax. Those are the number of things I've heard over the years, Addison, there's no reason to air her guilt."

"So I'll do what I can to protect her and in doing so, I protect me."

"That's my girl," he says with a smile.

chapter 28

"Come on, angel. We have to go."

"I'm comin'," I holler back. I spent the last couple of hours conversing with Cami, filling her in on our plan. She said it was a bit extreme, but that it should thwart the press from searching for more down the road. I had them push back the sound check so that I could finish up the press release for the day after our little escapade in New Orleans and I spoke with Mills about picking one of his guys to make the anonymous tip. He of course had a near panic attack because doing that could draw out a massive crowd, increasing the risks.

I gained so much respect for him in that moment that I promised to not do it again. He laughed and said the hardest part is going to be convincing one of the guys to call in the tip. I told him if it was too hard for them, we could use one of the roadies to do it. They'll do just about anything without asking questions.

"Come on, baby girl. We gotta run sound. We're down to less than two hours," Kyle shouts back as I do my tuck and fluff. I'm wearing my corset, the black skinny jeans that came with my super sexy blue top, and my purple Louboutins. My ribs are still sore, but doing better. I can tolerate the breathing because I could get it on. It's super soft on the inside, doesn't breathe well, but it also doesn't move around a whole lot either.

I take a deep breath, checking my make-up one last time and I go toward the front of the bus. I'm dressed early because we're meeting the new band and I won't have much time when we're done to get ready.

I come around the last little corner to see my guys standing there, side by side between me and the door, very impatiently. "You didn't have to wait," I say.

"Oh yes, we did. There is nothing better, well except for undressing you, than watching you walk around that corner when we know you're dressed and ready to go." Kyle grins.

"God, Addie, you look fucking amazing." Talon gives me his lustful look.

"I look forward to peeling that off of you later." Kyle looks to Talon and smirks. The look they exchange has me wanting to return to the bedroom with them.

"Alright, let's go you two," I say shooing them toward the door.

"Yes madam," Kyle teases.

As soon as we step off of the bus Talon turns to Rusty. "She's your responsibility." He nods and smiles.

"Yes, sir."

I roll my eyes. "I'm a grown woman, I can handle myself."

"We know," Kyle and Talon both say together.

I laugh and drop the subject as we walk into the venue. I can hear the guys on stage warming up, doing what they do best. We turn a couple of corners and then walk toward the stage. The set up here is interesting, but it works, and Dallas is one of our largest venues with seats for more than forty-thousand people. The venue was changed after the initial ticket sales sold out so fast. The event coordinator was able to get a different venue to sell more tickets. For as fast as the tickets sold out, 69 Bottles is playing some pretty small venues and I'd imagine for the next tour, there will be less stops, more shows and much larger venues.

We come up to the stage and walk on. The sound guy goes about setting me up with my mic and we go about our sound check.

Forty minutes later and we're done. We had a couple problems with the feedback, both Talon and I were having trouble hearing it, but we got it fixed and were able to wrap up. When we step off of the stage there is a group of five guys milling about. I'm guessing this is the band.

Introductions are made and the guys shoot their shit. One of the guys, the drummer, like Dex, is a dick. But there is something about him that I really don't like. He actually makes me uncomfortable and for the first time, I wish that Talon or Kyle was doting on me, helping push Mr. Creepy away from me.

I excuse myself and am thankful when Rusty follows me. I don't go to the bus, though that's where I want to go, instead I duck into Talon's dressing room. Rusty takes a look at the room and then lets me inside. He takes up guard outside my door and I take a seat on the couch. I try and shake off my nerves surrounding the guy from the other band. I didn't even catch his name, he just...I rub at my arms and the phantom creepy crawlies. I take a few deep breaths and calm myself down.

After about fifteen minutes, I'm joined by Talon and Kyle. "Baby girl, what's wrong?"

"Just nervous."

"About tonight?" I look up at Talon and nod. "Aw, angel. You'll do great."

"It's just a lot of people."

Talon smiles and comes to sit next to me. "When you're on stage do you honestly think about the crowd?"

I laugh, "No, I can hear them, but I usually can't see them."

"See, so why does it matter how many people are in attendance?"

I laugh. "I know, I'll be alright, just my usual pre-performance freak out."

Both the guys laugh and they change the subject. They start talking about the opening band and I don't pay much attention to them as I try desperately to remove my creepy feeling. By the time it's time to go on stage, I feel better. And I remind myself that I rarely saw Empty Chamber, I doubt I'll see these guys either.

While I am standing stage side waiting for the bands to switch out their gear and Kyle is off doing what he does right before the show, the band, Euphoric, comes off the stage and creepy drummer guy looks me up and down. His eyes are hungry and he licks his lips. I shiver and he smiles wide. Fuck!

Thankfully the guys start coming out. They throw out high fives and my guys come up to me. Dex, followed by Mouse and Peacock. Then Kyle wraps his arms around me and Talon cups my cheeks, kissing me. Right before I close my eyes, I catch creepy boy watching me. I try to block him out by closing my eyes, savoring Talon's warm lips on mine. It works and I'm distracted.

Talon proceeds with his new ritual of cupping Kyle's cheek and I pray to god creepy isn't watching, nothing like giving him ammunition for whatever he's after. "Go kick some ass," I tell Talon and he smiles. The smile melts my heart and he steps on stage. "How you doin' Dallas?"

And just like that the concert is off and running. I look down the hall and there isn't anyone there. I let out a sigh of relief. "You're really nervous tonight, aren't you?"

I nod because it's easier than lying. I decide to let Kyle and Talon in on our little issue later tonight. I take a sweeping look around and see Rusty only a few feet away and I'm comforted further.

The rest of the concert goes off without a hitch and just like Talon said, I completely forget the crowd and focus on Talon during our song. By the time we hit the greenroom, all thoughts of Mister Creepy are gone. Like Albuquerque and Galveston, once the VIPs are done with the band, I become their next focal point, again with pictures, autographs and conversation.

Once we're done we all pile into the cars headed for the bar. I'm excited and in desperate need of a drink. When we pull up, Talon turns to me. "Walk in with me. Help set up New Orleans." I look out and the reporters are in full swing out front. Apparently Euphoric is a news junkie.

"Sure." I turn to Kyle.

He smiles. "Knock 'em dead, panda girl." I lean over and kiss him.

"See you inside." He smiles again and the door opens. Talon elegantly climbs out of the car and he holds his hand out for me. I take it and slide from the car. As I stand up he wraps his arm around my back, holding me to his side. The flashes go crazy, igniting to a fever pitch when he kisses me.

Pulling back from me he says, "Let them run that headline."

I laugh at him and he tugs me toward the door. When we reach it Mills is standing there with a goofy grin on his face. As we pass he says, "About time you admit it." He laughs and we duck inside.

A couple of drinks into the evening I start to feel really woozy. It doesn't make any sense. I can drink a lot more than this and feel hardly anything. Talon is engaged in conversation with his guys. Kyle is talking to some chick and I can tell he's turning her down and she's pleading with him. She gives him the fake goofy laugh and I see him actually roll his eyes at her. I want to laugh, but I'm really not feeling good.

I stand up. Talon turns to me. "Where are you going?"

"Bathroom," I tell him and he looks at me a little strange, but doesn't comment. He smiles and goes back to talking to the guys. I know Rusty will follow me so I take comfort in that.

I head toward the back of the bar and the bathroom. Rusty sweeps the room and I stumble in after him. It's empty which is surprising with the crowd. I stumble toward the handicap stall. I feel a hand come around, covering my mouth, and another arm around my waist. "I knew you'd stumble in here. Now it's time to take what you've been flaunting all night." My eyes widen in fear. It's him, creepy drummer, but I am physically too weak to fight. I can't seem to make my limbs work, can't put my years of self-defense training to work. I'm at his mercy. He slams me against the wall, banging my head against the tile. The pain radiates through my body and I go completely limp. My mind turns zombie. I can see, but I can't comprehend what's happening to me, I've blacked out. I feel my corset being ripped apart.

All I can do is think, no, no, no, no....

chapter 29
talon

How long has she been gone? I look around and Rusty is missing, which means he followed her to the bathroom. I look over at Kyle and mouth, "Addison?"

He shrugs, then stands, pushing the chick off of him once and for all. He's rejected her more than a few times but she doesn't get the hint. "Mills," I hear him shout and in a moment Mills is there. "Get her off of me and we need to find Addison."

Mills escorts the lady away and talks into his hand piece. Then comes back. "She's in the restroom, Rusty is outside."

"She's been in there too long," I mumble mainly to myself. Something's wrong, she didn't look right when she left. She looked drunk and I know she hasn't drank that... I take off for the restroom and I can feel Kyle along with a couple of the security guys on my heels.

When I reach the bathroom door Rusty steps out of the way as I plow into the door. Fuck! "It's fucking locked." I slam my shoulder into it again and it won't budge. I slam my hand against the door. "Addison!" I scream. "Addison!" Something is wrong- she's hurt, she's fuck, something is really god damn wrong.

I slam my shoulder into the door one more time and it finally breaks the jam and I fall inside.

I see feet sticking out, Addison's feet. I push open the door and look down at her sprawled out on the floor of the handicap stall. I fall down beside her. There's blood on her face and hair, her corset is ripped open, her jeans shredded and pulled down to her..."NO! God, no, no, no! Addison." She moves her head and I let out a rushed breath. I pick her up, cradling her in my arms. I tap her cheek, trying to bring her around to me. "Addison, come on baby, come back to me. Come on, angel."

She moans and her head rolls from side to side.

"Call nine one one," I hear Kyle say to someone. "She's alive, but she's hurt."

"Addison, baby, who did this? Come on baby, stay with me."

"Dr..." I lean down closer to her mouth.."Dr...umme...r."

"Dex?"

Her head lolls back and forth in a lazy drugged motion, "Eufff..."

I look up into the petrified eyes of Kyle, behind him is Mills. "Find that son of a bitch."

"Who?"

"Eddie, their fucking drummer!" I shout.

After what feels like an eternity, the paramedics finally arrive, assessing her in the bathroom and then finally carrying her out on a stretcher. When they load her into their bus, Kyle and I try to climb in with her, but the paramedic stops us. "You can't ride."

"Fuck that, I'm going with her. She's my girlfriend."

"I'm sorry, sir. We can't let you in here." He pushes me back and then closes the door on me. One of our cars pulls up right behind us and the ambulance.

Beck is in with the driver, "We'll follow, get in." Kyle and I jump into the back of the car. Once we have a general idea where we might be going from our driver, Beck relays the information to Mills.

The cops had arrived at the same time as the paramedics. I refused to talk to them so Mills is dealing with it. Beck and Mills went in search of Euphoric, and magically the entire band disappeared from the bar after Eddie's stunt. Mills was directing cops back to where their tour bus is located. Hopefully if the cops get there fast enough the bus will still be there.

The drive behind the ambulance seems to take forever. Beck is in the front seat and Kyle and I sit in silence holding each other's hands, seeking comfort from one another.

"How the fuck did we not see this, how did this happen?" I spout off at random.

"Thinking about it now, she was so fucking nervous, but it wasn't until we were talking with the band before the show and she disappeared. Something freaked her out and then doing our pre-show kiss, she tensed up, but I didn't know why, she didn't tell me. When I asked about being nervous, she just nodded."

"Did she know him?"

He shrugs. "I don't know. But I got a creepy vibe from him too."

"She didn't look right when she went into the bathroom. I'd just assumed the adrenaline was wearing her down or she'd drank more than I thought, but she's drank so much more and been fine."

"Fuck!"

Beck turns around. "She was probably drugged."

"How the fuck did that happen?" I snap at Beck.

"Mills is looking into it. I swear to God, Talon, we will find out everything we can about what happened. She's like a fucking sister to me, dude. Do you honestly think any one of us would ever let anything happen to her?"

"Too late for that."

"Rusty says he checked the bathroom, looked in the closet and everything before she went in. There's a false back to the closet that leads straight into the men's room. Which we didn't know at the time, but no one was in there. He's one of our best men and I know he is kicking his own ass for what happened. He didn't fuck up, Talon."

I run my hand through my hair. "Fuck, I fucking know that. It's just, fuck, fuck fuck!"

Three hours and a shit ton of fucking coffee later, we've been joined by Dex, Mouse and Peacock, plus all the guards are standing watch over us. The news on the TV in the waiting room keeps replaying the scene of me and Kyle trying to get into the ambulance. "We need to get Cami on the phone," I say to Kyle, who's been on the phone since we arrived. He holds his finger up to me to wait a minute.

"Alright, thanks." He hangs up.

"Who was that?"

"The cops. The bus was gone when they got back to the stadium. They're looking for it on most of the routes on the way to New Orleans. Mills provided them with names and information. Assuming they show up in New Orleans, they can deal with them then."

"Would they seriously move on to the next show like nothing happened?"

Kyle shrugs, "Maybe, if they either don't know what happened, who did it, or even if anything happened. It's too fucking convenient for them to have disappeared already."

"God damn it. We've got to talk to Cami."

"Already done. The story should be shifting shortly." He looks up at the TV and sure enough, the Bold logo is on the TV behind a podium. Kyle and I watch as Cami comes to stand behind it and the reporters go nuts with questions. Cami gestures with her hands for them to calm down.

"I promise to answer questions when I'm done with my statement. Earlier this morning, around twelve fifteen central time, Addison Beltrand was attacked in the bathroom of a local Dallas bar following the 69 Bottles concert and is currently undergoing treatment at a local Dallas hospital. I am in close contact with the doctors as well as members of 69 Bottles in regards to her condition. At this time she is stable. We will continue to update you with more information as it becomes available.

"I am deeply sorry that this has happened to Addison and we are working with the police as best we can from here and I know the band, as well as their security detail are cooperating as well. Now, I will take a few questions."

Hands go up in front of the cameras.

"Go ahead," Cami says with a point.

"If the security detail is so cooperative now, what happened during the attack?"

Cami gives one of those 'I really hate you for asking that question' looks. "It is believed that Addison was escorted to the ladies room by a member of the staff, who then checked the bathroom before letting her inside. No one went in or out of the room during the time that she was in there. It wasn't until they found her that they discovered a false door in the back of a closet inside of the restroom. The closet led to the neighboring men's room with a door around the corner from the security guard. We're also under suspicion that Addison may have been drugged prior to the attack." She pauses, takes a sip of water, looks ridiculously sad and points to another reporter.

I zone out from the TV, not wanting to hear anymore. Cami is very good at what she does so I leave her to it. I just need Addison back in my arms, I need to see her. I stand up and start pacing. "How much longer is this gonna take?" I say aloud, but not really expecting anyone to answer the question.

We've been sitting here for some time with very little in the way of updates on her condition and it's driving me insane. They won't let any of us back there and after the way they treated us when we arrived, I'm surprised they're letting us sit here at all.

I close my eyes and all I can see is her on that bathroom floor, spread eagled, naked, and bleeding. So help me god if he fucking raped her, I will rip his balls off myself.

I turn to Kyle. "Get me the fucking label, now," I snap.

chapter 30

talon

"Talon? What's going on?"

"Who the fuck put us with Euphoric?" I snap at Seth.

"What, why?"

"You haven't seen the fucking news?"

"Calm down, Talon. No, I haven't seen the news, what's going on?" Seth says in a very calming voice.

"Their drummer attacked and possibly raped Addison tonight."

"Fuck!" The normally calming force of Seth is completely gone. "Where?"

I give him the details of what happened, "Fuck, Talon, I'm sorry. We had no idea."

"Judging from the way this bastard acted, this isn't his first rodeo. You might want to look into other incidents where they're involved. But as far as the fucking tour is concerned, they're done."

"You can't..."

"Like hell I can't do that, Seth. I will and I did. Either they go, or we go. You pick your fucking battle. They're going to be without a drummer when the cops catch up to them."

"How do you know…"

"Don't even fucking start with me on that. I know because she fucking knows. She was there, she saw him. She fucking knows who attacked her. That dipshit isn't exactly unremarkable, he fucking gave us all the creeps before this happened."

"Alright, we'll make some arrangements."

"Do not tell them until after the investigation is complete and that asshole is arrested. So help me god, Seth, if you fucking ruin our chances of catching this guy…"

"Relax, we'll work on it here on our end, set up someone else to play in their place for New Orleans and then go with it from there. Keep me posted on what's happening there."

"Be prepared, we might not make New Orleans. I won't leave her here."

"One step at a time, Talon."

"Yeah, okay."

Seth and I hang up. I start pacing again, relaying my conversation to the guys.

"I'm a fucking dick, but that asshole puts me to shame. I'd never, not in a million fucking years do what he did," Dex says. He's pretty upset about what happened.

"I know, man," I tell him.

"I can't believe they'd be cocky enough to show up in New Orleans," Peacock says.

"Here's the thing, I don't think this is the first time he's done something like this. I'd imagine that he's gotten away with it before, so he assumes he'll get away with it again.

Only he chose Addison verses some random groupie chick," Kyle says. He has a fucking point.

"If the band doesn't know, they will move on to New Orleans. It's just a matter of when they show up."

About an hour later Mills is on the phone, but no one can make out what he's talking about or who he's even talking to. At one point his eyes meet mine. "Okay, thanks."

"Well?"

"Three things. One, they're looking into Eddie's past. They've found several incidents in different states where he's been wanted for questioning for assault. In most cases, based on his alibis with the band, they've let him walk."

"Fuck!"

"Second thing, there is a witness at the bar, though they weren't in the bathroom at the time of the attack, they saw Eddie go into the bathroom, then emerge some time later. When he came out, he had a series of scratches on his neck. With the situation being as it was, at the time, they didn't think anything of it. But now, they're questioning this witness and the time frame fits with ours."

"Okay, that's," I swallow hard, "that's good. And what about the third thing?"

"They've pulled over the bus."

"Thank fuck!" I shout and Kyle is there next to me, he wraps his arms around me. I hug him back like my life depends on it. One asshat drummer about to be arrested, and now all we need is Addison to come back to us.

"The cops are going to need a full statement from her when she's well enough to talk to them."

Jesus, how many times is she going to have to relive this nightmare? I don't even want to know the answer to that question. Regardless, I wont let her relive it by herself, if anything, she needs us more now then ever before. But right now my hope is that this douche is pansy ass enough to confesses to what he's done, leaving Addison out of it.

"Let's get hotel rooms set up," Kyle says to Mills. "We need to stay here until she can leave, either the hospital or the state."

Mills gives him a small smile. "It's already taken care of. We're ready to take those who want to go now. Those who want to stay, of course can stay here."

"You guys go, get some sleep," I tell Peacock, Mouse and Dex.

"Hell no! We stay 'til we know she's okay or she leaves. She's a part of us and we never leave one of our own behind," Dex declares. Mouse and Peacock agree. I, on the other hand, go back to pacing.

Finally, after another two hours, it's sometime in the morning now, a doctor comes into the room. We all shuffle quickly to stand near her, probably scaring the hell out of her. We're not small men. "Who's Talon?"

"That'd be me." I step forward.

"She's asking for you, and Kyle?"

"That's me," Kyle says.

"Follow me."

Kyle and I look around the room, everyone nods and we follow after the doctor. "She's going to be fine," the doctor says once we're some distance away. "She's got a laceration on her forehead, and a bruised cheek, but other than that, she's alright. We're still waiting for tox results on the drug that was in her system. However, it's effects are fading fast but when I try to ask her about what happened, she says she can't remember. I'm assuming you guys know more than I do." The doctor looks from Kyle to me.

"We just know that she was attacked, we know who, and the police, I'm assuming, have arrested him by now," Kyle says. I'm too freaked out to talk, barely able to comprehend the conversation. All I heard is that she'll be fine.

"We're working on her discharge papers. Normally we're required to wait for the cops to show up, but we've been informed that it's okay to let her go."

"Our security team is working with the police. They'll be able to find us when they're available to question her. Besides, I don't think any of us would let her be questioned now anyway," Kyle tells the doctor who nods in understanding.

She comes to a halt and we stop with her. "Under the circumstances, she's a pretty brave woman. Take good care of her," the doctor says. "She right behind that curtain." She points to the curtain ahead of us.

Kyle pulls back the curtain, and I get an eye full of her in the hospital bed and my heart breaks. "Hey, big man," she says with a smile. Then she turns to Kyle. "How's my cowboy?"

Both Kyle and I move to sit on either side of her bed and grab for her hands. Neither Kyle nor I say anything. I just bring her hand to my mouth, inhaling deeply, pulling in her beautiful vanilla scent. I kiss the back of her hand. She moves her hand to cup my cheek and I lean into it. Her thumb strokes my cheek as she wipes away a tear. "Don't cry. Please. I'm okay. Honest." I look at her and she smiles. "I have a bump on the head, and a bruised cheek. That's all." She sits up in bed, coming very close to us. "Nothing happened," she breathes. "He pushed me against the wall, then the next thing I remember is that we were here. Nothing happened," she breathes in earnest.

Kyle and I both physically relax at her words. "Thank god," Kyle breathes. "I'm so glad you're okay."

"I'm a little shaken up, my head is still foggy, I am very tired, and I have a small cut on my forehead. All things considered, this could have been much worse. I'm ready to go back to the bus and get out of here."

Kyle and I both let out small laughs.

"We have to stay for a day or two. You need to talk to the police. Tell them anything you can."

"It was him, that drummer."

Both Kyle and I exchange looks. "You remember that?"

"Until he knocked my head into the wall, I was still conscious of mind. My body quit working, making it impossible for me to fight back. After that, I remember waking up here a little while ago. That's all, but it was him. I saw him briefly in the mirror before he shoved me into the bathroom stall."

"That's all you're going to need to tell the cops," Kyle says.

"That's all I can tell them." She shrugs.

About thirty minutes later, Addison has her discharge papers in hand and a pair of pale green scrubs that are a couple of sizes too big for her to change into. Kyle and I leave her to change and I head back down the hall to find the guys while Kyle waits for Addison. When I reach the guys, they all rush at me. I smile. "She's alright. She changing now and we can take her home. She has a cut to the head and a bruised cheek, but that's it." I look at everyone, emphasizing that really is all.

"Thank god," Someone says. "I'm so happy she's alright."

Before I can return to her room, Kyle and Addison join us in the waiting room. Everyone crowds around her, checking to make sure she's okay. I go to stand next to Kyle and wrap my arm around his back; I need a support system right now because I don't quite know how to handle all this. But it makes me certain of one thing. I really am in love with her.

chapter 31
addison

I still feel woozy, but I'm feeling much better. Talking to the guys, both the band and the security guys helps take my mind off of what happened. I look past the group and see Rusty standing off to the side. Why isn't he over here with us? "Excuse me, guys," I say and they all nod.

I squeeze between two of them, I'm not paying attention to who, and walk toward Rusty. I can see him visibly tense as I draw closer to him. "Please, relax," I tell him.

"I failed you," he says so sad that my heart breaks.

"You didn't fail me, Rusty. This is not your fault. You did everything right, you did nothing wrong, he just knew how to get around you. Please do not beat yourself up for this." I put my hand on his bicep. "I'm okay. It's a small cut and a bruise. Nothing else." His eyes widen in shock. "He didn't rape me, something stopped him, I'm assuming it was you or one of the guys, so in a way you saved me. So please, be happy that I'm okay and know that I will be far more careful in the future."

"I'm never leaving your side," he says, sadness is still in his eyes.

I smile. "I would expect nothing less. Come here," I say, wrapping my arms around his waist, giving him a hug. "All is forgiven."

"You're too kind."

"No, I speak the truth. Now let's get out of here."

He nods and we walk back toward the group, to a group of men with smiles on their faces as Rusty joins the party. Kyle and Talon come over to me. Talon leans down to my ear and whispers, "Everything okay?"

"Everything's great," I whisper back, releasing Rusty and wrapping my arms around the necks of my two men. "Now, take me home."

"Yes ma'am," Talon teases. "Let's go, guys."

We all head toward the entrance of the hospital. Me, Talon and Kyle are in the middle of one big circle. Protected.

We pull up in front of a hotel and I turn to Kyle in confusion. "Why are we here?" I ask him.

"Because the police still need to interview you. Once that's done, we'll get back on the road."

I pout. "I want to go to New Orleans."

I hear Talon laugh. "Angel, we will get to New Orleans in good time. For now, it's all about sleeping. You need to rest."

"I can do that on the bus."

"I know, angel, but please, humor us. You've been through so much. Let's just get you upstairs into a hot bath and a warm bed."

"Okay, but I just want to put it behind me, move on."

"Baby girl, we want that for you too, but right now I honestly think you're in shock."

"No, Kyle, I'm not. I'm not trying to brush it off, but the only thing that truly happened is that I got knocked in the head. I don't remember anything else, thank god, and it's just, I don't know, I don't know how to explain it but I just feel like I got into a fight with someone. Wouldn't be the first time and I doubt it will be the last. The only problem I am having with this whole situation is that I was completely helpless."

"What do you mean, angel?"

I sit down on the bed in my bathrobe. "I mean that whatever he gave me was like a paralytic. I was conscious of mind, slow, and sluggish yes, but I could comprehend who and where I was. But I had no strength, no ability to fight back against him. I'd tell my limbs to move and they'd do no such thing. That is the only part about this whole thing that bothers me."

"But he saw you naked," Talon says and I know he's having a really hard time handling this.

I look at him. "Being naked doesn't bother me, Talon. It's never been an issue for me. I've been to enough nightclubs and private celebrity parties where I've had my boobs grabbed more than a few times. Sweetheart, trust me. I'm going to be okay."

He comes to kneel in front of me, wrapping his arms around my waist, resting his head in my lap up against my belly. "I will never forgive myself if anything like this ever happens again."

I stroke my fingers through his hair to comfort him. The irony of the girl who was attacked comforting her boyfriend is not lost on me. Kyle comes to sit behind me, bringing his legs to my sides so that my back is pressed up against him. Though I know he doesn't intend for me to feel it, I can feel his erection against my backside.

His arms wrap around me, coming to rest on Talon's shoulders, his thumbs rubbing and comforting Talon. He's going to blame himself for this for a very long time.

"You mean so fucking much to me. I don't know what I would do without you," Talon says, his arms coming tighter around my waist. I start to cry. His pain is hard to bear and I slump back against Kyle.

"I got you," he whispers. "We got you. We will never let you go."

And like the floodgates being lifted, everything that happened comes washing over me, drowning me in a sea of tears, sadness, heartache and love. I love these two men and their pain is breaking my heart. Kyle rests his head on my shoulder, holding me and Talon tighter to him and I feel a warm wet tear escape his eye, hitting my collar bone and sliding down. I watch it as it falls between my breasts and down my body.

Every raw emotion I could possibly feel consumes me and I cry until my eyes dry out and I fall into a deep sleep cradled in their arms.

chapter 32

By noon, I was cleared by the cops. I was still exhausted but glad it was over. Apparently Eddie confessed to the assault, but given the circumstances, an attempted rape charge wouldn't stand up. So, he pled to a deal with the prosecutor. By late Sunday we were in New Orleans. I'd only slept in short sprints between talking to the detective and getting settled back on the bus, so when we got to NOLA, I ended up crashing in our hotel room for the night.

Talon and Kyle never left my side the entire time, which I was thankful for. Talon is still beating himself up over the fact that he knew something was off when I went to the bathroom. I told him that I honestly just felt sick, like I was going to throw up, and that I had no idea that I'd been drugged. Despite my best efforts, he still worries.

We spent all day Monday in bed watching TV, ordering room service and being lazy pigs eating everything in sight. By the end of Monday, things were starting to get back to normal. My headache finally went away and the bruise on my cheek was already starting to turn yellow and green.

We spent Tuesday walking around the French Quarter with Dex, Peacock and Mouse. The security detail was always in close proximity. I didn't drink any alcohol, which being in New Orleans is kind of a must, but most of my beverages came in sealed plastic bottles. Again, it was over the top, but I wasn't going to argue. I was feeling better come Wednesday but Talon asked me to not perform. When I asked him why, he said that he didn't want to put the extra pressure on me right now. Then he touched my cheek with soft fingers. I kissed his palm and agreed to stay backstage.

To avoid the issue while he was on stage, the band cut 'Your Eyes' from their set list. After the concert, Talon invited a couple of reporters into the greenroom before the VIPs were allowed in. He stood next to me and Kyle as we answered questions about how I was doing and when I would be back on stage. Talon said possibly Oklahoma City but at the latest definitely Kansas City.

When we weren't wandering the Quarter, or watching bad TV, Talon and I rehearsed the crap out of 'To Be Free'. I couldn't deny him anything with the light in his eyes anytime he brought it up.

When we got to Oklahoma City I wasn't feeling very good. I don't know if it was nerves or something else entirely, but Talon didn't let me back on stage. Told me to save it for Kansas and my mom. I couldn't argue with that.

Though our relationship as a threesome has blossomed dramatically since Dallas, those three little words haven't been exchanged and I'm starting to understand why. They don't hold a candle to the depth of emotion I feel when it comes to my big man and my cowboy. 'I love you' is trivial in comparison.

Cami has been hard at work, earning her paycheck in dealing with the press surrounding my attack which only seems to be growing. The fact that the rape charges didn't stick against Eddie had my panties in a bunch, but compliments of my new celebrity status, Eddie's picture was featured in just about every news outlet out there and over the course of the last week, several girls have come forward pointing fingers at Eddie as their attacker and rapist. It's a fair trade if you ask me.

As far as I'm concerned, emotionally, I'm fine. It honestly feels like a bad dream that disappeared the moment I woke up and I think the boys are finally starting to understand that and I'm more than thankful for it.

Kyle is doing amazing. Oklahoma City was hard for him because he knew his mom was so close. Kyle fought with himself most of the day about going and seeing his mother. Once it got to the point that he really didn't have time because the show was about to start, it was like a light switch flipped and he was perfectly fine. Without meaning to, mine and Talon's red carpet appearance at that bar, combined with the attack pushed all the Dan, Kyle and me triangle bullshit aside.

Now we are arriving in Kansas City and I get to see my mom in just a little while. I called her as soon as I could on Sunday, filling her in on all the details of what happened. She was freaked out of course, but she understood and didn't press when I told her I was honestly fine.

We arrive in KC around seven-thirty in the morning, which is great because I've made plans with my mom. Talon and Kyle were about to blow a gasket because I told them that I wanted to have lunch with her alone. Ironically, it's not the fact that it's my mom, it's because I'm leaving their side. Rusty and Beck, however, are another story. The excuse they used was the fact that I'm a celebrity now too and I need protection. I laughed, but agreed.

So here we are, in the car, Beck and Rusty are upfront, Beck is behind the wheel and we are on our way to meet my mother. We decided to meet at the restaurant, which is fine because it's attached to the mall where we plan to go shopping afterward.

When I arrive, I spot her in the back corner. Her eyes widen when she notices my two companions but the worry fades when she smiles wide. I go walking through the restaurant as quickly as my legs will carry me and she wraps me up in the biggest, warmest, most comforting hug I've had in a long time.

"Oh Addie, I've missed you so much," she says, pulling back to have a look at me. "And purple hair?" She laughs.

I forgot to mention that part. In New Orleans, in a moment of rage over what happened, I decided that it was time to change, so I brought out the purple and went to town.

"Some things never change." I laugh and we sit down.

"So how are you?" she asks. My mom is in her early fifties, very young with short black hair and glasses. I look a lot like her, except I enjoy the longer hair and, knock on wood, don't have the glasses just yet.

We talk all through lunch about everything. About the band, about what's happening with me and my whole new singing career thing and then we get down to the brass tacks of Talon and Kyle. I've talked about them a lot since Dallas because mom and I have been talking nearly every day.

"Honestly mom, they are two of the most gracious, loving, caring, honest guys I've ever met."

"Addison Lynae, are you dating both these guys?"

The question is not something I expected and it throws me for a loop. I sit there dumbstruck for a moment. She just stares at me, but she isn't angry. She's intrigued.

"Yeah mom, I am."

She kind of sits back, looking at me. "Huh, how does that work exactly?"

I smile and without giving away too many details, I fill her in on the three of us. My mom has always been open minded about a lot of things so I'm not surprised when she says, "Well, as long as they take care of my baby girl, then that's all I care about. You always have been high maintenance, no wonder you need two men to take care of you."

"Mom!" I nearly shout. "I am not high maintenance." I catch Beck snicker and I bust out laughing. "Okay okay, maybe I am a little high maintenance."

My mom laughs. "I can't wait to meet them," she says with a smile as we finish up our lunch.

Just as we're about to leave the restaurant, my phone rings. It's a number I don't recognize, so I answer with caution. "Hello?"

"Hello Ms. Beltrand. My name is Analese and I'm calling from Bank of California."

"Hi Analese, what can I do for you?"

"I'm sorry to bother you, but there has been a rather large transaction on your account that we just need to verify with you."

"Okay, I haven't used my account much."

"Oh, this is actually a deposit. We received a transfer in of over one point one million dollars." My legs go weak. "From Bold International, Inc. I see here that you have regular deposits from them, but never of this size."

"Uh, yeah, that's correct."

"Oh, wonderful. Well, then I will just make some notes here, and send you on your way. Thank you so much for taking the time to verify that with us and might I recommend coming by the bank to discuss alternative banking and investing options."

"Uh, sure, but I won't be back in town for about eight weeks. So I will come by then. Thank you, Analese, for your time."

"Oh absolutely, just looking out for our customers. Have a wonderful day, Ms. Beltrand."

"Thanks." I think. I hang up my phone and just sit there. My mom is hovering over me and I can see Beck and Rusty much closer than they need to be.

"Honey, is everything all right?"

"I...I think so."

"Who was that on the phone?" she asks, still concerned.

"That was my bank back in California. They were calling to confirm some activity on my account."

"Oh dear, is everything okay?"

I look up at her and smile. "Everything is beyond perfect, mom, really."

She looks at me, puzzled. I look to Beck and Rusty then back to my mom. "Mom, I think we should go back to the house."

"What about shopping?"

I smile at her. "We will go shopping another time. I need to discuss the phone call with you privately."

"Well, why don't we just go back to the car? I'm sure these two muscle men can wait outside. I really want to take you shopping."

I smile, "No, mom, it's my turn to take you shopping."

chapter 33

"Wha...?" My mom's stunned expression says it all.

"I got paid today for the two recordings Talon and I did while we were in Phoenix last week."

"And they deposited over one million dollars into your account?" I can tell she's having a hard time comprehending what I've said, which is okay. I'm not entirely certain I understand it either.

"Something like that. It's a ten ninety-nine thing, so I need to get with a tax advisor, figure out what I need to do tax wise, and a ton of other things as far as that money is concerned. I wasn't expecting it so soon." God, I'm rambling. "Look, the point is, I have the money now and once I have everything taken care of we can discuss some things. I'd really like you to consider moving to LA with me."

"Oh, why? I love it here. I have a job, friends."

"I know, mom, just think about it for me, will you?"

"Oh alright. Can we go shopping now?"

I laugh at my mom. "Yes mom, we can go shopping."

It's just before one when we enter Macy's and I call Kyle.

"Hey gorgeous."

"Hi sweetie. Couple things quick…"

"Absolutely, what do you need?" he says back.

"First, can we bump the sound check, or can the guys do it without me at four?"

I can tell he's talking to Talon when the phone drops away from his mouth. "She wants to know if you can run sound without her, or if you can push it back?"

I can hear Talon's reply, "Is she okay?"

"Yes, I'm perfectly fine. In fact I'm better than fine, but my mom and I are going shopping. I don't know if I can make it by four."

Talon comes on the line. "How much time do you need, angel?"

I smile. "Can we push it to five?"

"Of course. But you need to be here, otherwise I wouldn't care. We need to run 'To Be Free' a couple times. So five is the last possible time. We need to be clear by six thirty."

"I can definitely do five. And since you two knuckleheads have me on speaker phone, I miss you both."

"Aw panda girl, we miss you too. So hurry up and come back to us."

"I'll be there soon, and guys?"

"Yes, gorgeous?"

"She knows…" I just let the thought hang there.

"Knows what, baby girl?"

"She knows about the three of us and that we're all together."

"Baby girl, you didn't."

"No, she guessed, and she's perfectly fine. She can't wait to meet both of you, so put your game faces on."

"Oh shit." I hear them both say and I can just picture their shocked faces staring at each other.

"I'm standing in the middle of Macy's and I have plastic burning a hole in my purse. Can I please go shopping now?" I whine and beg.

It's Talon who replies. "Only if you're shopping with my plastic."

"Ha! I got paid today. I have my own, thank you very much." I laugh.

"Got paid?"

"Oh, let's just say I got a call from the bank about thirty minutes ago asking me if I was aware of a one million dollar deposit," I whisper into the phone. "Which of course I wasn't, but..." I shrug despite the fact that they can't see me.

"From where, baby?"

"Bold, it's the payment for the recordings."

"Oh, crap, that was freakin' fast," Talon says, shocked. "The boys will be thrilled, they can get paid too."

I laugh. Then whine, "Can I pretty pretty pretty please go shopping now?"

Talon and Kyle both laugh into the phone. "Have fun, baby girl, be safe. Stay close to Beck and Rusty."

"Aren't they supposed to stay close to me?"

Kyle laughs. "You know what I mean. Happy shopping, love," he tells me

"See you soon, angel."

We hang up. I look at my mom who is already piling up clothes for me to try on. I walk over to her, grabbing the stack. "I think you're the one who needs a new wardrobe, not me. Come on."

I hand the pile of clothes to the clerk and I take mom over to the woman's section.

"Addie, I can't let you spend this kind of money on me," my mom says as we're standing at the register with more than a counter full of clothes.

I put my hands on her arms. "This is nothing. You deserve new clothes and new shoes and anything else you want and for the first time in my life, I can honestly do this for you, so please, let me?"

"Oh all right." She smiles. "Did you say shoes?"

I bust into a fit of giggles, turning to the attendant taking care of my mother's load of clothes, "We're going over to the shoe department. Can you have someone grab me when you're ready for payment?"

"Yes, ma'am," the gal says and my mom and I head off.

While roaming around the shoe department I spot a black suede pair of Louboutins, like the purple ones I had and haven't gotten back from Dallas PD yet. They don't have the purple suede ones in my size, in fact all they have is a size four. Anyway, deciding that it is my turn to spoil myself, I buy them, along with a brand new Michael Kors purse that is black and big enough for my laptop. I also find a new messenger bag that converts into a backpack. I don't know the designer's name, but it sets me back over a hundred bucks. My other one is ratty and ready to be tossed out.

My mom ends up with six pairs of shoes, and combined with my shoes and two bags it all totals nearly three grand. I hand over my debit card, cringing. I've never in my life spent this much money in one transaction, let alone bought thousand dollar shoes. The card processes and I sign it. Thank god I didn't look like an ass with a declined card. I even had to give up my driver's license. I feel a little insulted. I'm not a damn hoodlum. Then Pretty Woman pops into my mind and I look down at my skinny jeans, thick studded leather belt and t-shirt. Pair that with the panda hat Kyle bought me in NOLA. It was so damn cute; he snatched it out of my hands and paid for it. It's got a cute cartoon panda face with big ears. It's knit, like a beanie. My big sunglasses are resting on top of my head. I tried to wear them inside, but it sucked. It was Beck's idea, but after five minutes, I couldn't stand that everything was so dark that I pulled them off. I stuck my tongue out at Beck when he scowled at me.

When you combine the entire ensemble I'm not the type of girl you usually see 'round these parts or expect to spend a ton of money.

Mom's clothes total more than seven thousand dollars. I had Beck and Rusty keep her busy so she didn't panic on me. Then all of sudden three men dressed in livery show up, talking to Beck and Rusty. They do their bodyguard thing and the gentlemen collect the bags from behind the counter and carry them for us.

Who knew that in a small suburb of Kansas City the Macy's would cater to the high class customer? Hmm, something to get used to? I mentally shrug.

We take mom's bags to her car. She insists on taking her stuff home and coming to the venue before the show. I offered to go with her and have the guys follow us and she refused. We hug and say good-bye for now and the guys drive me back to the bus.

When the car pulls up to the bus, my guys jump out and come over to greet me.

"Where's your mom?" Talon asks, looking into the car.

"She'll be here later. Said she wanted to go home, put her haul away and get ready for tonight."

"Well, let's get your bags," Kyle says going toward the trunk.

"Uh, this is it." I lift the two bags in my hand.

"What? You went shopping and that's it?" Talon laughs.

"I went a little overboard on my mom. Got her a whole new wardrobe."

"Well, alrighty then. Come on, panda girl." Kyle wraps his arm around my shoulders and tugs on one of my hat's ears as he leads me toward the door of the bus.

"What did you buy?" Talon asks as we climb up the steps.

"Some stuff for me."

Talon wraps his arm around my shoulders, pulling me in close, and he kisses my forehead before we head to our room. "Good for you, you deserve it. So what did you get?"

I smile and set my bags on the bed. "A pair of shoes, a purse and a messenger bag."

"That's it?" His disappointment is evident.

I laugh. "Yeah, it is."

"You were so excited to go shopping. I thought you'd come back with a semi-truck full," Talon says with a smile as he leans against the wall

"Well, I decided after I got off of the phone with you that my mom deserved it. I make good money at my job, but I've never been able to spoil her. I wasn't broke by any means but between my condo and bills, I can afford the things I want, but not like this. I've never spent this much money at once, other than when I bought my condo." I give a half smile.

"So show us, gorgeous," Kyle says with a bright smile on his face. He sits down toward the foot of the bed.

I pull out the messenger bag first, showing it off. "That means you can get rid of that ratty one?" Talon teases.

I laugh. "Yes, and if it will make you feel better, I'll even let you burn it for me."

Both of them laugh, then I show off my new purse. "That's a suitcase, not a purse."

"Hey now, you know a girl has to carry her entire life with her everywhere she goes. She has to have a bag big enough to carry it all."

Kyle rolls his eyes. "Your logic baffles me, but it's gorgeous. Perfect for you."

I pull out the box. Talon laughs. "Kyle, we've created a monster."

"Actually, I miss my purple ones."

"Oh," They both sober quickly.

"So I bought a replacement pair, only they didn't have purple so..." I flip the lid off the box, "I found matching black ones." There is a satisfied look of relief on their faces. "Am I missing something?" I ask.

"Well, we don't know when, or if your shoes will come back, so we ordered you a new pair."

"Awe, seriously? You guys didn't have to do that."

"Well, to be honest," Kyle says, "we didn't think you'd buy yourself a replacement pair so we took care of it. They should be delivered to Minneapolis."

"Well, thank you. I appreciate that, I love those shoes." I smile.

"We noticed," Kyle says. "I'm glad you bought yourself some stuff. I just wish you'd bought more."

"I will, next time I go shopping, in a bigger city with a better selection."

"Alright, panda girl."

"So did you have a good time, angel?"

I sit down on the bed next to Kyle, looking up at Talon. "I had a great time. I'm sorry it can't last longer."

"Maybe you should take your break here?" Kyle suggests.

"That's not a bad idea, but I have Sam still in my condo and I need to figure out what to do about that between now and then."

"Has she called you?" Talon asks.

"No, and I don't want to call her, at least until the last possible moment. I have security in my building so if something happens in my apartment, I will hear about it."

*chapter*34

"I need to get ready for the show," I tell them.

"We have plenty of time," Talon says as he sits down behind me. His hands come around my midsection and I shiver at his touch. Kyle comes to sit in front of me. His hands cup my cheeks.

"I think," he kisses me, "it's time," he kisses me again, "for an Addison sandwich."

I shiver. "What about the sound check?" I say breathless.

"We already did it," Talon says as he kisses my neck.

"What about our song?" I can't breathe, and if they keep this up, I won't be able to think.

"We know what we're doing." Talon kisses my neck again, this time with a full on open mouth kiss. "Besides, we can make this quick or we can take our time. We set up a rehearsal for you at six. Which is about two hours away." He kisses my neck again. Kyle moves off of my lips and onto my jaw and down the other side of my neck. "Since you're back earlier than you thought you would be, we have time." Talon goes back to kissing my neck while Kyle's hands roam over my chest, his fingers brushing my nipples.

"I, ah, I have to get dressed."

"You're gorgeous, baby girl. You could be ready in five minutes." His hand tugs on my nipples through my shirt.

"No I, ah... oh fuck, getting ready," I say as I grab the back of Kyle's neck, pulling him to me. My tongue slides into his mouth, caressing and tasting. Talon's hands roam, lifting my shirt up so that his warm hands are pressed against my stomach. I shiver in anticipation.

Kyle's kiss has stolen my breath and all of my ability to think straight. The next thing I know my shirt is coming up over my head, and Kyle's mouth takes a nipple, sucking and pulling it, while his fingers twist and massage the other. I writhe and my pussy weeps, soaking my panties.

Talon moves behind me, pulling his shirt over his head and he pulls me back against his chest. While he's pushing me backward, his hands roam down from my shoulders, toward my nipples, then he gets there and one of his hands brushes Kyle's cheek. Kyle tilts his head into his touch but doesn't release my nipple.

Talon's hands move down further, toward my belly button, my belt buckle and the fly of my jeans. Once he's undone the buckle, button and zipper, Kyle's hand slides light as feathers down my ribs and I shiver and squirm. "That tickles."

They both laugh and Kyle starts tugging my pants down. I lift my hips off the bed to make it easier for him. Talon's hands slide to my breasts, replacing Kyle's hands and mouth, pulling me right back in under their spell of sexual delight.

Once I am pants-free, Kyle stands up, pulling off his t-shirt and sliding his cargo shorts down his legs, his cock pops free and it is hard, ready for my mouth. I reach for it and he backs away. He shakes his head and I pout. Talon chooses that moment to twist my nipples, sending a shock wave of pain and pleasure straight to my pussy and I hiss through my teeth as I nearly explode because of it.

"She's ready," Talon says while helping me sit up. He slides from the bed and I'm left alone and naked on the bed. Talon slides his shorts down and his erection is free. I try and reach for it and he too denies me. "This is an Addison sandwich, angel." Talon climbs back onto the bed, right in the middle, and he lies down on his back. "Come, take me, baby." He gives me a salacious smile and I crawl across the bed to him. Reaching for his cock with my hand. Desperate to taste him. He stills my hand. "I love your mouth, I fucking love the way you suck me off, but this is not about me. Straddle me, facing me."

I moan. I don't get to ride him very often so I'm a little too eager as I climb on top of him. He smirks. I reach between our bodies, guiding the head of his cock against my wet slit. I coat his cock in my slickness as I line him up with my core. I slowly start sliding down onto him, teasing him along the way with slow little flicks of my hips as I suck him inside of me. I watch as his eyes roll up and my body shivers with love as he slides home.

I notice Kyle is reaching into our toy drawer as he pulls out the bottle of lube. "Oh fuck," I breathe. I know what he's going to do and my pussy clinches tight around Talon's cock. I grind against him, rubbing my clit against his pubic bone. "Fuck, argh." I explode into an orgasm I wasn't expecting and I collapse onto Talon's chest. His hands come up to stroke my back.

"That's our girl," he breathes and his voice vibrates his chest against my ear. I soak up the comfort I feel having him inside of me and his arms wrapped around me. Holding me, caressing me.

Then the bed shifts and I feel Talon spread his legs. I know that Kyle is crawling up the bed toward me. I moan when I feel a cold glob of lube against the tight bud of my ass and his hand is there, coating my entrance with lube. Getting me ready for what he plans to do. I feel one finger press inside. A thrill shoots through me and my muscles clamp down on Talon's cock.

As soon as one finger is in, Kyle adds another then immediately moves to push in the third. I feel Talon twitch inside me and my muscles spasm with his movement. Kyle begins to stroke along Talon's shaft from inside me. I moan.

We haven't gotten to this point yet with me. Though not for a lack of trying. We've continued with the butt plugs; deciding that Kyle would get to go first because he is equal in length to Talon, but thinner in girth.

He continues probing my ass with his fingers as I begin flicking my hips with Talon's rock hard cock still buried inside me. My eyes close to the pleasure as I continue to be assaulted by Kyle while sliding along Talon's shaft at the same time. I hear the lube open again, I tighten in anticipation of the cool gel and Talon's hands caress my back. "Relax, angel. If it's too much, or it hurts, we will stop." I nod on his chest and relax my hips. The motion sends Talon a little deeper into my sex and I moan. Kyle slowly extracts his hand and it is quickly replaced by the hardness of his cock.

I moan as the first bites of pain lick their way from one hole to the next and my pussy constricts. Kyle continues pushing himself into me. It's not painful. I feel full and his cock feels foreign but not at all unpleasant. Like they've done with the plugs, Kyle begins sliding in and out of me in short bursts. Talon remains still beneath me, but I can feel the twitches of his cock against Kyle's as he continues sliding inside.

The pleasure builds from deep in my pussy, radiating outward, reaching my toes. The sensation is so intense it nearly makes me come, but I bite my lip and moan, a good distraction until I feel Kyle's hips against my ass and I know that he is fully sheathed.

God, I am so full. Stuffed to the point of bursting. I flick my hips, my silent invitation for them to start moving. I pull myself up onto my hands, straightening my arms and I moan as Kyle pulls out.

The moment he begins to push back in, I feel Talon pull himself out. I cry out. The pleasure and pain is intense. I look at Talon. "You okay, angel?"

"Perfect. Don't stop," I say breathless and I begin to pant with each thrust in and each pull out. They gradually increase their pace and Talon grabs hold of my breasts, his mouth coming to a nipple and pulling it in with long licks. "Argh. Faster," I moan.

Both men respond to my command and begin pumping in and out of me like they need it to breathe. It doesn't take but five or six thrusts and my body locks down with an impending orgasm.

"Give it to us, baby girl. Give us your pleasure," Kyle groans behind me as he continues fucking my ass. Talon's hips are bouncing up and down on the bed and I am panting like a stripper on stage.

My body convulses, erupting in orgasm. Pain and pleasure, fullness and emptiness as they rock in and out of me in perfect harmony. Their thrusts become more demanding through each contraction of my muscles surrounding their cocks and they both call out my name as I feel their cocks jerk and unleash their flood of cum. It tips me over the edge once more and I writhe between them, milking them and sating my orgasm with their seed.

chapter 35

Kyle slowly pulls out first, but only after he fights to go limp at least a little bit. The loss of him buried in an untouched part of my body sends a shiver through me. Once Kyle has fallen free, Talon pulls out and I am rolled onto my side. Talon's naked chest is pressed against mine and Kyle's is pressed against my back. Wrapped in their love and warmth. "I love you," I breathe. I feel both bodies stiffen, and panic rocks through me as I realize that I've said those three little words. "It's hardly enough to express how I feel about both of you, but I can't find any better words," I say quietly.

Arms tighten around me, and I feel Kyle's nose nuzzling against my neck, at the base of my ear. "I love you," he whispers into my ear and I shiver with satisfaction.

I feel Talon's lips brush against mine. "Ditto," he breathes. "I know it's what I feel for you. I know I love you more than anything. I never imagined finding love, let alone a love as perfect as you are."

Tears spill from my eyes and arms are wrapped tighter. I can feel both Kyle and Talon letting the other one know they are there. Little touches and whispers against the skin. Kyle's hand comes away from my stomach and cups Talon's cheek in his hand as Talon's hand gently wipes the tears from my eyes. "These better be happy tears," he says softly. I nod.

"I just feel so engulfed by both of you. You're like air and blood, water and food. Everything I need in my life to survive. You're my lovers and my friends, and I can't do any of this without either one of you," I say, my voice cracking with emotion and I feel Kyle's lips on my neck, then I hear him inhale my scent, holding it within him before he slowly lets it out. "The love I feel for both of you is incomparable, but I don't know how to show it."

"Shh," Talon hushes me with his finger. "You show us every day."

"You don't need to find new ways to show us, baby girl. We know because we feel it too." He kisses my neck again and we settle into silence. I never wanted to be the first one to say it, but I know deep down inside they both felt it, they just didn't know how to say it.

When the words slipped free of my lips, it was too late to take them back, but I realized their conviction. I realized what it meant for me to say it and no matter what, I understood that my saying it didn't scare them, it only made it more real for them and that is the power of love.

I also know that they feel something for each other, whether it is the same as what they feel for me or not, I don't know, but it's there and in time they will come to realize it too. I know this now, it took me time to figure it out, but they will do the same.

"Come on, baby girl. It's time to go," Kyle shouts back to me.

"Coming."

Tonight I am wearing my new Louboutins, a pair of wide legged black pants and the purple halter tank that they bought me for Cami's dinner party. I look sexy as hell, but yet there is a very professional edge to my appearance tonight. Though it wasn't my intention. It just sounded comfortable.

I come around the corner to find my two lovers waiting for me. Though I don't get the 'my cock is going to explode' expressions I normally get, they are no less stunned. I pulled my hair up into a very messy yet elegant bun. Not wanting to mess with it tonight. Plus having it off of my back shows off my ink, which of course is always Talon's agenda. I also grabbed a hoodie. Hell, it's March in Kansas.

"Just when I think you can't get any more gorgeous you walk out in that," Talon says. "Your mom's here, so we don't want to ogle too long."

I smile and walk toward them. They both wrap their arms around me and I notice now that when they hold me they always seem to find some bare skin to touch. "Alright let's go," I tease and they both reluctantly let me go.

We step off of the bus to find Rusty and Beck standing guard and I can see Mills standing near the door. They are no longer taking chances when it comes to me after Dallas, and I'm one hundred percent okay with that. With my arms linked in Kyle and Talon's we walk toward the theater we're playing in tonight. It's a good sized venue with about twenty-five thousand fans waiting for 69 Bottles to take the stage. We rehearsed at six and it went amazingly well.

We're twenty minutes from Tender Souls taking the stage. They're the new band hanging with us now. Their lead singer is a chick, she seems really cool and if I could get my head out of Kyle and Talon long enough, she and I could be friends.

When we step inside I turn to Mills and ask, "Where's my mom?"

He smiles. "She's in the dressing room. Peacock, Mouse and Dex took the liberty of introducing themselves about two minutes ago, so I imagine they're looking for their relief."

"Oh no," I say, slightly horrified that Dex and the rest of the band are in a confined space with my mother. I pick up the pace a little and all five guys laugh.

We reach the dressing room door and I open it to my mother's laughter and I am comforted by that. All eyes turn toward us as we step inside. Kyle and Talon let me go first. "Hi Mom."

"Look at you, sweetheart. You look amazing."

"Aw, stop it, Mom, you're gonna make me blush."

She laughs again. "I was just chatting with Dex, Eric and Calvin." Oh thank Jesus, they used their real names.

"And you survived?" I laugh.

"Addison Lynae." Ah hell, that's the second time today she's pulled the middle name card.

"Lynae, huh?" The guys start teasing me and I can't help but roll my eyes.

"Mom, I'd like you to meet Talon Carver."

"It's a real pleasure to finally meet you, Mrs. Beltrand."

"Oh call me Lori, please. And it is great to meet you too, Talon. I've heard a lot about you." She smiles sweetly, takes Talon's hand and pulls him into a hug. It warms my heart to see it. "So if this is Talon, then this lovely young man must be Kyle?"

"Yes ma'am," Kyle says with a wide smile.

"Oh no, none of that."

All the guys laugh. Dex makes the first comment, "Well at least now we know why this one hates to be called ma'am." He laughs, and of course everyone else joins in.

"It's really great to meet you Lori."

"Likewise, Kyle. Alright Calvin, Eric and Dex, leave me with these three, I need to talk to to them." Oh no. I plead with Dex to stay, silently mind you, and I can see the pleasure in his eyes as he and the other guys leave the room. "Now boys, tell me, is she behaving herself?"

"Oh mom, seriously?"

"Yes." She grabs their hands and brings them back to the couch where she pulls them both to sit. I can see the worry in their eyes as they look at me. I shrug. "She's a handful that one. I'm so glad she has the two of you to take care of her. She needs good strong hands and you two seem to be doing an amazing job."

She dotes on them a little longer. She doesn't bring up Dan, but she does ask Kyle about his mom. Kyle being the good son that he is talks to my mother about his mom with nothing but nice things to say about her. I can tell Talon is a little uncomfortable with the conversation so I go to stand next to him and he wraps his arm around my hips.

My mom surprises me by turning to Kyle, "Doesn't that make you jealous?"

"Mom." I scold her with my eyes.

"It's alright, baby girl. No, Lori, it doesn't, which is how this whole thing works so well for us. You see, he is about to go on stage for two hours and during those two hours, she is usually standing backstage in my arms. We all get equal time. It's a work in progress, but it is working out so far."

My mother smiles wide. "Good, I'm glad."

"Lori, I hate to cut this short, but I need to go warm up and get ready for the show. Kyle is welcome to stay, though I could use his help. This way you can chat with Addie some more," Talon says. "If you stay through the show, we will definitely have some time afterward to chat."

My mom stands up. "I have a better idea. I know you guys have to get on to Des Moines tonight, and you're pretty busy these next few weeks, so when the tour is over, why don't the three of you come back to Kansas City for a long weekend?"

Talon and Kyle both smile. "That sounds like an amazing idea," Kyle says as he stands and my mom's face lights up.

"Wonderful, then it's a date. I'll set it up with Addison." Both of my very handsome men give my mom hugs and kisses on the cheek as they leave the room.

My mom turns to me. "Don't let them go."

"I have no plans to do that. I love them."

She wraps her arms around me, and despite my being much taller than she is, it is still the most comfortable embrace in the world. "We need to get you to your seat if you want to see the show. When it is over, I'll send Leroy out to get you and bring you back here."

"Alright, sweetie, let's go."

chapter 36

I introduce my mom to Leroy, who escorts my mom to her seat. I found out the other day that the bands are given so many seats to either give away or do with as they please. A lot of times they end up at radio stations for their giveaways or they're released for at-the-door sales which always sell out. There are always people who show up hoping for tickets and in some cases we have them. Tonight, we saved one for my mom.

Tender Souls is on stage and they're actually really good. I like their music and vow at some point during this journey to buy their album. They get a slightly longer set, at thirty-five minutes verses twenty-five. Which is good because they're great performers and the crowd takes to them. Tender Souls does an amazing job getting them wound up for 69 Bottles.

As they finish up their set, I notice a rather large group of roadies with them and I wonder just how popular they are. Then I wonder idly if it has anything to do with their lead singer. She's blond, from a box, and has a very school girl look about her. Tonight she's wearing a short red plaid skirt, much like the one I own, just less buckles, and platform boots. Her top is a shredded t-shirt over a tank top. It's rather grungy which is odd because their music is more alternative.

When their set is done, the change-over doesn't take but a couple of minutes before the guys are walking down the hallway toward me. I smile as Dex approaches. "See, I knew I'd grow on you," he laughs and kisses me.

"Like a bad wart on my ass, you're growing on me."

"Oh ouch, you wound me, love."

"Oh my god, whatever." I roll my eyes and then Peacock and Mouse hug me and kiss me. "Break a leg, boys."

They smile and step on stage.

Like clockwork, Kyle wraps his arms around me, holding me to him as Talon saddles up for his kiss. This time he pushes his erection against me and Kyle strokes it. His mouth falls slack and he lets out a silent moan of delight. I shudder. He takes my cheeks in his hands, kissing me with ferocious need. When he pulls back, he looks deep into my eyes. "I love you." I whisper, unable to stop it.

"Ditto, angel." He kisses me two more times.

"Go kick some ass." I rub my nose against his.

"See you on stage," he smirks and winks.

Kyle's arms tighten around me and I turn in his arms. I cup his cheeks, pulling my lips to his. I tease his lower lip open with my tongue and slide it inside. Our tongues dance with each other; I'm lit up from within. Ready, willing and wanting to take him right here and now. I pull back. "I love you," I tell him.

He smiles a very happy satisfied smile. "I love you," he says back to me and I melt into his arms just as the band picks up with their first song.

The arrangement has been altered for tonight and going forward. We're going to do 'Your Eyes' about thirty minutes into the set, then do 'To Be Free' about an hour and fifteen into it. Giving the guys a chance to take a breather and tonight is the debut of 'To Be Free'. I'm really nervous, but so excited because my mom is in the audience to see it.

Kyle and I dance backstage, enjoying each other's company while Talon does his thing until the sound guy shows up to set up my microphone. Once I'm all hooked up, the song before mine comes to an end and I can hear Mouse and Peacock teasingly play the chords of 'Your Eyes' and the crowd goes wild.

"Ladies and gentlemen, you're in for a very special treat tonight." The crowd erupts into cheers of 'Addison' and I can see Talon smiling wide. He cups his hand to his ear urging the crowd to get louder. I laugh nervously and Kyle hugs me close. "I can't hear you," Talon growls into the microphone. I can see Dex all but laughing behind his drums. "You want Addison?" Talon asks the crowd and their screams reach deafening levels. "Ladies and gentlemen, it is my honor and pleasure to introduce to you the one and only Addison Beltrand!"

The crowd erupts again and their energy is palpable. I can feel every ounce of it pouring into my veins as I walk across the stage. I wave to the cheering crowd as I come to stand next to him and he holds me to his hip.

"So what do you say, angel? Should we give them what they want?" he asks me out loud and into the microphone.

"I don't know, I don't think they're excited enough."

I can't see much of what's in front of me, but I can see the stands off to the side and everyone is on their feet, clapping and screaming. Talon gives the signal to the guys and they kick up with the full volume version of 'Your Eyes'.

Talon starts singing and I feel so animated tonight. I actually feel very comfortable on stage and Talon and I begin to move around. We only come back together for the final chorus, the crowd is singing along with us and it's crazy and trippy and oh my god, A-Mazing.

We finish out the song and Talon has a very shit eating grin on his face. He kisses me, hot and heavy right on stage and the crowd cheers us on. Finally, he releases me and I leave the stage with a wave and the band picks right up into their next song. I walk right into Kyle's arms and he holds me close.

"Wow, baby girl, that was amazing. It's starting to feel natural, isn't it?"

I nod. "I think so. Either that, or it's because my mom's here."

"Well, whatever it is, capitalize on it because when you're out there and you're performing, you light up the stage. Why you never wanted to be a singer is beyond me. But should you decide to make a career out of it, Talon and I will be right by your side," he says with such pride and love that I can't help but to kiss him.

Talon and the guys continue their rocking performance and I can tell by watching Talon that he's jazzed up and more excited the closer we get to 'To Be Free'. Finally the song right before starts to play and I get a little freaked out. I asked Talon to let me do something special before the performance, I haven't told him what, but he agreed without a second thought.

They finish out the song and the band clears the stage. They pass Kyle and me and I get a round of high fives as they walk past.

"Alright Kansas City, remember when I told you that I had a special treat for you tonight?" The crowd goes wild. "Please welcome back to the stage Ms. Addison Beltrand." The crowd goes insane again and I walk on stage to more cheers and screams and the excitement is flowing through my veins again.

"What's going on Kansas City?" The crowd responds wildly to me talking. "Are you guys having fun tonight?" They scream and holler some more. I look at Talon and he smiles wildly at me. I turn back to the audience. "Talon and I have a very special treat for you tonight. A never before heard treat, just for you, so if you're gonna video tape this on your cell phones, I pray you have battery life left." Talon laughs. I can hear him in the feedback, though he's some distance away from me, grabbing his chair and his guitar. "It is an honor and a privilege to be here with 69 Bottles and an even bigger honor to debut 69 Bottles' new single in front of a very special woman in my life who is sitting right over here." I gesture to my left and see her flinch so I know I've found her. "This one's for you."

I turn back to Talon who is smiling from ear to ear as he starts to strum his guitar. He takes it through the chorus once and then he starts singing. The crowd goes crazy, but settles quickly so they can hear him sing. I can't stop staring at how beautiful he is with his guitar in front of him. He finishes the first verse and the lights change to me.

Just like we practiced, I sing my part. Singing to the audience who is cheering and dancing. I can see my mom and I smile at her. Then the chorus picks up and Talon and I both sing our parts.

We go back to a verse for him and a verse for me. As I finish my verse I walk toward him and come to stand behind him as we finish out our song together and then Talon takes it home.

When he's done, the crowd gets impossibly loud as Talon sets down his guitar, stands and grabs my hand, pulling me to the front of the stage. The crowd starts chanting "we want more" and Talon and I look at each other before he looks back to the crowd. "The one and only Addison Beltrand," Talon says, raising my arm into the air. The crowd's roaring and my adrenaline is pumping.

I take a bow, and the crowd is crazy, bouncing up and down. Talon kisses me again, spurring them on even more before I back away from him, letting the distance separate us. He blows me a kiss as I duck behind the curtain.

chapter 37

"Addison Lynae!" I pull away from Talon and Kyle, feeling like I've been caught making out with a boy in the closet when I was fourteen. Don't laugh, it happened.

"Hi mom," I say sheepishly. We had Leroy bring her to the greenroom before we let the public in.

"Oh, wipe that look off of your face, you're not in trouble." I giggle. She comes up and wraps her arms around me. "You were absolutely amazing. I've seen the videos but they do not do you justice. You're beautiful and I loved every minute. And you guys," she looks at Talon and the guys standing behind him, "I'm impressed. I didn't know what to expect, but you put on one hell of a show."

I watch as all their faces light up. "Thank you, Lori," Talon says to her and she lights up.

"You're most welcome. You deserve it."

My mom sticks around for a few more minutes, praising me and the guys before she takes her leave of the room. I walk out into the hallway and into the crowd of people standing there. They start cheering when I walk out behind my mom and I fight the urge to blush at the praise of the waiting group.

I walk my mom out the back door to where her car is parked. "Addison, I had an amazing time tonight. You sing so beautifully and you looked like you were having a great time up there."

I laugh. "You know, tonight is the first time I really kind of let loose. It's scary being up there, but it is such an adrenaline rush."

"Then maybe you should consider their offers." She gives me that mom look.

"I am, mom, but right now if I sign with them, I'm done with these guys and I don't want that. I want to finish up my job and the tour with my band before I make any decisions and Cami, my boss, is keeping them at bay for me. We'll be recording both songs while we're in New York in a couple of weeks. Once I have a better idea of what kind of audience I'm going to gain, I'll decide." I lean against her car. "This might sound selfish, but I don't want to turn into some starving artist. I've made a hell of a name for myself at Bold and I hate to throw that away on the unknown, especially a whole new career."

"Oh, baby, I believe you would be a hit for a long time, especially after seeing what I saw tonight. They absolutely loved you."

I smile. "You're so sweet. They do love me, but what happens when I become me without 69 Bottles? They have such a following and my being included just might be a 'she's cool right now' kinda thing. There's just too many unknowns right now, but I promise to keep you posted on whatever decisions I make."

"Okay, baby girl," she says sweetly to me and then hugs me. "I miss you so much. Please, bring them after the tour.

I'd love to spend some time with you and with them. They're a couple of great guys, Addison, hold on to them."

"God, mom, I can't believe you're so…"

"Cool about all this?" she finishes my sentence. "Addison, you've been alone way too long. I know you love your job, but whether it's one man or a hundred…"

"Mom!" I scold.

"Well, hear me out. Whether it's one or a hundred, as long as you're happy, as long as you're breaking this wall you have around yourself, I don't care who you're with."

"Have I really been that bad?"

She smiles. "No, you just haven't been you. I understand what you went through with Dan, I honestly do, but it's not a reason to be alone for the rest of your life. If Dan really loved you, he'd want you to be happy. Whether it is with his brother or someone else."

"I didn't stay alone on purpose, it just happened."

"Oh sweetie, I know, but now is the time to live your life and I'm beyond the moon that you have two amazing men willing to show you what life is all about." I wipe the tears from my cheeks. "Aw baby, don't cry. Just live it up. Now get back in there, I think you have some fans to entertain."

I laugh and hug her again. "I miss you. I love you, mom."

"Love you too, sweetie. We will talk and then I'll see you, what, this summer?"

I smile and reply, "The tour is over in June. I'll know more closer to the end of the tour because the guys are due back in the studio, so we will need to plan it all closer too."

"Sounds great, baby." She hugs me again and climbs into her car. I stand outside and watch as she drives away. When I turn back toward the venue, I can see my bodyguards close by but Kyle is also standing just outside the door. I walk over to him.

"You okay, baby girl?" he asks with concern.

"Yeah, I just realized every time I see her, I miss her a little more. I want to move her to LA so she isn't so far away, but I don't know if she will."

"One day at a time, baby girl."

"I know. Why are you out here?"

He laughs, "You're not going to believe this."

I cock my head at him. "What?"

"No one will leave the greenroom. They're waiting for you."

"You're kidding me, right?"

He snorts, "I wish. I was sent out here to drag you back in."

"Well, then we better go."

Kyle wasn't kidding. I was all but mobbed the moment I walked into the room. Mills, Beck and Rusty were all over me, blocking me from the barrage of people. Talon and Kyle come to stand with them. Talon surprises me when he announces, "Alright guys, calm down. I promise you that she has time for all of you."

They all calm down and Mills begins moving them into a line and the party begins.

Two hours later and everyone is finally out of the greenroom. I've signed at least two hundred autographs and probably taken as many pictures. The guys all lined up next to me so that they could get me and then get to the others and back out the door again.

Climbing back onto the bus is a chore. I'm tired and my hands, cheeks and feet are killing me. I stumble my way back to our room. Kyle and Talon were taking care of some things before getting on the bus. We need to get on the road before too long so we're not going out.

I open the door and freeze. "What the...?" I grumble. The room is literally covered in flowers. Every surface has a vase full of red roses. The bed, the tops of the tables and down onto the floor are littered with rose petals. In the middle of the bed is a card that says "Addison" on it. The room smells so fragrant and vibrant. I reach for the card on the bed.

"What the fuck?" I hear Talon behind me.

"What's the ma...Addie, stop." I freeze on the bed. My heart is pounding wildly in my chest and I can feel my body shaking.

"This isn't...from you?" My voice falls to a whisper.

"No, come back off of the bed, baby girl. We didn't do this."

I pull off of the bed quickly pushing my back against the wall. I feel a hand around my wrist and I flinch. "It's me, baby, come here." I slide across the wall toward him.

"Mills!" Kyle shouts and then I hear him stomping across the floor of the bus. "Mills!" he shouts louder, but from further away.

Talon pulls me into his arms and wraps them around me before backing out of the room and down the hall. "We need to get you off the bus."

"What's going on?" I hear Mills say from behind Talon.

"We need a safe room, and you need to get into the bedroom. Someone's been on the bus."

Mills slides past us, his arm at his side ready to draw his sidearm. Talon moves me onto the couch and Leroy and Beck come to stand in front of us. Rusty follows Mills toward the back. He begins checking behind the bunk curtains. Nothing. He looks into the bathroom, nothing.

Suddenly the bus rocks to one side and back again and Rusty goes running back to our room. There is some shouting and another jolt against the side of the bus and I jump with each one. Talon continues holding me, rubbing my arm and whispering comforting words into my ear.

chapter 38

"This was the stupidest fucking thing you could have possibly done," Mills barks at whoever he has in his clutches. Rusty comes around the corner first.

"I don't know if you want to see this," he says to me and Talon, but mostly to me.

"Did you catch him?" I ask, and Rusty nods. "Who is it?"

"That's why I don't think you want to see this. The cops are on their way. We believe the situation is neutralized, but until we know for sure, you can't leave. So you can either cover your eyes or watch."

"Come on, angel," Talon says turning me toward him, patting his chest. "Don't watch, baby. Please." His voice is choked with pain and I want to hold him. Suddenly I feel Kyle behind me. "We got you, baby. We won't let anything happen to you."

Kyle and Talon sandwich me between them. I turn my face toward the wall. Being between them prevents me from turning, even if I wanted to.

There is some movement, some shuffling of feet, and I feel more than I hear because of how they have me protected. I close my eyes, concentrating on Talon's racing heart. I notice as it increases I can feel his hands tighten into fists at my side. This isn't good, whatever this is. The bus shifts and bumps as people climb down the stairs and then everything seems to settle again.

"He didn't see you, baby girl. He didn't even know you were here."

"Do I want to know who it was?"

"No, baby, you don't."

My gut tells me that I know exactly who it was, but the fact that he was hiding somewhere on the bus is all the more worrisome and I don't know how I feel about this. I don't know how I feel about all of this anymore. This is just too fucking insane. I burst into tears. Fear, panic, and a nervous energy rack my body. The only thing I know is that I'm not cut out for this. This is too much for me to handle anymore. I sob harder.

talon

"How long before we absolutely have to leave?" I ask Kyle after we put Addison to bed back in her old bunk. She's physically and mentally exhausted. Frankly, so am I. We came outside with Mills and Rusty so that we could talk without the risk of waking anyone up.

"It's about three, three and half hours so by one at the latest," he says. He's just as shaken over what happened as Addison and myself are.

Eddie, that fucker that attacked her, of all fucking people, it would have to be him. He was fucking naked. The image is burned into my mind.

"What the fuck happened, Mills? How did he get on the bus?"

"He managed to get past security at the fence. So we're working on that, but they're not our guys, so it's hard to tell. Then when he got to the bus, he told Ted that he had a delivery for Ms. Beltrand from Talon with specific instructions. Then Ted got pulled away with a mechanical issue on the other bus. No one noticed that he never left the bus.

"I found him in the closet. He was naked, waiting for his chance to strike. But you and Kyle interrupted it. So he stayed put. How he expected to get off of the bus, I have no fucking clue. But the bottom line in all of this is that he has a conviction of assault against Addison, add to that the stalking charge, plus he's violated his plea deal, and bail. He was arrested as soon as they released him for Addison's attack and charged him with rape of another woman. He was out on bail again. He wasn't supposed to leave the state of Texas. He's now been arrested here. I'm pulling some strings to ensure he doesn't get bail again. We will know immediately if he gets released again." Mills looks really upset about what happened. "Look, I'm recommending an additional four bodyguards to meet us in Des Moines this afternoon."

"Can you get them there that fast?"

"Actually, it was Cami's suggestion. She's already got them lined up and they will be on Bold's plane within a couple of hours. She's handling it because it was one of her employees that was attacked. These four will be assigned to Addison, but as a whole will be responsible for the band. Which means we will be able to have one of our guys at the gate, the door and then standing by the buses, as well as a team inside."

"Is four enough?"

"I don't think I can ever get enough bodyguards to protect her." Mills' voice is filled with emotion. "We've never had to guard the buses before, and frankly I never imagined anything like this happening, but going forward, we will prepare for the unimaginable. I'd rather have too many than not enough. We will also be making some procedural changes, including checking the bus before anyone boards. Even if we have someone standing outside."

I rub my hands over my chin. "Do we have room on that bus for four more bodyguards?"

"Comfortably? No. But one of the changes I'm implementing is placing one of us on this bus" he points to our bus behind us, "at all times. With the three of you in one room, there are two empty racks. We can move Mouse, Peacock or Dex back into that room and have a guard up front, or two. Oh and one of the guards Cami is sending is female."

"Then put her on this bus. Let Addison and her get acquainted and comfortable with each other. Plus that means that she always has one of hers with her," I tell Mills and Kyle nods in agreement with me.

"Alright, we'll make the arrangements. However, we're going to put Beck on here for the drive up. I'm waiting for confirmation from Cami on time of arrival for the guards. Once I know that, I will decide when we leave here. Now," he rubs his hand over his military short haircut. "How is she?" He nods his head in the direction of the bus.

"Freaked out, but I think she's okay. Nothing happened, and I think Talon and I scared her more than the flowers did. She assumed they were from us. Though I wish I'd thought of it, the flowers, not the pending attack," Kyle tells Mills.

I bump shoulders with him. "She won't go into the room until we're ready to go with her. The cops cleaned up the petals for evidence and Kyle and I have checked through the drawers and the closet looking for anything out of place, added or missing. So I'm hoping that he just came in, set up the flowers, stripped and climbed into the closet."

"The time frame fits because he showed up less than fifteen minutes before we came out. He would have barely had time for anything else before getting in the closet. I don't want to speculate, but I don't want to discredit anything..." His phone rings. He holds up a finger for us to hang on. "Mills."

I turn to Kyle. "How're you doing?" I wrap my arm around his waist.

"I'm fine. Worried about her, but I'm fine. It was a bunch of flowers and a note, which we haven't seen, which might be nothing. I'm guessing he was waiting for her to climb on the bed so he could pin her down, but we came just in time. I'm worried about her breakdown. She's barely getting involved in this lifestyle and look at what's happened to her."

I squeeze him close to me. "I know, but you also need to realize that this is all coming from the same man. The same sicko. He came back to finish what he started. Except he's not smart enough to know or understand that she is never left alone for long. We will have better tabs on him going forward if Mills' connection comes through. Honestly, I think it's my fault."

"Don't go there," Kyle says sternly.

"I can't help it. I mean, shit, Kyle, we're a bunch of guys. We throw punches without a second thought. We handle women, we rarely have to deal with men. We never have to think about this kind of shit. I didn't think that she would either so I didn't take the extra precautions I should have. We have four guards for four guys. We should have brought another one on as soon as she came on board."

"No. We didn't adjust to different events. Addison has been brought into the public eye with her singing, with her relationship with us, we didn't adjust to any of that. That's when we should have made the changes. We never had guards for her after all that happened. It's not our responsibility to make that choice. It's up to Mills, and he thought he had it handled and when he realized he didn't have it, he called for help. Please do not beat yourself up over this."

I lean into him and he holds onto me. "You're right."

"I usually am."

I laugh a little and Mills ends his call. Turning to us he says, "He's booked in. Pending extradition back to Texas, they can't release him. So he will stay in jail."

"Thank fuck."

chapter 39
addison

Waking up, I stretch and realize that I'm alone in bed, wait, I'm in my old rack. It takes me a couple of minutes to remember why I'm here, and then it all comes flooding back. I didn't want to sleep in the bedroom by myself and Talon and Kyle wanted to talk to Mills. Then get ready to leave Kansas City.

A beautiful, nearly perfect night shattered into millions of pieces with a few dozen roses. I don't know who it was that put the roses in the room; I just know that they were still in the room when I'd gone in there. If it hadn't been, once again, for Talon and Kyle, something worse may have happened. I lost it last night. Overwhelmed by the prospect of this being the kind of shit that I'm going to have to put up with if I take on this whole "celebrity" thing.

I roll over on my bunk, I can feel the bus moving and the hum of the engine as we travel toward Des Moines. I look at my watch and it's eleven thirty. Jeez, I slept a long time. I sit up and...

My heart breaks. Kyle is asleep, sitting up, leaning against the wall. Why is he on the floor and not on the bunk, or why is he not sleeping in bed with Talon? I slide off of the bunk, trying to be quiet. I don't want to wake him just yet. Once I'm done in the bathroom, I'll wake him up and bring him into Talon's room.

I leave the room and catch Mills asleep on the couch in the galley. I have so many questions for him, but I need to take care of business, put Kyle to bed and then I can talk to Mills.

When I'm done, I go back to my old room and when I come around the corner I'm shocked to see that Talon is asleep on the bottom bunk. They didn't leave me. My heart melts a little more. Talon is pressed against the wall, leaving plenty of room for me to crawl in, but I'd rather be wrapped up in both my men.

I go over to Talon and run my hand through his hair. He jumps. "Hey angel," he says softly as he opens his eyes.

I put my finger to my lips, then point to Kyle. He smiles. "Come on, let's go to bed." I can see worry in his eyes. "It's okay, big man."

"Are you sure?" he whispers.

"I'm positive. Nothing bad has happened to me in that room. In fact, it's an amazing room when the two men I love are in it." I give him a small smile. "Come on, I'll get Kyle."

"What time is it?" he asks as he throws the covers off. I smile when I notice he's in his boxers and he's hard.

"Like eleven forty."

"We shouldn't be far from Des Moines."

"We can still sleep. Come on." He smiles and gets out of the bunk rather awkwardly. His hulking size is nearly too much for that tiny bunk.

He goes out of the room and into the bedroom. I turn to Kyle and cup his cheek. His eyes fly open. "Hi cowboy." I smile.

"Hey baby girl, you okay?"

"I'll be better when I'm wrapped up in my guys. Come on, let's go to bed."

"You sure?"

I want to roll my eyes, but he doesn't know that I've already woke up Talon. "Absolutely. Talon's in there already."

"Okay," he says sleepily and gets up off of the floor. He wraps his arms around me. "You okay?"

"Better now." We walk to the bedroom and Talon is pulling back the sheets, which I notice have been changed and a different comforter is on top.

"We threw them out," Talon says as he notices what I'm looking at.

"You didn't need to do that." Talon and Kyle exchange a look. "What? Don't baby me about this. I let you do it so I didn't see who it was, but I won't let you keep secrets from me."

"It's not a secret, baby girl. Neither Talon nor I could stand the sheets anymore. So we changed them out. It was more for us than you," he says sheepishly.

"Well, okay then."

"Besides," Talon adds, "the other ones were a little..."

I laugh, "messy?"

Both guys laugh and the invisible weight is gone from all of us. "Climb in, baby girl." Kyle gestures toward the bed. I reach for the hem of my tank-top. Kyle's hands still my motion. "If you do that, we... shit Addison, you know we won't be able to help ourselves and I'm not sure..."

I put my fingers on his lips, "Shh. I know what I'm doing and what I want." His eyes are full of love and devotion. "Nothing happened to me. It was a bunch of flowers. I don't know any more details than that, so the idea of trying to process what happened isn't even a thought in my mind. I lost it last night because I've been thrown into this wild world and it is so overwhelming for me. The one thing I know, without a doubt, is that I love you and I love Talon. You're my rocks, you keep me grounded and you keep me safe, and more than anything, you help me forget it all. I want to forget, I want to be so lost in you and Talon that I forget my name. Are you going to deny me that?"

He shakes his head and kisses my fingers. Talon comes to stand behind me, wrapping his arms around me, grabbing the hem of my tank-top in the front and pulling it up, over my head. When he's done, his hands slide into the waistband of my pajama bottoms, pushing them just past my hips so that they fall to the floor in a silent rush.

Kyle brings his hands to my face, holding me gently so that he can bring his lips to mine. He kisses me, his teeth nipping at my bottom lip, pulling it into his mouth. Talon's hands slide up my stomach and he cups my breasts. He takes my nipples between his fingers and presses his erection into me. Kyle slides closer so that his erection is pressing into my front and I shiver.

Kyle pulls back from his kiss, "What do you want, baby girl?"

"I want you, inside me. I want Talon inside you," I breathe as Talon continues tweaking my nipples in his fingers. I watch as Kyle's eyes widen and his whole body radiates excitement at the idea of being taken by Talon. "I want Talon to claim you as his," I moan.

Kyle looks at Talon with desire and lust in his eyes.

"Anything for you, angel," Talon murmurs against my neck, kissing and licking his way along my shoulder.

"You have to do it for you. This isn't always about me," I respond as the pleasure rocks through me.

"Oh, believe me, angel, I want to be inside of him almost as much as I want to be in you." I shiver as his breath caresses my shoulder with warmth.

I remove myself from between the two of them and I slide up onto the bed. I lay down with my head on the pillow. They're both watching me so I begin caressing my breasts in my hands. Writhing against the flood of sensations between my legs. I let one hand slide down my stomach, cupping my mound and my finger begins strumming my clit. I moan and my eyes close in bliss.

When I can focus on them again, I can see Talon and Kyle each stroking their cocks as they watch me play with myself.

"Fuck!" I call out, "I fucking need you."

Kyle slides up on the bed, coming to rest between my legs. I lift my knees up, spreading my pussy wide for him to watch my moving fingers. He watches as I stroke my pussy.

"Fuck yourself, baby girl. Let me watch you fuck your pussy," he says huskily and I quickly slide my middle finger into my core. My body explodes with pleasure and an orgasm begins to simmer just out of reach. I continue sliding my finger in and out as Kyle strokes his cock. I look over to Talon who is watching us with rapt attention. Then he reaches into the drawer for our bottle of lube.

Kyle moans. "I can't take it anymore. Move your hand so I can fuck you."

"Oh yeah," I groan as I remove my hand. Kyle takes it, bringing it up to his mouth. He begins licking and sucking my fingers clean.

"You taste like heaven," he moans around my hand. The head of his cock probing gently at my sex. I reach down with my other hand, grabbing hold of him, stroking him, lining him up to slide home. "Mmm, impatient aren't we?"

"Yes!" I moan.

chapter 40

"Take me, please," I beg. Kyle smiles, putting my hand back at my side. He steadies himself on his hands and slides inside of me hard and fast. "Ahh!" I moan and he begins sliding in and out of me. My body is alive with sensation as his cock rubs my g-spot.

My pussy clenches around him and he moans. I feel the bed move and look past Kyle to see Talon coming up behind him. Talon rubs his hand on Kyle's back and he arches into the touch.

"Lean forward, sexy," Talon growls to Kyle and I'm delighted that Talon has finally given Kyle his own little pet name.

Kyle leans forward, falling to his elbows on top of me as he continues sliding in and out of me. Kyle's lips land on mine and I wrap my arms around him, holding him to me. He grunts and moans and I know that Talon is beginning to prepare Kyle and my pussy responds, clenching around Kyle as he tells me, "Come for me, baby girl."

I explode around him and he pounds into me harder, milking my orgasm. As I calm down from my explosion, I feel Kyle still.

I look into his eyes and he's frightened. I caress his back, helping him relax. "Kiss me," I breathe and he doesn't hesitate. His lips land on mine. The kiss is hard at first, but then he softens into my lips, and my hands continue stroking his back.

"Argh!" he cries out.

"Kyle, you okay?" Talon asks.

Kyle hisses through his teeth. "Yes. Don't stop."

I shudder with pleasure knowing exactly what Talon is doing as I feel Kyle's cock twitch inside of me. I wish I wasn't so pinned down by him. I push my feet into the mattress for leverage and I begin to slowly slide my pussy along his cock. Kyle cries out with pure pleasure. I continue pumping my pussy along his shaft. He lifts his hips, pushing back into Talon, giving me room to continue riding his cock.

"How you doing, Kyle?" Talon asks him and I look into his eyes and I can see them rolling with pleasure.

"More," he moans.

Talon takes hold of Kyle's hips and looks down at their connection and I feel Talon pull back, then back in. "Fuck! Fuck! Fuck!" Kyle growls. Talon nods to me and I go back to working my hips along Kyle's shaft. "Fuck, too m...I'm gonna come," he moans and I slow my pace.

"Better, cowboy?"

"Mmhmm," he moans and I can feel Talon's thrusts because he is driving Kyle into me deeper. I'm ready to explode again already but I bite my lip, hoping it will be enough to hold it back. I don't want to come, not yet, because I will make Kyle come and I want him to savor this a little longer.

I slowly lower my hips back to the bed and Kyle brings his knees up under my thighs as he sits back onto Talon's cock. Talon groans. "Your ass is so tight. It feels so fucking good around my cock."

Kyle's breathing portrays his pleasure above me. His eyes are closed, his mouth is open and he is panting with each thrust of Talon's cock into him. His cock slides in and out of my pussy and I can no longer hold it in.

"Kyle, I'm gonna...agh fuck...I can't..."

"Let it out, baby girl. Come for me. Come for Talon."

Oh fuck, I explode, shattering, convulsing, clenching, squeezing, milking.

"Jesus," Kyle moans and I feel him erupt inside me. "Harder," he moans and I can feel Talon pump into him harder, working toward his own release. "Fuck, your cock, it's fucking...agh!" He continues panting and I can still feel spurts of cum from his cock shooting into me.

Talon stills and Kyle takes over, thrusting into me, his ass pulling on Talon's cock buried inside. Both men moan above me. Kyle is working feverishly to make Talon come. "I need it. Fuck, Talon, I need you to come."

Talon begins matching Kyle's thrusts. Each thrust forward by Talon is met by a backward thrust by Kyle. When they pull apart Kyle slams hard into me and another orgasm is racing through my veins, my heart is pounding, blood rushing, fire burning and my orgasm is on the surface. My legs tremble, my body locks down.

"Talon!" Kyle moans and I hear Talon's animalistic cries as he thrusts hard and fast into Kyle, his orgasm taking him, taking Kyle into his own second orgasm. My pussy is clenched so tight, it squeezes around Kyle's cock sucking him deeper into me. I shatter into another orgasm and my body falls limp on the mattress. Kyle collapses on top of me and Talon leans forward, wrapping his arms around Kyle and rubbing along my arms.

Talon kisses Kyle on his shoulder. He looks at me and smiles. I know I have this ridiculously glorious, sated, mind blown smile on my face. "Ky, I've got to pull out."

Kyle nods and Talon shifts. With a series of grunts and moans, Talon extracts himself from Kyle and Kyle plops out of me, limp and satisfied.

"I'll be right back," Talon says, donning a pair of shorts before he leaves the room.

"How you doing, cowboy?"

"Hmph."

"Is that a good thing?" I ask and he nods slowly. "How was it?"

"Amazing," he mumbles against my breast.

"So we'll be doing that again?" He nods, nuzzling his face between my boobs.

"You smell so good," he mumbles and I shiver as his warm breath covers my nipple and dissipates into coolness.

"I'm so proud of you," I tell him as I stroke his back. "You did it. You were ready and willing."

"I knew that if it felt half as good as when you took me with that toy, then I'd be set. I just had to get past the initial invasion."

I smile. "It's pretty intense, isn't it?"

"Mmhmm."

Talon comes back into the room. I look over at him and he has something in his hand. A towel, I think. He climbs up onto the bed behind Kyle. "I'm gonna clean you up, cowboy." He says gently and I smile at his use of my nickname for Kyle. Talon smirks at me. "What? It fits."

I giggle and Kyle jumps. "It stings," he says with a hint of pain.

"There was a little bit of blood. Kyle, I'm sorry, I didn't…"

"Hey," Kyle moves his hand around, reaching for Talon, "It's alright, big man. I'm okay."

Talon finishes cleaning Kyle and Kyle slides off of me, plopping onto the bed next to me. "Now if you don't mind." I watch as Talon slides up between my legs. "I'm gonna take our girl."

I moan as Talon begins pushing the head of his cock inside me. Talon's lips wrap around a nipple, licking and sucking it into his mouth. I writhe under him, moving my hips to help. He starts pounding harder and I can feel his hands reaching for mine. There is a hunger in his eyes, an animalistic hunger and I melt. "Take me, Talon, take me hard."

Talon brings my arms together over my head. Holding me down, using his thighs to bring my hips up higher, adjusting the angle of his thrust and I can feel the head of his cock pounding deep within me and I moan. His thrusts increase in rhythm and he lets my hands go. Rearing up, he pushes my thighs wide and toward my chin, lifting my pussy higher as he pounds harder.

"Fuck, fuck fuck, Talon!" I scream as my orgasm overtakes me and my pussy erupts, sending my orgasm squirting from within, soaking his abs.

"Oh fuck!" Talon moans as he pounds harder into me, keeping the same angle. "You're gonna do that again," he growls and immediately I can feel a new orgasm building, playing with the surface, tightening my sex and hardening my clit. His actions are slamming his cock inside and his hips are stroking my clit with each thrust.

"Oh fuck oh fuck oh fuck!" I scream as I explode, sending my orgasm squirting from my body once again and

Talon explodes inside of me. He calls out my name as he grinds out his orgasm in long languid strokes.

chapter *41*

I'm standing in our bedroom, blow drying my hair in an attempt to get ready for tonight when Kyle comes in. "Hey, panda girl."

"Hey, what's up?"

"How much longer do you think before you're ready?"

I stop the blow dryer. "What's up?"

"Nothin', we're just wondering how much longer before you're ready. There are some people here for you to meet."

I scowl at him. "Who?"

"Don't worry about it." He looks worried.

"Kyle, what's wrong?"

"Nothing, baby girl, honest. We'd just like to talk to you."

"Who's we?" I ask him.

"Talon, me, Mills, Beck & Rusty. We're going to make some adjustments to the security staff. We don't want to leave you out of it and Mills has some news for all of us, but he won't say until you're ready." I walk over to him and wrap my arms around his waist.

"Give me fifteen minutes. Let me finish up my hair and then I'll be out."

He rubs his hands along my back. I'm wearing a t-shirt that's got a row of oval holes down the middle of the back. It's also very low cut in the front. I'm wearing a pair of skinny jeans and I plan to pull my hair up over my left ear with a flower clip. The hair dryer helped with the curl. He bends down and kisses me sweetly.

He leaves shortly after that and I finish up my hair. I'd already done my make-up because I wasn't quite sure what I wanted to do with my hair. Once I'm done, I slip into my black Louboutins that I bought for myself. I'm still not wearing a bra, because my ink while healed, is still very tender. So I've donned the pasties once again. Something I think Talon and Kyle enjoy taking off of me at the end of the night.

After this afternoon, I've realized we've reached a new plateau in our relationship and it's time to bring Talon up to Kyle's speed and I have a plan, but it's going to require Kyle's help. I hope to talk to him about it while Talon's on stage.

I leave the bedroom, closing the door and walking toward the front. I can hear talking, but I'm not paying much attention when I come around the corner to see a woman dressed much like Mills, and three additional faces I don't recognize.

"Hello," I say hesitantly.

"Addison," Mills says, "I'd like to introduce you to your new bodyguards." I stop dead in my tracks.

"What do you mean 'your'?"

Mills, being the wonderful professional that he is, cracks just a little bit at my tone. "After what happened last night, I realized that the four of us were no longer enough for the six of you." Six? Oh, he means Talon, Dex, Mouse, Peacock, me and finally Kyle. "When we just had the four band members and Kyle, plus the guy you replaced, the four of us were more than enough. We didn't have to worry about Kyle as much as we do now, and we certainly need to worry about you." I flinch. "I didn't mean, ah hell, Addison, I didn't mean…I just mean that we screwed up last night and probably back in Dallas somewhere along the way. When I called Cami, since she's your rep, she was very concerned, and insisted on sending out your own bodyguards. She values you as her employee and she will not see you hurt."

I slide into the couch under the TV. "Cami insisted on sending you a team. They arrived here about an hour ago and I've been briefing them since. We're not doing this to scare you, we're not doing this to make you angry, we're doing this to keep you safe," Rusty says behind Mills.

"Safe I can understand, but I certainly don't need four, one would do," I tell them, though my irritation with this situation is rising. If it had been anyone else sent to fill this role, they certainly wouldn't be doing this.

"We have four, and we've had four brought in because we can utilize them to not only protect you, but increase security for the band. We will now have the staff we need to mind the buses, the venue, hotel rooms, and even help to provide shifts."

I nod, still confused. "Who was it? The guy last night. Who was he?" I ask and everyone hesitates, long enough to piss me off. "Damn it, don't, you held it from me last night and up until this minute I didn't want to know, but whoever he was has you guys scared shitless that something is going to happen to me. So, who was it?"

I am met with some pretty long faces and they obviously don't want to tell me who it was. "I can go ask Leroy, I'm sure he'll tell me." I stand up.

"No, Addison, sit down," Talon says and he comes over to me. I sit and he crouches down in front of me. "Before we tell you, we need you to know that what happened will never ever happen again. We also know why it happened and while it doesn't make it right, the proper steps are in place to ensure it doesn't happen again."

"Who was it, Talon?" I whisper. "It was Eddie, wasn't it?"

He pulls back from me. "How?"

"A hunch. So am I right?"

"Yes," Mills says, "He came here in an attempt to finish what he'd started in Dallas. But in doing so he violated the terms of his bail by crossing state lines. He violated the terms of his plea deal by attempting to make contact with you. The Dallas prosecutor has dropped the plea deal and it is going to court. Seeking the maximum for assault, stalking and attempted rape."

I look at him. "I thought they couldn't prove... Oh god."

"He was naked when I found him. His intention was for exactly what happened to happen. He wanted you to climb onto the bed so that he could trap you there. Talon and Kyle interrupted his plans. He figured by the time he was done, the deed would be done and he could go to jail satisfied." Mills looks at me with pity and my blood boils.

"I do not need your pity, god damn it. I am a grown fucking woman."

"Addison," Kyle scolds.

"What, Kyle? I'm not a helpless child. At least last night I wasn't drugged. I could have fought back. Don't treat me like I'm a god damn child." I stand up, because there are far too many men in my way. "I don't need to be treated like a fucking egg that's going to break if I'm handled too roughly. So until you can talk to me like I'm an adult, I will not have this conversation and I don't appreciate decisions being made on my behalf without consulting me first. So you can take you're posse and go to hell."

I storm to the bedroom, slamming the door shut and locking it. I fall face first onto the bed and scream.

Am I being childish? Yeah, I probably am, but fuck them. Everything is being done for me and I have no say one way or another. I wasn't given a goddamn choice last night about whether or not I wanted to see the asshole who'd put flowers everywhere. They put me to bed instead of letting me discuss what happened, why it happened or even the fact that someone was sending bodyguards. Kyle and Talon couldn't be bothered to tell me and Kyle dodged my questions when he was in here.

There's a knock at the door. I don't respond.

chapter 42

talon

"Come on, man, it's time."

"Where is she, Kyle?"

"She won't answer the door, so I don't know."

"I don't know if I can do this without her backstage."

Kyle rubs his hand on my back and I slouch into him. As much as Addison comforts me, Kyle does the same. "You've done it for years without her. I think you can handle one night without her being there."

"What about the song? Fuck, they're gonna want the song and I can't do it without her, either one of them. We really fucked up."

"That's just it. I don't think that we did, Talon. I think that she's overwhelmed by everything that's happened to her since she's gotten on this bus. I mean, think about it, us is just the starting point, then the whole singing thing. That really was never her life's dream, Talon, and you, me, the guys, we all pulled her into doing it, forced her to do it. Then she gets drugged and attacked, and then her attacker comes back. That asshole has tainted her entire celebrity experience. Imagine how you'd feel if shit like that happened to you."

Fuck, he has a point, as always. "I can't say how I'd handle it, the odds of having something like this happen to me are slim, I'm a guy. Women, especially gorgeous women such as Addison, are usually the targets of crimes like this. I wish I knew better why she's so upset. I wish she'd talk to us."

"I'm upset," Kyle and I spin around to see Addison approaching. "Because nobody told me anything, no one discussed anything with me. You all just took it upon yourselves to decide what was best for me. A hoard of bodyguards? I feel like I'm being smothered and suffocated by everything with no way to express myself." She takes a deep breath. "I don't think you understand how all of this makes me feel inside and I don't know how to tell you so that you can fully understand or without speaking about things we've already talked about. Like the fact that I am a very independent person, so to go from independent, to no independence with the two of you, to having my life controlled for me, puts me into a position that I want to fight back. It makes me feel defensive and I don't like it. So you need to find a way to understand the fact that I have a say in what goes on in my life. Do we need more bodyguards? Yes, we do. If Mills thinks that we need four, then we need four more bodyguards. But everything has happened to me and no one else, so I should have a full say in what happens next." She folds her arms and leans against the wall by the TV. She's defensive and I don't blame her. "The ball got dropped, I got caught in the crosshairs, and I don't like it, but I will deal with it better when you're upfront and honest with me about what's happened."

"Baby girl, we didn't skirt anything."

"Kyle, you did, in the bedroom. You were given a chance to tell me what was going on and you dodged me. Prior to that, instead of putting me to bed, you could have included me; you could have woken me up, like I asked. Instead you went about your business and then fell asleep at my feet. We lay in bed for nearly an hour, not saying much of anything, you could have told me then. But that's not the point. The conversation could have happened like it did, without the audience of four new bodyguards who no doubt think I'm a big whiny baby right now."

I scowl at her. "Does it ever occur to you that we were protecting you?"

"From what? Because I think I handled the whole Eddie situation in Dallas pretty well and I had doctors and nurses telling me what happened to me, without the sugar coating. I broke down and lost it last night because I didn't know, at the time, whether last night was the work of a madman or an insane fan. I didn't know if I was the target of an attack, or if whoever was out to hurt one or both of you. I lost it because in the midst of all of this, I'm losing myself." She starts crying and my heart breaks. I take a step toward her, intent on comforting her. She puts her hand up, stopping me and I feel like my heart is being ripped from my chest.

The breath rushes from my lungs. "Angel, I..."

"Talon, please. I need a break."

"What? No," I argue.

"Talon, listen to me. I am overwhelmed. I am splintering and shattering into thousands of pieces because I don't know what to do. I was sent here to do a job, to handle your public relations, to deal with the headlines, to handle your social media, to make sure that everything stayed intact. I am failing at my job because I am too wrapped up in the two of you. I haven't even checked my email today. I haven't even seen what's been going on in the world because I'm so caught up in this bus. Because I can't keep my hands off of you two. It's not a bad thing, believe me, but it seems like everything else is consuming the real reason why I'm here. What I'm being paid to do. I can't not be around you and Kyle. It killed me to deny you access to the room, but I needed to have time to myself. To handle my emotions surrounding what happened last night, what happened earlier, and how I can handle this without losing my cool again. I don't like feeling like this. I don't like having everything so out of my control, it scares me. It scares me to the point that I want to run to the airport because it's safer back in my condo in LA. But I can't run. I can't because I've made a commitment to Bold, to Vicious, and to the two of you. I fucking love the two of you so god damn much it scares the hell out of me. So talk to me, be honest with me, communicate things with me, not to me. Communication and honesty is what our relationship is built on, and that was shattered today. This conversation is not over yet, I will not deny you your chance to argue or agree with me, but we are out of time. We need to get inside for the show."

Neither Kyle nor I say anything to her, allowing her her chance to breathe. She walks past us and down the steps off the bus. No doubt right into Victoria.

I look at Kyle. The fear in his eyes matches my own. "We can't lose her," he says to me.

"We won't. We will fix this, we will make this right. I promise you." I wrap Kyle up in a hug and he hugs me back. It's not the same as hugging Addison, but the comfort is none the less there.

chapter 43
addison

"Addison, I'm Victoria."

I try to tamp down the emotions running through me. "Hi Victoria."

"You can call me Tori. I know that I'm probably not your favorite person right now, but I am here to protect you."

"Well then, come on," I say and I walk toward the backstage door. I see another one of the men standing near the entrance to the venue, and I'd noticed another one of the guys near the door of the bus.

"I'd just like to say that I'm sorry we were pushed on you like that earlier. We had no idea you didn't know we were coming."

"Tori, it's not your fault. There have been a lot of things over the last few weeks and it's all come crashing down on me."

"If I can speak freely?"

I stop and turn to her. "Might as well."

"They love you, don't be too hard on them. I know that you think they're babying you, but they honestly just want to protect you," she says very straight faced and I'm a little shocked that she's aware of our relationship. "You have no idea how highly Mills, Beck, Rusty and Leroy speak of you, do you?" I shake my head. "Not to mention your boyfriends. My point is this, your attack in Dallas and what happened last night are exactly the things that any decent man wants to protect a woman from and even some women like myself. So you may think they're babying you, they're not. They're protecting you."

"You're awfully insightful into the personal inner workings of this group for just arriving here."

"Cami cares about you too," she says. "She's the honest to god reason why we're here. She doesn't want anything to happen to you, as a friend and as an employee of Bold. She'd do this for anyone. In fact she has in the past for other employees. The men you've been dealing with are just as broadsided by Cami's actions as you are. So remember that the next time you want to go off the handle. Regardless of what you think, they all care about you."

I close my eyes, fighting the urge to cry again. For as much as I cried in that bedroom you'd think I'd be cried out, but apparently I'm not. I've already re-done my make-up once. I don't need to do it again. "I appreciate your advice and I will consider the things that you've said." I do my best to not sound like a bitch, I'm pretty sure I fail. "But you might want to get to know me a little better before you go spouting off things that you have no real clue about. When it comes to what's inside my head and in my heart, you don't know me. So please don't pretend like you do until you actually do." I turn to walk away and she grabs my arm.

"Despite what you think, I care about you too, it's my job."

"Then do your job," I say, pulling my arm from her hand and walking toward the venue. As I approach the door, the other guy opens it and I can see straight toward the side of the stage. Standing guard around two doors are Beck, Rusty, Mills and Leroy.

I need a damn minute alone. I can hear Tender Souls on the stage and I know I don't have much time. I walk toward the guys. "Which room can I go into, alone?"

Mills opens the door behind him and I slide into the opening to find a bare dressing room. I plop onto the couch. Why am I so damn emotional all of a sudden? Fuck, this is just ridiculous, and it's getting out of hand.

I don't agree with what they did, allowing new guards to show up without my knowledge, but in the same token, I don't think they were given much of a choice. I can picture Cami telling Mills that he doesn't have a choice. But I think Mills also realized where some of their weaknesses were and when the opportunity presented itself he took it and ran with it.

I put my head in my hands. God, I'm such a fucking idiot. I've treated everyone like shit and they don't deserve to be treated that way, but the point still remains.

I can hear Tender Souls winding down their performance and the crowd getting excited for 69 Bottles to take the stage. If I go out there before they take the stage, I have to play the happy go lucky one and I don't know if I'm capable of that. Then I remember Kyle and Talon and the fact that they've done nothing wrong. They've only ever loved me, proven that they love me, over and over again. I stand up, straightening my shirt. Fidgeting with my hair. "Get your ass moving, Addison," I say to myself as I grab the handle of the door, swinging it open. I step into the hallway.

I turn toward the stage and see Kyle standing there. He gives me a half smile, the fear and worry is evident in the way he's holding himself. I start walking toward him, but I can feel Victoria not far behind me. I turn around, facing her. "Back off. I'm backstage, there are only so many ways out of here and they're all being guarded."

She puts her hands up. The one thing I liked about Rusty was that he was always there, but I never noticed him. This one is another story.

I turn back toward Kyle who has a smirk on his face. I smile at him and he lights up. I come to stand in front of him. He takes my cheeks in his hands and kisses my forehead. Disappointment runs through me and I know all too well why he did it. I've made a huge mess of this and I need to figure out how best to fix it.

I turn around just in time to see Dex. Talon sees me and smiles a small smile but he too is broken by what I said on the bus. I don't take it back and I won't, but I need to find a way to right the ship.

Dex comes up to me and plants his wet sloppy kiss. "They really love you, you know. Stop being so hard on them." I stare at Dex in shock. "But I'm always here if they piss you off too much." Annnd...Dex is back.

"Keep dreaming, Dex." He laughs and moves away.

Peacock and Mouse come in for their hugs and kisses. "He's a mess. Give him some extra love," Peacock says into my ear. Then him and Mouse step onto the stage.

Talon is now standing before me. I wait for Kyle to wrap his arms around me and he doesn't. Pain and fear runs through my veins. I turn around to him. He's terrified. I take his cheeks into my hands. "Just because I am upset does not mean that I do not love you, it does not mean that

I do not care about you, and it certainly does not mean that I do not want to be with you or Talon. I love you, and if anything I love you even more." I let it drop, releasing his cheeks and I turn around to find Talon standing close to me.

He takes my cheeks in his hands. "Never leave me. I can't handle this now, I can't deal with it. I will die without you, Addison Lynae." He brings his lips to mine in a warm, passion filled kiss. Kyle's hands wrap around me with his hands moving slowly, comforting and engulfing me in love unlike anything I've ever felt in my life. Talon's tongue licks along my lips. The love, the pain, the joy, the desire, it all ignites within me like nothing I've ever felt before. Tears streak down my cheeks as Talon dips his tongue into my mouth, stroking my tongue. He uses his thumbs to wipe away my tears. "Please don't cry, angel. You cannot push us away that easy," he breathes and kisses me again, wiping my tears once more. He backs away toward the stage, and with each step backwards my heart grows fuller, my chest pounds harder.

My love grows stronger.

When Talon takes the stage, I turn to Kyle, burying my face in his chest, breathing in his scent. Holding him to me as hard as I can, like if I let him go, I won't be able to breathe.

"Shh, baby girl, I got you. We got you, we will never let you fall."

chapter 44

The concert is one of Talon's best. Our duet of 'Your Eyes' goes amazingly well and the crowd starts cheering wildly for 'To Be Free'. When it comes up in the set, our performance is filled with so much raw emotion that it sends tears to Talon's eyes. When we finished, he kissed me with so much love and passion that I considered putting my plan back in motion for after the show.

But then I realize that we can't screw away our problems.

The greenroom is met with much of what happened in Kansas City. I join the line of the band, signing autographs and taking pictures. It takes us two hours to get through the entire line. Sometimes I wonder why the guys stick around. They can leave at any time. There is nothing in the VIP ticket that guarantees autographs and pictures, but it is a tribute to 69 Bottles' reputation and their love for their fans.

I leave the guys to their business and head back to the bus. Tori is on my heels but at a distance. When I reach the door of the bus one of the other bodyguards I haven't met, unlocks the door and asks me to wait before I can board. Tori stands with me.

I turn to her. "Once your men are free, bring them to the bus, I want to talk to them all."

"Yes ma'am."

"I am no ma'am," I tell her, "I am Addison, or Addie, no ma'am nonsense. I am hardly old enough, and if I'm older than you, I'll be surprised."

"Absolutely, Addison." She smiles a little. I smile back as the guy who boarded comes back off of the bus.

"All clear."

"Thank you." I climb on board and go for the fridge. I can really use a drink, but we don't keep alcohol on the bus. It is a moving vehicle after all.

I get to the bedroom and grab my new messenger bag and my old bag. I want to switch them over. I go back up to the galley and grab a seat on the couch. I plug in my laptop and start pulling stuff from my old messenger bag. My planner, my folio case, along with my iPad, which is dead, and a ton of loose papers. I need a binder to put all this stuff in.

I start setting up my new bag while my laptop loads. Once it is up and running I open my Facebook page. I need something mindless for a few minutes and there are over two thousand new friend requests, notifications up the wazoo and too many messages to count.

Looking along the left side of the screen I notice a new line, "Addison Beltrand". I click the link. The scene switches and then finally a pop up. "You've been added as an admin to "Addison Beltrand" do you accept?"

I click yes. "Holy fuck!" I have a musician's page on Facebook and it has... "Fuck me." Over three hundred thousand followers. Notifications up a storm, messages, etcetera. Okay, this will take far more time to sort out than I have time for.

I open my email and flip back to Facebook. For Pete's sake, it's going nuts. I click on the notifications, most of them say "so and so tagged you in a post" I click on one of them from a few minutes ago.

It's a picture, taken tonight. The tagline reads... "I got to meet the amazing, talented and gorgeous Addison Beltrand at #69Bottles #DesMoines Concert! Made my year."

I decide to make her day a little more with a comment. "It was great meeting you tonight, thanks so much for coming."

I click on a few more links of "so and so tagged you" some of them are videos, pictures and comments regarding the concert tonight. After about five minutes my email finally stops bouncing with incoming mail, I close the window and flip into my email.

I begin the tedious process of sorting, Trinity, Cami, Bold related emails, my news alerts, 69 Bottles news alerts and finally am left with a few random emails, which based on the preview are junk, so I delete them. I click on Cami's folder. Scanning the subjects, I land on some from last night, after the event happened.

I open it. The email is explaining her plan, sending bodyguards, explaining that Bold employees are valuable and if for no other reason than to protect a valuable Bold asset. I take a deep breath. If I'd read my email, been doing my job, I wouldn't have freaked out on everyone earlier, but again, I was in bed, having steaming hot sex with two very sexy men. I shiver remembering Talon taking Kyle.

I flip through a couple of other emails from Cami, most are Bold business, congratulations for the amazing Kansas City show. She even sent a couple of the videos. Then I finally come to one that says Facebook.

"I know you don't use your personal Facebook much, but you have no doubt been inundated with friend requests from fans, so I went ahead and had a musician's page set up and had you added as the admin. It is your site to control, but I, along with Trinity and Vincent retain control as well. Have fun with it.

"Oh and we've also created a Twitter account, which has already been verified and an Instagram page which have all been tied together. Facebook will post to Twitter, Twitter and Instagram to Facebook. I recommend downloading them to your phone so that you can Tweet from time to time. Share pictures etcetera. You know the PR drill, for now, we will let you run it."

That's the gist of the email. She prattles on a bit about other social media things, but I am well versed in what I should or shouldn't do with social media. She also provides the passwords to Twitter and Instagram.

"This is really happening, isn't it?" I say to no one and I don't get a reply.

I continue scrolling through her emails and find one with the subject "assistant?"

I open it.

"We're sending Raine to New York to meet with you. We're finalizing your schedule for the time that you're there and right now it's packed full and I think things would be easier for you if you have someone to help you out. Though she is my assistant, she's more of a decoration around here, and she is very good at what she does. I think she can be put to better use helping you."

"Well, okay then," I mutter. Maybe she has a point, but I shouldn't be given an assistant because I'm not doing my job. If I spent time doing my job more and Talon and Kyle less, it wouldn't seem like I'm not.

The bus jerks a little and I look to Tori and her men coming up the stairs. I close my laptop. "Hi Tori," I say.

"Addison, let me introduce you to Bruce," She gestures to the biggest of the three men, how apt, "Troy," the cutest of the three, "and Casey."

I stand up and walk around the table, taking their hands. "Pleasure to meet you guys. I apologize for earlier and I appreciate you going to work without knowing who you were protecting."

"No problem, ma'am," the cute one says and I watch Tori stiffen and I laugh.

"Troy, right?" he nods. "My name is Addison or Addie, I don't answer to ma'am."

"Yes ma'am, I mean, Addison." He blushes.

I laugh. "I understand it goes against anything you're taught, but I am hardly old enough for ma'am."

Bruce is bald, not by age but by razor and he is huge. His bicep is probably bigger than my head. Troy is slimmer, but no less bulky with reddish military short hair. And Casey is a little more wiry, kind of like Kyle. He's muscular, but in sleeker ways. They're all at least six feet tall. Tori is a tall brunette, slim, but she has some muscle and she stands about five ten or even five eleven. She has wider shoulders than I do, but less hip and ass than me.

"So explain to me what happened when I came back to the bus?" I ask.

"We're required, by Mills, to lock the bus doors when no one is on board, but regardless of the doors being closed and locked and guarded, we will be checking the bus to be sure that no one is on board who doesn't belong. Once someone is on board, their bodyguard is to stand by with the original guard. It's a safety precaution to make sure no one else gets on board.

"We also have a guard with the event security at the gate. This is to ensure no one who isn't supposed to be here gets past security and the gate closes fifteen minutes after showtime and opens for exits only ten minutes before show end. If anyone tries to leave through the back door prior to that time, they're told to go out a normal door or wait. Crowd control really," Tori tells me.

"So what happens when we go out after a show, the next one for example?" I ask, I really don't need to know, but I think I am entitled to know the processes.

"We will divide the guards, sending no less than two, in advance, to the venue to review their security protocols, this will happen before the show starts. Once everyone is in the greenroom following the show, those same two guards will go ahead to the venue. Ensuring security procedures are being met, and the safety of everyone's arrival. We will always leave two guards with the buses and the remaining six of us will be on hand at the bar."

"Who's primarily responsible for me?" I ask.

"That would be all of us," she says and I look at her. "Everything we do revolves around you and your safety, Addison. However, outings will involve me and one other guy, whether it's one from Mills' team or my own."

"I like Rusty, if you're going to pick one of Mills' team. He's been my shadow for a while and I'm comfortable with him. So until I get fully comfortable with you, I ask that you bring Rusty along. Though I don't go very many places."

She nods. "As you wish."

"I'd just like some more time to get to know everyone. I've been with the other guys for over two weeks, and I'm comfortable with them, so I imagine the same will happen with all of you. Lastly, I have a firm request, and by not honoring this request can lead to your dismissal." I look at all of them. "If I ask you a question, especially procedure, problem or otherwise business related, I expect an honest, immediate response. Do not beat around the bush. I am not made of glass, I need to know. If something happens, a security threat, and I have to be whisked away, I expect an explanation."

"Yes, Addison," Tori says.

I look to Bruce. "Yes, Ms. Beltrand."

Then Troy and Casey both confirm their yeses. "Thank you. I also agree to notify you if at any time I feel uncomfortable and need your assistance. In an incident where talking isn't exactly possible, do you have a signal?"

"Thumbs down, if it is an immediate need. If it is an uncomfortable need, tug on your ear."

"Like this?" I tug on my earlobe.

"Yes, though you can be a little more subtle."

"Okay, that is something I do from time to time, a nervous fidget. So can we add something to that?"

"How about this, do it like you'd normally do." I do. "Okay, your hand opens up. If it is something that you need our help with, keep your hand near your face after you do it. You can do something like this." She tugs on her ear, then crosses her other arm across her body and then rests her arm against it. Keeping her hand near her face. It's a casual gesture and shouldn't alert anyone other than my security staff.

"Perfect, I can do that."

We continue our conversation for a little longer and then they leave. I notice that the guys still haven't come back yet. I text Kyle.

Me: Where are you guys?

Cowboy: They're having a meeting about tonight and then tomorrow.

Me: how much longer?

Cowboy: a while, why?

Me: come help me with something. I'm on the bus, bedroom.

Cowboy: on my way.

chapter 45

"Hey baby girl, what's up?"

"I need your help."

"With?" I turn around, three things in my hand, I show him. His jaw drops. He swallows hard. "I...um, how?"

"Well, I want you to get me set up for Talon. I figured you could um, help me to help him."

"Absolutely. What do you want me to do?"

I tell him and we go to work.

Two orgasms later and I'm all set. Lying on the bed, naked. Kyle's cock is in my mouth, I'm sucking and working it with excitement, waiting rather impatiently for Talon to show up.

"Ahh!" I moan as Kyle pulls on the purple cock protruding from my body. Though the Feeldoe didn't elicit as much excitement within when I saw it, it's still sexy as fuck. Kyle's cock in my mouth is serving as a great distraction from looking at it.

I continue licking and sucking, toying more than putting forth solid effort in getting him off. I want him to save it for Talon. I told Kyle my plan and he was more than excited for it. Talon hasn't had a chance to experience my cock and I want him to feel it with Kyle underneath him.

"Angel?" I hear Talon shout.

I pull Kyle's cock from my mouth. "In the bedroom," I shout and take Kyle's cock back into my mouth. He tugs again on my cock and it sends a shot of pure pleasure through my body.

"Addie, are you..." Talon stops dead in his tracks as he opens the door. He stands there completely dumb struck and I smile around the head of Kyle's cock.

I turn toward him. Kyle's hard-on in my hand, his hand on my purple dick, "I'm great." I smile. "Come here, big man."

I can see a visual as his mind clears. "We need to talk."

"Is it about earlier?" I ask him, losing focus as Kyle strokes along my shaft, tugging it and pushing it back just enough that the bulb shifts against my g-spot. "Or is it something else?"

"Earlier."

I smile. "Then it can wait."

"But, Addie..."

"Listen, I've come to a realization and right now, I am craving you so bad that I want to fuck you. I promise that we will talk, but right now, I am desperate to be inside you." I moan as Kyle continues pushing and pulling on the toy that is giving me immense pleasure just by being stroked. "Please," I beg.

His answer is removing his vest, then his t-shirt. I watch as he unbuttons his fly and slides his jeans down his legs, springing his rock hard erection free. "I can't say no to you," he breathes. He sounds almost disappointed that we aren't talking.

"I promise, we will talk," I reassure him and he nods as he kicks off his boots, shedding his jeans completely and climbing onto the bed. He goes straight for my toy. He takes it from Kyle with a smile and he wraps his mouth around it. Pushing it down, the ridges stroke my clit, the bulb slides against the plug in my ass and I moan, pulling Kyle's cock back into my mouth with gusto.

Talon and I continue sucking, licking and stroking the toys in our mouths. I am however, rewarded with little dribbles of Kyle's delicious pre-cum. Talon slides up on all fours and he begins stroking his cock while he licks and sucks mine. I moan at the sight of him between my legs.

Kyle pulls back from me, moving off of the bed and walking toward the foot of the bed. He taps on one of Talon's legs to get him to spread wider and he does. There is a flash of terror in his eyes. That is, until Kyle lays down on his back, pushing himself between Talon's legs. Talon lifts his hips, giving Kyle better access to what he's after. I can barely see what's happening but I watch as Kyle takes Talon's dick from his hand and begins stroking it for him. I watch as Talon's eyes roll up into his head with the pleasure Kyle's mouth is bringing him.

Talon begins stroking my cock a little harder and a little faster, igniting my orgasm and sending shivers up my spine. With my hands free now, I stroke Talon's hair, encouraging him to suck faster and he does. The ridges bounce along my clit and the bulb moves up and down, in and out slightly. "Fuck!" I moan and Talon's eyes turn white. "Don't stop," I moan and he continues, my legs lock up and my orgasm rolls through my body, seizing my muscles and shooting off fireworks behind my eyelids at the same time that I hear him groan.

He comes off of my cock and moans as Kyle continues sucking him. I watch as Talon's hips begin to bounce up and down slightly and I know he's close. "Jesus, Kyle, fuck!" he moans.

Kyle groans as Talon erupts in his mouth. Kyle swallows him down, stroking him, milking him and I nearly come unglued watching it.

Kyle slides out from between Talon's legs. Talon rolls onto his side. I roll the other direction so that I can get up. I can't actually sit with either device. I pull myself up onto all fours, then come up on my knees. I hear Talon hiss through his teeth as he takes in the sight of me. "Fuck, angel, that's so goddamn hot."

I look at him through hooded eyes and he groans. I put myself in position, on my knees at the head of the bed. Using my pointer finger I gesture for him to come to me and he does. Crawling to me face first. I don't understand why until he runs a wet, flat tongue over my nipple and I tremble as pleasure ignites once again. "Turn around," I command.

He obeys, having done this with Kyle, but Talon is a little more excited about it. Though I know he's never done this, anytime I play with his ass, he's loved it. Kyle is standing at the end of the bed. "Come here, cowboy," Talon says to him. Kyle smiles.

"Oh I will, but not yet," he says with a satisfied smirk on his face. "I want to watch our baby girl fuck you."

I shiver with Kyle's dirty talk. He doesn't do it often, but fuck, it's hot when he does. I reach over for the bottle of lube and Talon readies himself. Spreading his legs to either side of mine. I put a cold drop of lube right on his entrance and he jumps slightly, but he settles quickly.

I begin working the lube around the tight ring of his ass and he moans. I continue playing, probing only with the soft pad of my middle finger. With my other hand, I rub his back. I can see him clenching and releasing. "If it's too much, just tell me and I'll stop," I tell him.

"It feels so good," he moans. I can feel his hand come to his cock, and start stroking it.

"Don't you dare take that orgasm from me, Talon Carver," I say and he stops. "Good boy," I praise him and watch as he shivers with anticipation. "Are you a switch, big man? Do you like to be mister tough guy or do you like to submit to me?"

I slide my finger inside. "To you," he moans and I continue fucking his ass with my finger.

"Good boy," I say stroking his back. "Fuck my finger," I tell him and his hips begin rocking back and forth. I look at Kyle who has his jaw on the floor while he watches me. I begin probing with another finger, pushing it inside.

"More," Talon cries out and I begin working a third into his ass and he moans, rocking his hips against my hand.

"Greedy boy, are you ready for my cock?"

"Argh, yes," he groans and I begin lubing up my purple cock. Coating it with a nice layer of lube.

I extract my fingers. "Come down a little lower, big man," I say and his knees spread wider and his hips fall toward the bed. I begin pushing the head of my purple Feeldoe into his ass and he moans. I pull it back out and the ridges caress my clit and I moan. "Fuck, your ass feels amazing," I tell him and he pushes back a little onto me. "Easy, big man, I don't want to hurt you."

He stills and I go about pushing in and pulling out in little spurts. Talon begins to pant while writhing beneath me.

I'm finally all the way inside and I stop. "How's my big man doin?" I ask and he moans. "Do you want me to fuck you?" I ask, surprised by my own brazen questions.

Something about having him under me, taking my cock is the most empowering thing in the world.

Kyle comes to the side of the bed. He hands me a towel so I can clean my hand off as I begin pumping in small, excruciatingly slow thrusts. I toss the towel and Kyle climbs on the bed near me. He kisses me with ardor. "You're so fucking beautiful," he says as his hand caresses one breast and then the other.

His kisses move down my jaw and the thrusting is sending me close to orgasm. Kyle pulls a nipple into his mouth, sucking on it and I moan. He pulls back, letting it pop free and I moan as the cool air brings both my nipples into hard peaks.

Looking down my body I can see my purple cock sliding in and out of Talon and it's beautiful. My hard nipples and breasts framing the perfect view. I moan.

I slide back into Talon all the way. "Big man?"

"Mmm," he moans.

"Lift yourself up. Kyle is going to crawl under you. He's going to take your cock into his mouth, and you can have his."

"Ahh," he moans as he shifts around. Kyle goes to work, awkwardly sliding in underneath him. Talon can barely contain himself from taking Kyle into his mouth and my heart swells with how far my two big men have come since we started this relationship.

Their strides spur me on and I begin sliding further out of Talon before thrusting back in. He moans and I can see his body shaking with pleasure. Now that Kyle has him in his mouth, it won't take him long to come and I want to get off too.

"Faster." Talon moans, sucking Kyle back into his mouth.

I begin thrusting faster into Talon. His moans and pants become more frequent and my orgasm is building, spreading desire through my veins. My clit hardens and the ridges of the Feeldoe dance with each thrust and pull. The bulb inside pushes and pulls and my muscles clamp down on it.

"Fuck me," Talon moans, "I'm coming." He cries out. I pound into him harder, bringing my orgasm to a head and I cry out his name as I explode.

Talon's animalistic cries fill the room and I can barely hear Kyle as his orgasm takes him.

chapter 46

I slowly pull out of Talon and he groans more than a few times. I take satisfaction in what I've accomplished tonight. Now it's time to reward Kyle. Poor guy only got a blow job. Once I've pulled out of Talon, he falls to his side. Freeing Kyle. Who reaches up to my pussy and helps me by pulling my cock free. I shiver. Kyle smiles up at me. Then he begins tugging on my butt plug. I push out slightly helping it come out. We went with the biggest one we have because I have more in store for my guys.

As predicted, Talon is watching as Kyle extracts my toys and his cock is still rock hard, ready for number three. Once Kyle has me free, he sits up. Getting off of the bed, he throws on a pair of shorts and I grab the bottle of lube. Sliding over to Talon, I take his cock into my mouth and he shudders.

"Fuck." He jumps a little with each pass of my tongue over the underside of his head. "What are you doing, angel?"

I smile around his erection and show him the lube. I pull off his cock and it flops to the side. Fuck, he's huge. I take the lube and pour a good amount in my hand. I sit up, rubbing it between my hands, warming it. Then I put my hands on his cock, lubing him up.

I continue stroking him until he is good and hard. "Kyle's had enough today," he groans.

"This isn't for Kyle."

His eyes pop open and I shift. Straddling him reverse cowgirl. I put my feet under me to give me some leverage and I reach between my legs. I take hold of his cock and rub the head along my back entrance. He groans. Once I have it in position I begin lowering myself onto his cock.

"Fuck!" I moan. "You're fucking huge." But my voice is dripping with pleasure as I continue sliding down. I feel his hands come to my ass cheeks, helping me balance myself and stop my shaking legs.

He gives me tiny thrusts in and out, working his cock, spreading me open, filling me full until I've taken all of him in my ass. I grind against him and he groans. "Fucking a, Addison."

My name on his lips sends a thrill through me. I sit down on him, stilling to adjust myself. I lean back, placing my hands on his chest and I slide my feet out from under me, holding them tight to his legs as a shot of pain shoots through me and I wince. "Easy, baby girl," Kyle says as he comes back into the room.

I begin slowly sliding my hips up and down on Talon, the pain I experienced quickly turns to pleasure as I take him inside of me. "Argh," I cry out as pleasure sky rockets. "Kyle," I moan. "I need you inside me." I watch as Kyle watches me riding Talon. Then he comes around the bed, climbing carefully onto it. He reaches for my pussy.

Stroking my clit and sliding fingers in and out of me. The pleasure is so intense I bite my lip, saving my orgasm.

"Let it out, baby girl. Give it to us," he says softly as he slips two fingers deep inside me and I clamp down on them. My muscles lock up and I can no longer move. Talon quickly takes over sliding in and out of me.

"Fuck me, Kyle. I need your fucking cock," I cry out and looking down my body I watch as he lines up the head of his cock with my core. Talon slows as Kyle slides in. The slow pace is maddening. "Fuck me!" I groan. "Take me."

This is it, this is what I need, what I crave, what I'm addicted to. Having them, taking them and being so wholly taken by *them* in every way possible.

Neither one of them hesitate. Kyle slides in and Talon pulls out. The dual sensations are intense, add to that the fact that Kyle has taken a nipple into his mouth and it's mind-blowing. My arms begin to tremble. Kyle wraps his around me. He stops sliding in and out. "Relax, let me hold you," he says and I do. He's holding me up. "Move your arms." I do and he gently lays me on Talon's chest. Talon can no longer move, but his hands go to work caressing my body, pulling on my nipples and Kyle begins fucking me in earnest. I cry out. I am so full of Talon and Kyle's pounding that another orgasm builds. "Talon?" Kyle groans.

"Oh yeah," Talon says behind me and Kyle thrusts faster and harder into me. I explode, clenching down, shattering into thousands of tiny pieces around their cocks and their love.

Kyle pulls out first, then moves to help Talon and I roll over. I have no strength left in my body and Talon knows the only way to pull out safely is to turn me on my side. He does that, then slowly he sits up, pulling out of me. He's gone soft so the extraction is gentle. "So three is your limit," I tease as he pulls free of me.

He laughs. "Yeah, maybe. Don't move, angel, we'll clean you up."

"Good, because I can't move."

They both laugh and go about helping me clean up. A shower would be best, but I refuse to be carried naked for one, and for two, I couldn't stand once I got in there. Talon comes back into the room with a wet washcloth and a towel. He spreads my legs and begins wiping me from front to back. Both of them have shorts on, though I know they won't stay on. I see Kyle has a shirt in his hand.

Once Talon is done cleaning me, he puts my legs back together and takes the towel and washcloth back to the basket between the guys' bunks and my old room. There is a washing machine on the other bus, which I didn't know until like, yesterday.

"Can you sit up?" Kyle asks and I groan. "I just want to put a t-shirt on you. We really are going to talk tonight before anyone gets any sleep."

I groan again and find the strength to sit up. Kyle is right there with a t-shirt that isn't mine, it's one of Talon's white shirts. It's huge on me, but I don't complain because it smells like him.

When Talon comes back into the room he has three bottles of water. He hands one to Kyle, then opens another one, handing it to me. "Drink up, angel." I do as he says and I drink back a good third of the bottle before I come up for air. I was thirsty.

Both Talon and Kyle sit on the bed with me. We're all cross-legged at this point, they're shirtless and in boxers, and I'm bottomless and in a t-shirt. Oh the irony.

"Now, it's our turn to talk," Talon says and I shiver at his tone. He's dead serious. My heart stops.

chapter 47

"We will never keep you from doing your job," Talon says straight up, no beating around the bush.

"I know, and you don't," I tell them both. "I make the choices that I make, but it's hard sometimes to let you and Kyle go."

"But us clinging to each other isn't good either," Kyle says. "We all need to find a distance we're comfortable with."

"I know, and I meant what I said, but I didn't mean it as harshly as I said it. Yes, I feel like I'm suffocating, but it's because I feel like so much is going on behind my back. When things happen that involve me, it is important for me to know what's going on. For my sanity sake." I take a deep breath. "I also overreacted. Which boils back to doing my job first, and my boyfriends second. If I'd done my job, I would have known before the bodyguards showed up that they were coming. I would have had a better, clearer explanation that made perfect sense to me. Instead, I got a pity trip from Mills and it pissed me off. I understand better now why the pity trip, but I didn't know it then."

"What are you talking about, panda girl?"

"I had an email from Cami, explaining to me why she was sending bodyguards. They were coming whether Mills wanted them or not. She was sending them to protect a Bold employee and when I talked to, or rather scolded Victoria on my way into the venue after giving my little speech, she told me that I am not the first employee Cami has provided security services to. So again, knowing the story first would have cut back on my reaction. For that, I am deeply sorry."

"But it's brought us to a point in our communication that we obviously needed to get to," Talon says. "I'm not going to lie. I don't remember everything you said, I just remember the things that hit home the most and that was you needing a break. Then I come back to the bus and you were ready for me, waiting for me and I honest to god did not know what to think." He scrubs his face with his hands. "If you need a break from me, from Kyle or from both of us, then we need to talk about it, not fight about it. We need to discuss what we can do as partners to work through the need you have for a break."

"I don't need a break exactly. I just need to be in charge of certain aspects. I need to know what's happening when my security is involved. I'm not made of glass, guys, and I promise I will not break."

"You looked pretty shattered last night," Kyle says sadly. "It nearly killed us to see you like that. We let you be because we both know and understand independence and we understand how you feel about it. We didn't know how to help you and we made a choice to leave you alone." Kyle takes a drink of his water. "Our other option was to push you to talk, and after what happened today, I think we made the right choice. Mills asked us to not discuss the incoming bodyguards with you. He wanted to do that, which is why he slept on our bus last night, but you came back to the room next door and pulled us both into the bedroom. The rest is history, but by the time we were done, Mills was briefing the new team. Which is his job; it's what Talon pays good money for him to do."

"I also pay him to keep us safe and that didn't happen," Talon grumbles.

"Don't go there, big man," I tell him. "What happened last night was no one's fault. Things happen, and it's unfortunate that it took what happened to realize our weaknesses. I also know that Mills agreed to the bodyguards because he wasn't afraid to ask for help." I run my hand through my hair. "What happened in Dallas was a freak accident. I mean, protocol was followed and I was still attacked." I watch as both of them flinch, "You stopped it, you recognized a problem and you solved it. What happened last night was at the hands of a man obsessed. So now with all new security and the new protocols they have in place, the chance of something happening again is slim to none. So at this point my security is a mute discussion."

"I agree," Kyle says.

"So you're okay with the security team now?" Talon

"I am," I nod, "I spoke with Tori and then met the rest of the guys. We discussed a few things, like trouble signals, who my primaries are, the fact that Tori is moving onto the bus. Speaking of, did you know that Peacock, Mouse and Dex all elected to give her my old rack?" They both shake their heads. "Well, they did. She didn't move in tonight, but by the time we leave Minneapolis, she'll switch over. I also know that I'm not allowed to go anywhere without a tail and I put Tori in her place about following too close to me."

"When did you do that?" Kyle asks, suspicion in his eyes.

I laugh, "As I was walking to you before the show."

He bursts out laughing. "I wondered if that's what that was all about."

I giggle, "She wasn't too pleased with me, but it was one of the things I loved about Rusty tailing me. I never knew he was there, but yet I always knew where he was. We worked great together, which is why I told her tonight that until I get completely comfortable with the new guys, Rusty is to come along anytime I want to go anywhere without the band, like shopping."

They both laugh. "Thank god for that," Talon says and I scowl at him.

"You went shopping with Kyle all on your own in Phoenix."

He laughs, "Sort of. I utilized the personal shopper at the store. I gave her sizes, she picked stuff out and Kyle and I decided what we liked and didn't like."

"Oh my god, and here I thought I had a totally heartfelt wardrobe," I tease them both with a laugh.

"We picked it out, we just didn't spend the hours looking for it," Kyle says with a smile on his face.

"Well okay then." I nod my head.

"So are we okay?" Talon asks, his voice is shaky with concern.

"Come here," I tell him and he crawls over to me, wrapping his arms around my waist and laying his head in my lap against my stomach. Oh god, no wonder I'm a damn mess. "We're absolutely okay." I run my fingers through his hair. I look at Kyle who looks sad. "Come here." He comes at me, wrapping his arms around my neck and knocking me over. "Yes, we're okay, I promise you we are."

It isn't much longer after we giggle our way into forgiveness that we crawl under the sheets. I pull the t-shirt over my head so that my boys have their skin on skin contact they seem to crave so much. Ironically, this time, they're each cupping the breast closest to them. I roll my eyes and try not to laugh at their choice of body part, but it works and at nearly two in the morning, we fall asleep quickly.

chapter 48

Today is Sunday, and we're on our way to Minneapolis where we will play at First Avenue, which is one of the leading venues that started a lot of major bands in the past. It's a small venue, only housing fifteen hundred people, but the stop is worth it because the tickets went for premium pricing. It is also our first stop where we will be spending some time in a hotel. I am in need of a bath.

When I wake up, the guys are still sleeping, so I crawl out from under them, throwing on Talon's t-shirt and a pair of pajama pants and head into the bathroom. I check my watch and it's only nine-thirty, which gives me plenty of time to take care of business.

Once in the bathroom, I do exactly that. Only this time I have to pull out my birth control. I've been on NuvaRing for a few years now, it works great because of the higher dose of hormones and with my PCOS, I need it. And not to sound gross or anything, it's not there when I reach to pull it out.

I remind myself that I've had sex with two very well hung men and it's probably been pushed higher. I dig a little deeper and I find nothing. Well shit. I know I put it in three weeks ago. As is my Sunday ritual.

Having PCOS is no fun sometimes, but I've been able to regulate it with birth control, though I don't always bleed very much. Which is why I take it out on Sunday and put a new one in the following Sunday, but I've never had sex with it in. Though I had no intention of doing so, I asked all the questions when she first prescribed it to me.

I try to push it to the back of my mind, the main concern is the fact that I'm going to have to ask one of my guys for help. If I can't find it, that means that either I will need to visit the doctor to have it removed, or it fell out and then we have a major issue.

The likelihood of getting pregnant for me is less than a ten percent chance. I have one semi functioning ovary and the other is completely blocked by cysts, which are checked regularly, so don't panic on me. Believe me, I'm doing enough of that myself.

I put my hand on my stomach and I'm bloated, which is normal. I'm a crabby ass bitch right now, which is a good sign of me having PMS, and I'm an emotional mess. So for now, I'll wait.

When I'm done, I sit down with my laptop at the table. Instead of jumping into my email, I log into Facebook. More friend requests, over three hundred new notifications and messages. I go into the settings to see if I can turn off friend requests, also, making sure the page is private so that people can no longer contact me though this page. I have a new musician's page and they can friend me there. Once that's done, I hop over to the page and there are no less then another ten grand in new likes since I saw it last night. Jeez. I guess I'm more popular than I thought.

I look through some of the notifications and the majority of them are people tagging me in posts and pictures, which is great. I click on a few of them and surprisingly, I remember meeting a lot of these people when I see the pictures.

There are a ton of them that say they can't wait to see me in...fill in the city and it warms my heart. I log into Twitter with the credentials given to me by Cami and I can see that I have more than ten thousand followers and that I am following about fifteen people. I click on the following and smile.

Cami, Tristan, Mick, Beau, Travis, Trinity, Vincent, Talon, Dex - oh lord -, Mouse, Peacock, 69 Bottles, Vicious Records, Kyle, and finally I'm thrown by the last one, Bryan Hayes. I click on his pictures, enlarging it to reveal a picture of The Bryan Hayes, one of country music's biggest names right now. Then I notice that he's following me. I click back and see that everyone I'm following is among those who are following me and I smile.

Then I click over to the Mentions section and holy shit, there is a lot here. Mostly large groups of new followers, which I turn off. Looking only at the @ Mentions.

It's a lot of the same, can't wait to meet her, met her, so on and so forth, until I come across a tweet from Bryan Hayes. "Dying to see @AddieBelt69 in Minneapolis 2nite, she's amazing, would love to sing with her. #69Bottles"

"Holy fuck!" I nearly shout.

"Unless you're dying, shut up, love." Dex grumbles from behind his curtain in the bunks.

"Bite me, Dex," I call back to him.

"Stop threatening me."

I roll my eyes and he pops his head out from behind the curtain. "Seriously though, you good?"

"Fucking fabulous!" I stand up, grab my laptop, disconnecting it from the wall and go bounding back to our bedroom. I shut the door behind me. "OHMYGOD!" I all but scream, both of them jump about a mile high off of the bed. "You're not going to believe this!" I jump up on the bed, making them bounce a little more.

"Baby girl, what time is it?"

"It's after ten."

"Oh," Talon says. "You all right?"

"No, I'm over the fucking moon!" I squeal.

"Oh lord, what are you so excited about?" Kylè says, playfully covering his ears and plopping back onto the pillow.

"Bryan fucking Hayes is coming to the show tonight!"

Kyle's eyes pop open, "The Bryan Hayes?" I nod.

"Country superstar Bryan Hayes?" Talon asks.

"The one and only."

"So why does that make you so excited, I thought you loved rock music," Talon teases.

"I love rock music, and classical and country and pop and oh hell, just about anything but I *love* Bryan Hayes. But that's not why I'm excited." I open the laptop to the bigger version of the Tweet. "Read it, read it!" I squeal.

"Stop shaking it, baby girl. We just woke up. How long have you been up?"

"Like forty minutes, I haven't even had coffee yet."

"Oh god," Talon says, excited. "You're kidding me right, he said this?"

"Uh huh. He's following me on Twitter too."

"Since when do you have Twitter?"

"Oh fucking read the Tweet, cowboy, please?" I beg.

Talon is staring at me in shock.

"Holy shit!" Kyle exclaims. "Holy fucking shit, baby girl, that's fucking, wow." He looks at me with love.

"I knew you'd make a name for yourself," Talon says with a big wide grin on his face.

"Oh my god, now I'm fucking nervous."

"About what?" Kyle teases, "Tonight's show?" I nod. "Oh baby girl, forget about that, you always do anyway, stop fretting about it. And give me a fucking hug." I laugh and fall on top of him, hugging him. Talon comes up behind me, sandwiching me between the two of them.

"I'm so proud of you, angel," Talon says then kisses my cheek.

The excitement of that tweet overrides all thoughts of birth control and missing rings.

chapter 49

Shell shock... that's about all I can say right now. After I got done freaking out over the tweet and the boys helped me freak out a little more, they too are very excited; I got into my email. There was an email from Cami that reiterated the validity of the tweet. She told me that Bryan would be stopping by before the show to introduce himself. I squealed again when I read that and the boys thought I'd lost my mind.

"What? Just because I don't fangirl over you," I say to Talon.

He puts his hand over his chest. "I'm offended, you don't fangirl over me."

"Oh for crying out loud. I fangirl over you, I just get to fangirl over all the parts no one else gets to see." I give him a wide eyes 'so there' look.

He busts out laughing. "You don't fangirl, you worship."

"See, so which would you rather have..." I put my hands up all prissy like. "OHMYGOD it's Talon Carver..."

then I start pawing at him, "or" I get onto my knees and bow to him, kissing the bed, "I'm not worthy."

He's still laughing. "Neither," he says, "I prefer you worshiping me in bed."

"Oh, I do that too." I wink at him then go back to my email.

Cami's email goes on to say that I can commit to a duet with Bryan Hayes, but it cannot be recorded until after my contractual obligations are completed with 69 Bottles. I shrug, it's fine with me. I won't pull back from this tour for anything.

"So what's the plan?" I ask Talon and Kyle when I close up my laptop a few minutes later.

"We should be at the hotel shortly. Mills will get us checked in and take care of all that stuff. We have sound check at two, which isn't giving us enough time here to get ready before the show." I look at my watch and it's after twelve, and I'm starving. "First Avenue isn't that far from the hotel, so when sound is done we can come back here, or you," he looks at me, "You can pack up your outfit for tonight and get dressed there."

"You mean actually use a dressing room for once?"

Kyle snorts a laugh. "Would certainly give you more room. The show starts at six and we do not have Tender Souls tonight. So we have to be ready to roll by five forty-five."

"I'll pack up a bag and outfit, I'll get ready there. I can go jump in the shower now, get my hair dried so I can style it later." The guys nod. There's disappointment on their faces. "What?"

They both come at me, tackling me to the bed, engulfing me in a tangle of arms and legs, and they start kissing and licking along my jaw. "Oh no, you don't." I feel hands creeping up Talon's t-shirt. Sliding along my belly toward my breasts. They're both doing it at the same time like their hands are tied together. They both reach my breasts and find my nipples at the same time and my back arches. "So not fair."

They twist and tug, then push the shirt higher and they start licking and sucking. Having two mouths, one nipple each, is an intense sensation. My pussy pulses with need and my body shivers in delight. Now that my nipples are in their mouths, their hands slide back down my stomach and into the waist of my pajama pants. "No, no, no," I whine without conviction. They both suck harder on my nipples and I moan. "Shower...get read...oh forget it," I groan as one hand makes contact with my clit and the other slides into my sex. Flicking and fucking me to the point of near explosion.

Their actions don't let up. Fingers moving, tongues licking, mouths sucking. My orgasm ignites on the surface and my blood is racing in my veins. "Fuck." I jump with a flick on my clit, sensation exploding, orgasm building. "Argh!" I moan and explode, shattering into thousands of pieces under their touch.

Kyle backs up and Talon pushes me onto my stomach. Then I feel someone pulling down my pajama bottoms and I lift my hips to help. Once I am missing bottoms, they lift my hips into the air. Spreading me wide. That's when I feel the head of Talon's cock pushing inside of me and I moan. I know it's Talon because Kyle is crawling onto the bed in front of me with his cock in his hand, stroking it. Just as Talon slides in all the way, Kyle rubs the head of his dick on my lips and I open, sticking my tongue out, I let him take the lead.

Talon is sliding in and out of me, quickly building me back to another orgasm. Kyle takes my cheeks in his hands as he guides himself into my mouth. Something wet and warm hits me on the tight ring of my ass, then I feel Talon rubbing and playing with my hole as he thrusts in and out of my sex.

Being filled in all three holes at once is too much. Kyle continues fucking my mouth, while I suck and swirl at irregular intervals. Talon's pace increases with his cock and his finger isn't letting up as he strokes in and out of me. My skin is raging and sensitive, goosebumps form, my nipples harden and my legs stiffen. Both men recognize the signs and step up their pace, desperate to come with me.

I moan around Kyle's cock, sucking and fucking. Talon's forward thrusts send Kyle's dick deeper. I feel full, I feel used, and I feel loved all at the same time. I explode into a body shattering orgasm. I can feel Talon overcome with his own orgasm and my tongue is treated to Kyle's salty goodness.

Both men pull out of me as I come down from my orgasm. I collapse onto my chest, leaving my ass in the air. That is until Talon stretches out my legs. "We're not going to wear you out, angel."

I look at Kyle for reassurance and he smiles, the effect is comforting, telling me that it's okay. I'm not sure how I feel about that, but I feel the bus make a series of turns and then come to a stop, so I know we're pulling into the hotel.

I lay there for a little while longer. "I'm spending tomorrow in the bathtub," I groan as I find the strength to get up. Talon's shirt is so big that I could walk around in it and nothing else, so I use it to cover myself up. No need to feed the animals any more than I did without even knowing it.

"You can do whatever you want, baby girl," Kyle says. "We don't have to be anywhere until Tuesday afternoon. We have the signing at the Mall and then we take off for Chicago right after."

"That's right. I'd nearly forgotten. I wouldn't mind going shopping at the mall though."

"We figured you might. But that means you can't spend all day in the bathtub tomorrow. Better to shop without time constraints, right?" He laughs.

"True. Okay, then I'll just spend three hours in the tub."

They both laugh. Talon bends down and kisses me on the head. "You can do whatever you want, angel."

"Good, I'm going to go shower." I grab my towel from the hook on the wall and head toward the bathroom, nearly running into Tori and knocking her over.

"Oh, hi Tori."

"Hi Addison."

"Everything okay?" I ask.

"Fine, just coming to get you. We're at the hotel."

"I figured. I was gonna jump in the shower real quick."

"The rooms are already ready. You can shower there if you want."

"Oh, um, alright." I turn back toward the bedroom.

chapter 50

Okay, this is heaven. I'm so glad I decided to shower in the hotel room. Three rainforest style shower heads is like standing in the rain, just much warmer. I had all of my bags, clothes and everything brought up to the room. The guys thought I was nuts, until I told them that I needed to organize some stuff and send clothes to the laundry and dry cleaning since we were going to be stationary for a couple of days.

They don't argue with me and I see them doing the same thing. They're also going to be cleaning the bus during these couple of days. It will be nice to have some more clean clothes. I have plenty but my options are running very low.

When I come out of the bathroom, I jump. There is a bunch of stuff lying across the bed. "What the hell?" I walk closer and see that it's clothes, outfits, stuff I've never seen before.

"Kyle? Talon?" I shout, looking over the clothes. I really like what's lying here, I pray to god it's from them.

"Yeah, baby girl?"

I point to the bed, "What's all this?"

He gives me a Cheshire grin. "Well, the silver box is your replacement purple Louboutins. The rest of it is stuff Talon and I bought and had delivered here to the hotel. Pick an outfit for tonight," He tells me and I look over the clothes.

There is a green plaid shirt with suspenders. With it is a very low cut, square neck black, cap sleeve t-shirt. It would look great with my platform boots. Good thing I shaved.

The one next to it is a red dress with various black stars, devils, and swirls. It's a spaghetti strap at the top and where the straps come into the dress there are two black bows. This would look amazing with my black pumps.

The one on the other side of that looks like a jump suit, but by looking at it closer, I can tell it is going to be more of a snug fit. There is another layer to it, it's a lace full length, down to the floor, tank top that goes over the tank top jumpsuit. I like this one the best. And it would look amazing with my black Doc Martins.

"Decisions, decisions," I say aloud and Kyle laughs. "Well, I don't know which one I want to wear. Any suggestions? Favorites?"

"I'm bias." he says straight faced.

"Why's that?"

"Well, I picked out the red dress. So of course I'm going to say that. Talon picked out the black two piece number and we both liked the skirt." He shrugs. "It's going to be chilly tonight."

I laugh, "So I'm screwed either way?"

He laughs too. "Yeah, probably. But you know we'll keep you warm. I think Talon has a solution for that," he says just as Talon comes into the room. He's carrying a black wool, thigh length peacoat. It has a really large, deep hood on the back.

"This might help. Though the legs might be an issue," he says laying the coat down on the bed. "Did you decide?"

I shake my head. "Well, we will get them hung up again for you and thrown into the garment bag to take with us. We're running out of time," Kyle says, making a point of pointing out my current towel attire.

"Okay, leave the coat. I'll be ready shortly. I need to blow-dry my hair and find some clean clothes."

They both come over and kiss my forehead before leaving me to get ready to leave for sound. They take all the clothes with them, except the coat.

Twenty-five minutes later and I'm clad in a pair of flare jeans and a 69 Bottles t-shirt. I forgot that I'd stuck it in there and I figured since we had the fangirl conversation earlier, that I'd go to sound looking like a groupie. Which in a way, I am. I throw on my tennis shoes and throw my make-up, hair stuff, black pumps, platform boots and my Docs into my duffle bag. I don the coat, button it up so they can't see my t-shirt yet, and throw my duffle and messenger bag over my shoulder before going into the sitting room.

Kyle is the only one there. "Hey panda, you ready?"

"I hope so. If I forgot something, I can send someone back here, right?"

"Absolutely."

"Where's Talon?"

"He went ahead with the band. There's a problem with one of Dex's drums and it will take him and Talon to get a new head on it."

"Ah, okay, I'm ready."

He takes my bags off of my shoulder and throws them over his own, then wraps his arm around my waist, leading me from our suite into the hall where Rusty, Victoria and Casey are waiting for us. They're all dressed in black with black cargo pants and black t-shirts, which I wouldn't mention, except for its not their usual show attire. They're usually in dress pants and t-shirts and a jacket of some type. Casey and Tori are wearing their guns in thigh holsters and Rusty has his tucked into a holster on his belt, where it always is, but not normally so visible.

"What's the deal with the heavy armor?" I ask.

Kyle bumps shoulders with me, shaking his head. It irritates me, but then Tori answers. "We're always packing."

"Why so visible?"

"New procedure is all. We're trying to be more visible," Tori tells me.

"Okay then."

I notice that Casey stays in the hallway and doesn't come with us. I feel sorry for him, standing by in the hallway all night. The doors are locked. But then I remember what happened on the bus and decide not to feel so bad for him. If we don't have someone standing by, then anyone in the hotel with a key can get into our room. Both incidents are perfect examples of how people can be bought and then pulled away from their post in seemingly innocent fashion. So instead I take comfort in Casey staying behind.

Once we get back to the lower level, Rusty steps out first, sweeping the hall, then Kyle and me, and finally Tori brings up the rear. I'm not sure about all this stuff. I liked it better when we just were the way we were. But I can't doubt their due diligence in ensuring safety, problem is, they wouldn't be doing this with Kyle.

"You alright?" Kyle asks me.

"Yeah, I just think this is all a little extreme."

"Better to be safe than sorry, baby girl. Just let them do their job and try your best to ignore them. The only reason you're noticing is because you have a better understanding of the danger that you didn't have before. In all honesty, nothing's changed. This is how they function around Talon, Dex, Mouse and Peacock."

"Alright, I will try and remember that, and try even harder to ignore them."

He smiles and we walk through the hotel door.

"Addison, Addison, Addison," Flashbulbs, more screaming, more questions.

"What the hell?" I whisper.

Rusty has my door open and I slide in, sliding across, making room for Kyle. It's not until I'm inside that I realize we're in a limo and Tori slides in behind Kyle, then goes to sit behind the driver. I can see Rusty walking toward the passenger door and climbing in. As soon as he's inside, the car takes off.

I look at Tori, "What the hell was that?"

"The hotel location was leaked; at least I'm assuming that's the case. We will set up for a parking garage return. We didn't have time to make the change before they showed up."

"Well, there goes shopping tomorrow," I grumble.

"Why?" Tori asks.

"I don't want to deal with this while I'm shopping."

Tori smiles, "That's what we get paid for, darlin'. If you want to go shopping, you will go shopping and we will do it quietly."

Kyle squeezes my thigh, reminding me that he's there. I look at him. "Whatever you want to do, we will make happen. None of us want to see your personal life affected by this. So we will go shopping tomorrow. Talon will be coming along so we will turn some heads no matter what. We will likely cause a crowd, but we will be doing it."

I smile at him. "Alright." I lean over and put my head on his shoulder as we ride to First Avenue.

chapter 51

When we got to First Avenue, Talon fell over with laughter when I took off my coat. Which, of course caused everyone else to look at me too. Dex had a proud smirk on his face. Then the groupie comments started. I just rolled my eyes and stuck my tongue out at them when it was appropriate. When I told Talon I was just being a fangirl he enveloped me in his arms and kissed me with fervor. Sending my head spinning, my heart racing and my breathing nearly stopped all together. "I like you as a fangirl," he smirked and went back to helping Dex.

The sound check went awesome. I love the smaller venue. Though it reminds me of a bar, without a bar, it's pretty awesome just the same. Playing First Avenue is like a rite of passage in the music industry as evidenced by the number of major stars lining the walls back stage. Prince, of course, is nearly everywhere and his presence in evident by my purple dressing room.

I did my hair stick straight tonight. I wanted something different, and I pulled it back into a ponytail that is sitting high on the crown of my head. Because my hair is thick, there is a lot of it cascading down my back and over my shoulders. I decided to go with the red and black dress, not because Kyle picked it out, but because it works great with my hair and I'm rocking my black pumps.

I'm finishing up my make-up with another coat of lipstick when a knock rattles my door. The knob turns. "Addison, there is someone here to see you," Tori tells me.

"Who is it?"

"He said you're expecting him."

"Bryan Hayes?"

"That's him." I lean into the mirror, smile, check my hair, and decide that I won't get much better than this.

"Okay, let him in."

"I'll be coming in with you."

"Does he have security with him?"

"Yes."

"Okay then, but if his security staff stays out, so do you."

"Addison, I don't work that way."

"Tori, he's Bryan frickin Hayes."

"Yes ma'am," she says and I don't correct her this time. This time it's warranted; I need to know that she understands who her boss is.

She opens the door to someone who isn't Bryan, and they step inside. "Ms. Beltrand, I'm Kevin, Mr. Hayes' bodyguard. If you don't mind, I'd like to take a quick look around and then I will leave you to Mr. Hayes."

"Hi Kevin, go ahead." I stay standing where I am. I let him look around, there isn't much in the room besides a couch. He does his check and then goes back to the door, nods and then steps aside. Standing in front of him is Bryan

Hayes. He looks a lot younger than I imagined based on pictures I've seen of him and damn, he's good looking.

"Ms. Beltrand, I'm Bryan Hayes," he says as the door behind him is closed.

"Please call me Addison." He smiles a beautiful smile.

"Good, call me Bryan. It's a real honor to meet you, Addison." He extends his hand and I take it.

"I should be saying that about you." I smile. "I have to say, I'm glad you're here to see 69 Bottles tonight."

He laughs nervously. "Oh, I didn't come for them. I came here to see you and I can tell you right now that the videos don't do you justice." He gives me a full, gorgeous smile.

"Ditto."

"Listen, I stopped by before the show because I wanted to introduce myself. Our people seem to be pretty excited about my tweet the other day."

"Did you mean that? What you said?"

He smiles again. "Absolutely. I have my people working on it, but I understand you're under contract with 69 Bottles. But when the tour is over, you're a free woman." He blushes slightly.

"I am, technically, but you do understand that my singing with 69 Bottles was a complete fluke."

He laughs, "I've heard the story, but I don't care. You have an amazing stage presence for one, and for two, you have an even more amazing voice. Anyone would be honored to have you sing with them. Myself included."

"I can't say one way or another, but I can tell you that I won't think twice about it. I'd be honored. I'm one of your biggest fans." I blush.

"Really? A sweet rock chick like you enjoys country music?" He cocks his head.

"I like all kinds of music. Including rock and country, but rock is where my heart is. I've followed you since you first stepped on the scene. I knew one day you'd become something amazing." I smile.

"You have good taste then. Listen, I'm going to let you finish getting ready and I'm going to go get into my seat for the show."

"I appreciate that. I will be in the greenroom after, then I believe we're headed to an after party. If you'd like to join us."

He takes a step toward me. "I'll consider it, but..." he hands me a card, "here's my email and phone number. Let's talk some more."

"Don't you have people to handle this kind of stuff?"

He smirks. "That's not why I gave you my number." He winks, "It was a pleasure, break a leg tonight, Addison."

"No pressure or anything."

He laughs, "None at all, you'll do great." I extend my hand to him, he takes it, bends down and kisses the back of my hand. "Thanks for seeing me," he says as he lets my hand go.

"Absolutely, thank you again for coming."

"Anytime," he says as he opens the door and walks out into the hallway. Tori sticks her head in.

"You good?" I nod, dumb struck. "It's five forty-five."

"Thanks, I'll be out in a minute." She closes the door and I fall into the chair in front of the vanity. Breathing heavy. "That was intense," I breathe then try and pull myself back together.

Once Talon is on stage, after our ritual, I turn to Kyle. "Hey baby girl, you okay?"

"Nervous as shit."

He laughs. "Why?"

"Bryan Hayes is in the audience."

"How'd you know?" he asks.

"Because he stopped by my dressing room."

"Oh." I can see sadness creep into his eyes.

"Why the long face?" I ask.

"Because he stopped by and we didn't think to."

I roll my eyes, "he stopped by to introduce himself, let me know that he's serious about the duet and that he's looking forward to tonight's performance."

"Well that's awesome, I guess."

"Only thing is, he didn't come to see 69 Bottles, he came to see me."

"That's what I was afraid of," he mutters.

"It wasn't anything like that, not really. Just that he wanted to see if I'm as good in person as I am on the videos. That's why I'm nervous," I tell him. "Wait, are you jealous?" He tries to hide it and fails. "Kyle Black, you can't be, oh baby, no, it's nothing like that, not for me. I can't help it if he likes me, but I can help where it goes and it will go nowhere. I love you and I love Talon and the two of you are what I want. No one and nothing can come between that."

"He's a good looking man," Kyle says.

"You're better looking. Now explain something to me, you get jealous of Bryan Hayes, but yet you can watch Talon and I having sex, that doesn't make much sense to me."

"That's easy," he says, "we're all together. I know that when Talon gets his time, like today, I will get mine later, and vice versa. Plus, we all came into this relationship together, we work together, we sleep together, we love together."

"Do you love Talon?"

He doesn't answer right away, making me nervous. "Kyle?"

"Yeah, I do. But I don't know if he loves me back."

"That bothers you, doesn't it?"

"Yeah, it does. It's different with you. You knew it, probably before I did, that I loved you, but wasn't ready to say it. I was okay with that. With Talon, it's different. I love him, I'm in love with him as much as I'm in love with you. I just don't know how he feels about me."

"Have you tried talking to him?"

He snorts, "No, that's not something I know how to bring up with him."

"Do you need my help?"

He looks over my shoulder. "Maybe, but you've got sound coming in. We will talk about it, I promise." He kisses me chastely. Then whispers, "I love you, panda."

His voice is so soft, it melts my heart. "I love you." I kiss him sweetly and he shivers.

"God, I love you so much," he breathes and our conversation is broken when my mic shows up.

Once I'm hooked up, Kyle starts dancing with me. He's working on pumping me up for my performance and it's working with just the right amount of excitement.

They finish up the song right before 'Your Eyes' and the band starts in on their subtle, low volume version of the song and the crowd of fifteen hundred people goes nuts.

"And now Minneapolis, the real reason you're here tonight." Oh my god, I blush. Kyle laughs. "It's an honor to introduce to you Ms. Addison Beltrand." Kyle quickly kisses my cheek and I step out on stage. I wave, and the crowd goes nuts.

"How you doin, Minneapolis?" I say and they scream a little louder. "You ready for some fun?" The crowd starts jumping around and cheering as the band fires up their full volume rendition of 'Your Eyes' and Talon and I set the roof on fire.

The show goes on, until I'm called out again for 'To Be Free'. There is something special brewing between Talon and I on stage tonight and I'm pulled deeper into his voice and his trance as we sing our song. There is a deep, carnal craving that forms in the pit of my stomach. Something I've felt before for both Kyle and Talon, but this time, it's different. With Kyle's confession of love for Talon, the craving intensified. Talon learned that he was capable of loving me and he does it very well. He's rough. He's gentle. He's strong and driven. No matter how many times I have him, how long I get to keep him; this craving will never go away. I'm suddenly very eager to get back to the hotel.

chapter 52

At the end of the show, Talon makes an announcement about the signing at the Mall of America Tuesday at six. The crowd gets really excited about that and it makes me excited to know that we just might have more people there than originally thought. The signing is to celebrate the release of the album and it also kicks off their string of public appearances that will continue throughout the tour. Including TV and radio spots. Which means we will be limiting the after parties. We will need to leave as soon as the show and greenroom activities are over.

When we arrive at the after party there is a long line outside of the club, along with a media line that goes crazy when Talon and I step out of the limo. Tonight is the first night that Kyle comes with us because the rest of the band is packed into the same car.

As a band, they agreed to humor the paparazzi and pose for pictures along the way. Many cameramen refuse to take pictures without me in them which I find strange, but the band just pulls me in. We laugh and smile and then we finally duck into the party. Which is in full swing.

The music is pumping, the crowd is dancing and the alcohol is flowing. After 'To Be Free' was done, Kyle and I chatted about the party. I told him I didn't want to drink and he tried to talk me into it. I was firm in my decision because frankly it scares the crap out of me. I stick to bottled water and I have a great time just chatting with the guys and the people who come up to talk to the band. I get my fair amount of praise, but I keep the chicks off of Kyle because I refuse to leave him alone this time. I think Talon misses both of us because it isn't long before we're pulled into the inner circle.

Talon gets pretty drunk, which is a first; he doesn't normally drink like this, but I don't say anything, what right do I have? Plus, he's been really good, not drinking, not partying, he deserves a night out. I noticed that even when I wasn't around him, the girls seemed to stay at bay and I'm impressed, maybe it's finally getting around that he's taken.

We close out the bar around two in the morning and when we pile back into the limo, the guys are pretty wild, but they're having a good time. Even Kyle is getting in on the action. A contact drunk. I feel it too, but I'm not feeling that good so it's hard to get too into it. About thirty minutes after we arrived at the bar, I got really tired and very achy, almost like I'm catching a cold, but I don't think much of it and do my best to ignore it.

When we get back up to the room, Talon is acting strange. He's drunk— I get it—but, I don't know? Something's off. "Talon?"

"Yes, angel?"

"Are you feeling okay?" I ask.

"I feel amazing, why?"

"You just seem a little off."

"I'm drunk, so what?" he says with a hint of anger.

"I don't care if you're drunk, Talon. I just worry about you," I tell him.

"Well, don't."

"What the fuck...seriously, Talon?" I say.

"You picking a fight with me tonight? After you spend time alone in your dressing room with Bryan Hayes."

Whoa. "Talon, don't..." Kyle says but he's interrupted by Talon.

"You're okay with the fact that she was alone in her dressing room with another man?" Talon's words are slurred together.

"Talon Carver, I can't believe you...Jesus, you fucking think I did, oh my god! I'm not going to argue about this while you're drunk. Because it's nothing to be arguing about."

"Like hell, it's not."

"Talon, no, it's not." Kyle tries to step between Talon and I. Which of course drives my anger level higher. "You're throwing stones for nothing, Talon. They had a conversation about his tweet."

"Then why did I find this in her bag?" He pulls out Bryan's card. With his email and phone number on it.

"Why were you in my bag?" I snap.

"I wasn't, it was hanging out. Why did he give you his number, Addison?"

I pull the rubber band from my hair. "Because he wants to do a duet with me. Because he wants to further discuss it with me."

"He has people for that shit, people that need to talk to your people, not you two talking to each other."

I see Kyle stiffen and he looks at me. I hadn't told him about the card either, but I saw no harm in it. I know damn well that what happened between Bryan and I was completely innocent. "Honesty and communication. I've never lied to you. I'm not lying to either one of you now."

"Bullshit," Talon says.

"Talon!" Kyle snaps at him. "What the fuck, brother, what the god damn hell are you doing?"

"Doing what I do best," Talon says and slumps into the couch, but I am too pissed off, too fucking hurt to give a shit.

"A few hours ago, I was beyond excited to get back here, to spend the evening with the two men who mean the world to me. Who I love more than anything and will do anything for. And I get back here to this." I spread my arms wide. "I've done nothing wrong. You're so goddamn jealous of the fact that someone else wants to sing with me that you're blind to the truth. Tonight, I am invoking my safeword." I turn on my heel and walk straight into the bedroom where I turn, grabbing both doors. Just as they close I see Kyle's shattered look and my heart breaks. I close and lock the doors.

I strip out of my clothes, throw on my pajamas, scrub my face and climb into bed.

During one of our late night talks that turned to sex, we discussed safe words, mainly for the fact that Talon likes to get rough with me and I fucking love it, but we decided I needed a safeword. I told them I didn't need one, but that I should be entitled to have the ability to do exactly what I did. Invoke it and neither one of them can do a damn thing about it. If I invoke it, I get the bedroom on the bus, and the guys have to find somewhere else to sleep. They're not allowed to knock, attempt to get in, or attempt to contact me via cell until I was ready to come out. With the exception of food, in which case, if I left the room for the bathroom or food, all I'd have to do is say is 'safeword' and they couldn't approach me, talk to me, anything until I was ready. We all agreed that it would be allowed to be used by all of us. With the same no contact rules.

Though the no contact is only allowed to last for twenty-four hours. After that, those locked out would be able to try and make contact, try and talk it through.

This is the first time it's ever been used and I'm the one using it because of Talon and it is killing Kyle in the process. At least I talked to Kyle about Bryan's conversation, so with any luck he can talk some sense into him. Or get his drunk ass to bed to sleep it off.

I wrap my arms around a pillow and I shiver because I'm cold. I'm tired, and I'm alone.

chapter 53

The part about this whole fucking mess that pisses me off is he made an assumption, instead of talking to me about it. He just assumed and pissed himself off because he was afraid of the possibility. Couple that with the fact that sleep, while usually my friend, has become my enemy.

I've tossed, I've turned, I've lain still with my eyes open staring at the ceiling. Now it's seven in the morning and I'm up, sorting through my clothes. Piling up what needs to be dry cleaned and what needs to be washed. When I have the dry clean bag for the hotel stuffed full, I take it to the front door. Standing outside are Mills, Rusty and Tori.

"Good morning, Addison, everything alright?" Tori asks.

"No, but nothing for you to worry about." I hand over the bag and tell them that I'll have my laundry ready shortly. "I want to go to the mall today," I tell them all and no one looks surprised.

"What time?" Mills asks.

"What time does it open?" I retort.

"Uh, we'll have to find out, but I'm assuming nine or ten. So what time would you like to go."

I look at my watch and it is nearly eight. "Let's shoot for leaving around ten thirty."

"Will the guys be joining you?" Rusty asks.

"No," I say without further explanation.

"They wanted…"

"If they want to go, they can make their own arrangements. I am telling you mine."

"Yes, Addison," Tori says. "We'll be ready."

"Thank you." I slip back into the suite, closing the door quietly. When I turn around Kyle is standing at the end of the hallway. "My safeword is still invoked," I tell him and his face drops. "I am not mad at you, it has nothing to do with you, but I need to be alone for a while." He nods sadly. "You're still my cowboy." I give him a sad smile and he lights up a little bit. I walk up to him and place my hand on his cheek and he leans into it. "When I get back, after he's sobered up, and with any luck realizes what an idiot he's being, we will talk. But he is not allowed to buy me anything or do anything other than talk when it comes to what's happened."

"I understand." He kisses my palm.

"I appreciate you sticking up for me last night." I pull my hand down. "I'll see you later." I turn to walk away.

"I love you," he tells me and I stop.

I turn my head toward him. "I love you too, cowboy." That gets a small smile, but my heart is breaking knowing that I am inflicting unnecessary pain on him, but I can't allow time with one, when I'm pissed off at the other. "Go back to sleep."

"I can't. I can't sleep without you."

"That makes two of us, cowboy. But try, now that you know that I'm not mad at you, it might make it easier."

He nods and I walk across the sitting room to my bedroom. I notice that I can't see him from where I'm standing, which actually breaks my heart more.

kyle

"Addison." I jolt awake. "Addison? Where'd you go?" I can't see Talon but I can hear him. Then I hear the door to the suite open. "Where is she?" he asks whoever is in the hall. "Fucking great!"

I sit up, throwing my legs over the side of the bed and look at the clock, it's after twelve and Talon is frantic, which tells me that he's either realized his fuck up, or he's wondering why he woke up in the second bedroom next to me. I scrub my face.

"She's not here," he says.

"I figured. Where is she?" I ask.

"She went to the mall with Tori, Rusty and Casey." I hang my head. We were all supposed to go together and my heart aches knowing that she went alone.

"We were supposed to do that together," I grumble. Even more pissed off at him than I was last night.

"What the fuck happened last night?" he asks, and my blood boils.

"You, you're what fucking happened last night, Talon. She invoked her safeword because of you. Because of you, she's out shopping by herself. And we can't call her, we can't text her, we can't even fucking talk to her until she's ready to talk to us."

I look at him. "I got too drunk last night."

"I'll say. Everything was going great until we got back here. You fucking went through her bag, then threw it in her face."

"I didn't...honest to god, it was hanging out."

"So fucking what, Talon. You can't do shit like that to her. It's not fair. You flew off of the god damn handle because some guy gave her his number. A guy, mind you, who wants to sing with her, a guy who wants a professional relationship with her to record a song. You all but accused her of cheating on us, which you know damn well that wasn't the case."

"Fuck!" he growls and puts his head in his hands.

After a few minutes of him beating himself up internally he pushes away from the door jamb and goes into the bathroom. A few minutes after that I hear the shower start.

I pick up my phone, hoping for a text or anything from her and there is nothing, at least not from her. I have a bunch of emails from the label, discussing changes to the New York schedule, the schedule for tomorrow's signing at the mall, the radio station spot in Chicago Wednesday morning, etcetera.

I pull up my texts.

Me to Addison: Not violating safeword. U R not in vicinity, just need 2 knw u r okay?

Addison: I'm fine, shopping, be back between five and six. He awake yet?

Me: Yes, and he's pissed, desperate to talk to you. I'll keep him at bay.

Addison: Thnx cowboy. :-*

I take a lot of comfort in the fact that she's not mad at me, but I'm pissed off because I have to suffer at the hands of Talon's mouth, jealousy and temper. I wish there was some way to actually talk to him. I knock on the door, open it. "You hungry?"

"No," he snaps back.

I step into the bathroom and pull open the glass door of the shower and he's facing away from me. "Listen to me. I am not the one for you to be pissed off with right now. You're the one you should be pissed at. Do not take this out on me. I am suffering just as much, if not more than you are because she safeworded because of you. Remember? I'd already discussed what happened with her, and rather than fucking talk to her, you let jealousy win out. She can barely handle the two of us, what on god's green earth made you think that she'd ever consider cheating on us?"

He doesn't answer. He just hangs his head. I strip out of my clothes and climb into the shower with him. He jumps slightly when I touch his shoulders. I begin to massage his shoulders, down his arms. He turns around, putting his head on my shoulder and I can feel the silent sobs wracking his body. I rub his back. "I don't want to fuck this up, I can't fuck this up. She means everything to me."

"You know, she's not the only one in this relationship."

His head comes up and I can see his eyes are red from crying, which is likely why he snapped at me in the first place. "I know," he says as he brings a hand up to cup my cheek. A thrill runs through me and he places his lips on mine. Kissing me with gusto and I melt. Fuck, this shit is heady, and too much with him sometimes, but I don't stop kissing him back.

When he pulls back I breathe, "I love you." He stiffens, his body trembling slightly. "I know, it's alright." I reach up to cup his cheek in my palm. He relaxes. "I know what it means to you for me to say that, I know that you probably don't feel the same way. But I needed to say it. I need...." I am cut off by a finger at my lips.

"Shut up, Kyle." My heart sinks. "I...I don't know if I can, or am ready to admit it to myself yet."

I kiss his finger. "It's okay," I breathe and he moves his finger. This time, I take his head in my hands, bringing my lips to his and push him against the shower wall. He's already hard, and was hard when he turned around. I press into him, our cocks trapped between our bodies and I explode with desperate need. I feel his cock twitch under me and I know he needs this too.

"Let's go to bed," I breathe and he nods.

I pull him from the shower and wrap a towel around myself and dry him off. When I stand up, he reaches between the gap in the towel, taking hold and stroking my cock upward. My legs shake and my balls draw up in pleasure. "I need this," he breathes against my lips and a new wave of pleasure rocks through me.

chapter54
kyle

Talon and I make our way, clumsily, to the bed where I fall down on top of him. Our mouths haven't stopped moving and I can feel emotions pouring into me. I know, in some strange way, that this is his way of telling me he loves me. He can't say the words. Even when he says them to Addison, I can tell that it's a struggle for him, but he does it because he knows how it makes her feel. I don't need to hear it from him. His kisses, his touches, his everything tells me what I need to know.

I straddle him. The action causes our cocks to rub together and he groans into my mouth. "What do you want, Talon?" I growl.

"You."

"You have me," I counter.

"No, I need you, inside me." He brings his hand down around my cock, stroking it with his need and I close my eyes, my mouth falling slack from the pleasure he's eliciting in me. My need to be in him grows hotter.

I reach between us, taking his cock into my hand and I stroke up and down gently. "Fuck!" he moans and he thrusts his hips up. I sit up to watch our hands dance along each other's shafts. It's fucking gorgeous to watch. I try to slide down, to take him into my mouth, but he won't let go. "Come here," he breathes. No command, no dominance, just a simple plea for me to do what he wants. I lift my leg over his body and crawl on my knees toward his mouth. His hand never leaves my erection as I do. He turns onto his side, wrapping his mouth around my cock and my balls shrink up tight. I reach for his erection and he stops me with his eyes and a subtle shake of his head.

I don't argue with him. He has some idea in his head and I need to let him roll with it, but it spurs on the idea that he's doing this to show me what he really feels about me and I shudder with pleasure at the idea. He continues licking and sucking along my shaft. Then his hand moves south, taking my balls and massaging them, letting his finger dip further towards my ass and I'm too close to coming. "Talon?" I grunt. "I don't want to come in your mouth."

He lets up on my cock, shifting so that he can roll over onto his stomach. "Take it. Take me," he says with a deep gravel in his voice and my desire to take him overtakes my thoughts.

"I'll be right back," I tell him with a caress of his back, down along his cheeks and his thigh. I leave in search of the bag, and I find it in Addison's room. Opening it I see our plethora of toys wrapped in their own little bags for protection and I find a bottle of lube and quickly go back to the other bedroom. Talon hasn't moved in my absence and he looks at me through heavy eyes as I approach the bed. "You're sure?"

"I've never been more sure of anything," he says as he lifts his hips. With his head and chest still planted on the bed, he reaches back and spreads his cheeks wide, an invitation to take him. Claim him. I saddle up behind him, between his feet and once I'm situated, I can feel his feet touching my calves.

I begin working a glob of lube around his hole. Gently rimming him with my finger. He groans and pushes his hips up further, his own invitation for more. I continue gently massaging the tightness, slowly working one, then two, then three fingers inside and he's thrusting his hips. I reach down and grab hold of his balls and he cries out, "Take me, Kyle. Take me and tell me I'm yours."

I'm shocked by his blatant yet sweet command, and I realize that this isn't about me. My craving for him to love me has turned into his own desperate craving for me. This is about him. He needs to feel me. He needs to feel my love for him and sex is the only way he knows how. I am past the point of no return. I will give him what he needs because I need it too. I have to know that his ability to do this with me, and just me, is about us, not about our relationship with Addison. This is our moment to be with each other and for me to satisfy my craving for his love. For him.

I begin retracting my fingers, releasing his balls, and begin to work a healthy dose of lube along my cock. He lowers himself onto the bed. Pressing his cock between him and the bed and I press the crown of my own erection gently against his entrance.

He doesn't tense up, he simply relaxes into what I'm doing and I feel a sense of pride in this moment, a sense that he is honestly capable of doing this with me. With little thrusts, I work myself inside of him. Each stroke sending waves of pleasure through my body. Igniting an orgasm. One that's capable of tearing me apart. But I don't stop. He needs this, I need this, *we*, need this. Once I am sheathed inside of him, I pause, giving him that moment to adjust. Then I begin sliding in and out of him. My thrusts are slow, but deliberate and he is rocking with me. As his pace against me increases, I increase my own. I grab onto his ass and he arches his back, pushing himself against me and I use my leverage to begin sliding in and out of him harder and faster.

He doesn't tell me to stop, he is moaning with my thrusts and I can see the pure pleasure on his face as I take him, take him for me, for him, and for us. "Fuck me, damn it, Kyle don't stop," he groans and I pound into him harder. With each thrust, my orgasm ignites hotter and brighter. "Fuck! Fuck! Fuck!" He grinds against me, taking me, milking me as he shatters, his body convulsing under me and I explode inside of him.

Once I can finally move again, I begin extracting myself and he moans. Teasing him, I push back in. "You want me to take you again?"

"Yes," he groans and thrusts his hips against mine.

This time I take him harder and faster. It doesn't take him long before he's coming again and I follow shortly after. Soft and sated, my erection no more, I lay down on him. Holding him to me as my dick falls free. "That was intense," I breathe against his back.

"That was amazing," he says. "I really fucked up with her, didn't I?" he says with such sadness that I almost want to cry.

I sit up and rub his back. "She needed time. I think you hurt her more than anything. You made an assumption that simply isn't true."

"I realize that now."

"She was so excited to come back here last night. She asked me over and over again if we could leave. She teased the living shit out of me at the club, and then we came back to what happened. I sat by the door for over an hour after I put you to bed. She was crying and it broke my heart."

"I'm sorry I hurt her, and I'm sorry I hurt you."

I lean forward, brushing his hair from his eyes so that I can look at him. The angle is bad so I decide to lie down next to him. "You only hurt me because you hurt her. You said some pretty accusatory things last night and she had it right. Honesty and communication is the foundation of what our relationship is built on. You were being honest about how you felt, but rather than talking about it, you accused her of lying to us."

"Fuck, I don't remember that."

"Well you weren't exactly forthcoming with it, but when she brought up honesty and communication, she said that she's never lied to us and that she isn't lying to us now, you told her 'bullshit;'."

"Fuck, fuck, fuck. I don't know how to fix this," he says.

"Well, I think you need to talk to her. Talk it out. You can't fuck it or buy it away. You've got to find it in yourself to talk to her about what happened, how you feel, why you feel the way you do. Believe it or not, Talon, she's a very brilliant woman who would rather talk it out than piss it all away because you got pissed off. Whether it takes ten minutes or four hours, you've got to figure it out."

"I know, shit, I know, I just," he growls in frustration with himself that he's in this position, but I can't imagine him not figuring out a way to do this.

My cell phone rings. I get up and pick it up from the nightstand. "It's her," I whisper and watch relief wash over Talon's features. Her calling means she's ready to talk.

"Hi baby girl."

chapter 55
kyle

"Get him together. Mills is standing by waiting until you're ready. He'll bring you to the mall."

"Are you sure?" I ask her.

"I'm tired of being alone, I'm ready to talk. We will sit down and have a late lunch, early dinner and we will talk about this," she tells me, I can hear a lot of background noise so I know she's still in the mall.

"Wouldn't you rather talk to him alone?"

"Yes, but this is between the three of us and we need to all discuss it. I will give him his chance to say his peace and if he'd rather do it alone, I'll afford him that. But we need to talk. So I'll see you when you get here?"

"We'll be on our way shortly."

"Thanks, cowboy."

"I love you," I say without thinking.

She sighs. "God, I love you too, both of you."

We hang up.

"What was that all about?" Talon asks, he's anxious.

"She wants us to come to the mall." He flinches. "She wants us to sit down, eat and talk."

"Not the appropriate place for it," he mutters.

"No, it's not, but it is also neutral ground. She's taking away the ability for us to turn it into sex, and forcing us to actually talk," I tell him and he nods. "Mills is already on alert, preparations are made. We just need to get ready."

"I need to shower," he grunts as he gets up.

I look down at my naked form, "Me too."

"Well then let's go," he says, gesturing for me to join him.

addison

We need a restaurant. Mills just texted Tori letting her know they were in route. I look at the directory and there are several to choose from. "Crave," I tell Tori. "That's where we'll go, provided it's quiet enough, plus controllable."

"Sounds good." Looking at the map I can see that it's on this side, opposite corner from where I'm at, and on the same floor. I just left a store called Ragstock, which was actually pretty awesome. They have both new and vintage clothing, their prices are below what I would normally spend on clothes, but damn, I found some great stuff. Spending less than five hundred dollars, I have at least another suitcase full of clothes. Keep this shit up and I'm going to need a bus just for my clothes.

"Tori?"

"Yup?" She turns back.

"Do you think, if I can get a hold of some boxes, that we can ship some of this stuff back to LA before we leave?"

She shrugs. "I don't see why not."

I picked up a few things in Ragstock for the guys, some t-shirts mostly. They don't wear much else besides jeans and t-shirts anyway. Though there is a Harley Davidson store, maybe I can find something there for Talon. Kyle, on the other hand...I start to ponder ideas as we walk. It's Monday mid-day in the mall and it's busy, but mostly tourists like myself, and I've only been recognized twice. Then again, I'm here by myself, which might change with Talon in tow. Although, Dex, Mouse and Peacock showed up a little while ago and they're wandering around somewhere. "How are Dex and them doing? Any problems?"

"Not so far," Tori tells me.

"Good." I smile and we keep walking. This area is mostly filled in with restaurants and when we come to the middle of this side of the mall, I can see the amusement park that occupies the center. Only in Minnesota does an indoor amusement park make sense. Too bad I'm not into all that, it could be fun with the guys.

As we approach Crave, there are people inside, but not a lot to get excited over. Tori and Casey look through the windows, trying to figure out the best spot to put me to meet the guys. I notice in the far left corner, it's a little darker and more private. I point and Tori nods. "Let me handle the hostess," she says and she goes over to her. Tori can be very intimidating to a lot of people, which probably helps make her good at her job. I notice the woman checking a few things, then talking back to Tori. She then picks up some menus and leads Tori and Casey to where I pointed.

I walk up to Rusty, "What are they doing?"

He chuckles, "Just checking out the area, looking for ways in, ways out, and making sure no one else is back there. Mills will be showing up with Beck, giving us six, which is a little excessive for inside the restaurant. Odds are Mills will send one or two of us to meet up with Leroy and Bruce." Troy is the only one missing in the equation and I'm assuming that he is on hotel duty.

A few minutes later Casey comes out, gesturing to Rusty and me to go ahead and come in. We do, and I'm seated quickly, facing the front of the restaurant. I don't need to ask why this is. Better to have me facing front than Talon doing it. Though I'd imagine they'd like me on the other side with Talon, which I can't do because I have to be able to look at him while I talk to him. I notice that Casey goes back to the front of the restaurant. Rusty takes a seat at the bar not too far from me, and Tori is a couple of tables ahead, she's sitting of course, not to look suspicious or anything. I can see Casey through the window leaning casually against the railing. We're on the corner with Macy's and I entertain the idea of going in there when we're done eating.

The waitress comes toward Tori and she stands up. Talks to the girl, probably scaring the crap out of her and then lets her pass. "How you doing today? My name is Amber, I'll be your..." I look up at her and she stops talking. Her face lights up in recognition.

I warn her, "If you start going all freaky fangirl on me, there are two bodyguards that will escort you away, and find another server. So take a minute, take a deep breath and try that again." I watch as she visually tries to calm herself. "I will have a glass of water and an apple juice. Now, I am going to warn you, I will not be here alone. So I am going to give you a heads up, allow you to freak out in the kitchen before you come out again. I will not be dining alone."

"No way...he's coming?" I nod. "Ohmygod, okay, okay...water, apple juice, got it."

"Oh, and Amber."

"Hm?"

"Do a good job and we'll make sure it's worth it." I smile at her and she lights up.

"Yes ma'am," she says as she turns back toward Tori and the kitchen. No doubt to freak out some more.

Rusty comes over to the table and asks me, "What did you tell her? It would have been more fun to watch her freak out." He laughs and I join in with him.

"That's easy, I didn't want her totally freaking out when Talon sat down. Besides, it was more fun to watch it like that. Because I know, no matter how much she prepares herself, she's still gonna freak out."

He laughs, "They're in the building."

"Jeez, that was fast."

"Traffic was good?" He shrugs and sits back down.

Amber returns with my drinks, sets them down and asks, "Can I get you anything else while you wait?"

"No, I'm good. Doing better?" I ask with a smile.

"Much, thank you. I was at the concert last night."

I smile. "That's why you recognized me so easily."

She nods with a smile. "My boyfriend got me tickets for my birthday, but he couldn't do the VIP thing. I'm off at three tomorrow so I was gonna try and go to the signing."

I smile widely at her. "Not that we don't want you there, but maybe we can spare you the long lines before we leave today."

"That would be awesome. Thanks, Addison."

Amber turns to leave and nearly runs right into Kyle. "Sorry, darlin'," Kyle says. "You alright?"

"I'm good, thanks." She sidesteps Kyle and I can tell when she gets an eyeful of Talon because she pauses before continuing. Good, she saw him, now she can freak in the back and return.

The guys don't think much about it and I stand up, Kyle wraps his arms lovingly around me. "Missed you, baby girl, you okay?"

"Tired, but good. You?"

"Better now." He kisses me on the cheek and slides into the seat across from me, and he slides all the way over.

Talon comes up to me. He's hesitant. I open my arms and he cuddles right into me. I hear him sniff my hair as he wraps his arms tightly around my shoulders. He kisses my forehead. "I'm sorry, angel," he says sad and sweet. I know he means it.

"Apology accepted, but we're still going to talk."

He kisses my forehead again. "I think that's best," he says, surprising me. Talon isn't much of a talker. When he takes his seat, I look at Kyle. His expression is silently asking me if I'm okay. I nod slightly and sit back down.

Amber, being the diligent waitress that she is, shows up with water. "Hi I'm Amber, what can I get you to drink?"

Talon points at my glass. "It's apple juice." He cocks his head but doesn't say anything. I'm not a soda girl and I'm not in the mood for coffee, I've already had a turtle mocha from Caribou.

"I'll have a coke," Talon says.

"I'll have one too," Kyle chimes in.

"Can I get you guys any appetizers to get you started?"

"Whatever she wants," Talon says gesturing toward me.

I look at her, I smile and she takes a silent deep breath. I nod and wink. "I'd love the lemon garlic wings, please."

Kyle notices our little exchange and I shrug it off. "How about two of those?"

"Absolutely, anything else for now?" Amber asks. She seems to have gathered the nerve to talk to Talon without issue and I commend her for that.

"No, Amber, I think we're good," I tell her when Talon doesn't say anything. He hasn't said much but he can't take his eyes off of me.

"Okay, I'll be back with your drinks." She leaves the table.

"What was that all about?" Kyle asks.

"She was at the show last night. She recognized me, and freaked out. I warned her Talon was coming so that she could freak out in the back. If she keeps this up, you," I look at Talon, "owe her a picture and an autograph."

He laughs, "she isn't freaking out because of me angel."

"Ha! You didn't see her take a deep breath, she's freakin out alright, and it has nothin to do with me." I take a sip of my apple juice.

Talon laughs. "Alright."

"Besides, she was going to come to the signing tomorrow after working here all day. I figure I'll save her the time standing in line. She can have an exclusive with the ever elusive Talon Carver."

He snorts. "We could get the rest of the guys here."

I shake my head. "You do that and ninety percent of the mall will show up here. Just let it go." I wink at him.

Before we can begin talking we all dive into our menus, making our choices. Amber returns with drinks and refills, and then comes back with our wings.

"I'm sorry I was a dick last night," Talon says out of the blue, and I look at him. Pain is etched on his face. "I just, I kinda just freaked out."

chapter 56

"Talon, you freaked out for all the wrong reasons. You knew that Bryan Hayes was coming to the show. You knew about the tweet, you knew that the conversation could be possible, so why would it surprise you that he gave me his number and email address?"

I watch as he scrubs his hands through his hair. He doesn't say anything and Kyle sits quietly. I can tell by the way their arms are aimed toward each other under the table that there's a good possibility Talon is pulling strength from Kyle, holding his hand. "I think that I freaked out because I…I thought maybe we don't make you happy."

Oh my god. "Talon, have I ever given you that impression?"

He shakes his head. "That's why I woke up feeling so stupid this morning."

"So you understand that I'm not interested in anyone else?" He nods. "Then if you understand that, why did you freak out on me last night?"

"It was all too convenient and I let my mind run wild with possibilities. I feel...I feel like I, we're," he gestures between the two of them, "not good enough for you."

A tear escapes my eye. Just as Amber arrives with our food. She sets it down quickly, asks if we need anything else, and when we decline she leaves again. Her arrival is enough to distract me.

"Does it ever occur to you that I feel that way sometimes?" He goes to say something and I stop him. "Hear me out, please?" He nods. "Before I came into your life, you slept with how many women? Don't actually answer that because, yeah, I don't want to know. But you've gone from one, two or sometimes three different women a night, at least while on the road. Then I come onboard, you fall in love with me and you don't think I worry that I might not be enough for you?"

"I never thought about it like that," he says sadly.

"Just because I might feel that way, I don't freak out about it. I don't worry about it because you've given me no reason to worry about it. I'm with you all the time, and when I'm not, I know that Kyle's with you, and if neither one of us are with you, I think Dex has enough respect for me to keep you in line. Add to that the fact that I honestly believe you don't want to hurt me and you know stepping out on me will do just that. Not to mention that it will hurt Kyle. I have a lot of faith in that. If I'm wrong, tell me now." I take a drink of my water and watch him carefully.

"I'd never do it, I couldn't do it. I love you too much. It tears me apart thinking about it."

"Then, before you accuse me of something that isn't true, talk to me. We'll work through it. Raise your concerns and we'll talk about it. Don't just make an assumption, get drunk and then hold it over my head. I invoked my safeword because I was being attacked verbally by you, because you were unreasonable and not listening to me. We'd still be arguing if I hadn't gone to my room."

"I was drunk, angel."

"And you got drunk because you assumed, rather than asked."

He scrubs his face. "I did. I was wrong and I'm sorry. I don't know what else I can say to you to let you know how sorry I am. I feel awful, and I want to fix this, so tell me how to fix it."

I smile, "you can't fix it Talon, what's done is done, all you can do is think before you act going forward. The next time you think I've done something, or you feel like you're losing your head, talk to me, tell me, tell Kyle, bring it up, we'll talk about it. Even if it means you have to write it down or text it, breaking the ice. But when you break it, you need to be prepared to explain it. Be ready to discuss it and I promise to be open-minded and not fly off my own handle, like with the bodyguard incident. Okay? We all have some learning to do with this relationship, we have growing pains and these are some of them. Nothing's changed about how I feel about you or how I feel about Kyle. You can't push me away that easily." I smile sweetly.

I see the burden in his eyes lifting and Kyle looks lighter too. "Eat," I tell both of them and we dive into eating, the mood shifts more back to normal with each bite.

About halfway through our food, the silence is almost too much. "So what did you guys do today?" I've never seen two men blush as red as these two do. "You didn't?" I squeak.

Talon laughs. "We did."

"Oh?" Color me shocked. "Who?" Talon gestures to Kyle then back to himself. "No!" I say shocked. "And I wasn't there." I mock pout at both of them.

Both guys look upset. "Is that okay?" Kyle says, "We've never set those kinds of boundaries and I told him I loved him and it..."

"Wait, what?" I look at Kyle. "You told him?"

"Is that a bad thing?" Talon says.

"That depends, did you say it back?"

Panic washes over Talon. I can see him visually lock up. "He doesn't have to say it," Kyle says. "I know how I feel, I've told him, and as long as he knows how I feel, I'm confident when he knows he's ready to admit it, he will." I wish I had Kyle's confidence. "But my telling him led to what happened," Kyle says with a satisfied smile.

"Well, okay then. Talon?" He looks at me. "It's okay, Kyle and I know. We don't need you to say it." He smiles softly, the look is almost childlike. "Was it good?" I ask with a smirk.

Talon smiles a very satisfied smile. "It was amazing," He says so light and carefree, that Kyle perks up a little bit.

"Really?"

Talon looks at him with all the love he can't say out loud, and I watch Kyle melt.

We finish eating and Talon honors Amber with an autograph and a couple of pictures with me and Talon, plus Talon, her and me. Then we decide to do some more shopping. The experience is certainly one to remember. The guys are great at picking out outfits for me. Beyond hilarious actually. Especially some of the more risqué stuff, but in the same, I love that they enjoy my body that much. All in all, I ended up spending over eight grand in Macy's and Talon was pretty peeved when I told him I was paying for it.

"Big man, listen to me, I am capable of paying for all this."

"That's not the point, angel. I want to."

"I understand, but is this 'want to' because of what happened last night?" He doesn't argue, so I continue, "Then you're absolutely not going to pay for this. Talon, I don't need your money or for you to buy me things to show me you love me. If you want to buy me things, do it because you want to, not because you feel guilty."

"But we picked out most of this."

I smile. "If I didn't love it, I wouldn't buy it and most certainly wouldn't let you buy it either."

"I just don't..." he stutters.

"I understand you feel the need, I honestly do, but I know how you feel, I don't need you to buy me stuff to show me you love me. I need you to hold me, kiss me, make love to me, talk to me, be with me. Besides, I'm already going to have to ship a bunch of stuff back home." He laughs. "I'm serious, or we're going to need another bus just for my clothes."

"Oh baby girl, don't tell him that, he's liable to buy another bus."

"Or a trailer."

"Oh for crying out loud, I don't need a bus or a trailer for my clothes, I just need to decide what to keep and what to send home."

"Alright, baby girl, we'll get you some boxes," Kyle says with a roll of his eyes. "I will never understand clothes and women."

I snort. "For such a loving person, I'd think you'd understand," I tease him.

He laughs. "No. That's one thing I'll never understand."

"Ah, but don't you want your panda girl to look good?"

They sandwich me. "We always want you to look good, angel, but you can do that naked too."

chapter 57

As we finish shopping and walking around the mall some more, I am reminded of why it is that Kyle and Talon mean so much to me. Though Talon's drive to buy things for me, to show me he loves me, comes from his mother and the things she did when he was a child, it doesn't make it any less easy to accept his natural inclination to do so. But the fact that he feels so compelled to do just that, warms my heart.

Over the past few weeks, everything in my life has been shifted, twisted, turned, tossed and then finally righted itself once again. I've never been happier, even when I couldn't sleep last night, I knew it would all work out in the end, it had to. Everything that's happened so far has honestly happened for a reason, and whatever those reasons are, I'm dying to know.

Kyle is my lover. Strong, caring and passionate. Always desperate to find new ways to make me happy, both in and out of the bedroom. He's strong and independent, but like me, he has a craving for Talon that only Talon can satisfy. I think that barrier was breeched today when they were able to truly be with each other, alone.

Kyle's admission to Talon is a huge step in the right direction for our relationship. An admission that was long overdue. I'm thankful that Kyle took advantage of my imposed safeword break to break down that wall between the two of them. Though I am sad I wasn't there, I'm not jealous; in fact it's a testament to their relationship that they could do it without my guidance. It's also proof positive that they don't need me all the time. That they care enough for each other to turn their relationship from friends to lovers.

It's also proof to myself that I can handle the idea of being jealous. Knowing that they did something, without me, should have me pea green with jealousy, but it doesn't and I'm confident that it never will.

Talon shattered a brick wall today. The wall that he carries inside of him all the time. Though he is tough, domineering and sometimes overbearing, he's discovering better who he is. Though no matter what, I pray to god he never loses that edge. When he takes me roughly, and especially when he is commanding Kyle and me, it's the hottest damn thing in the world. I crave it, I'm starving for it.

We have a very long way to go in this relationship, but once again, our ability to talk about things, right our overturned ships, and move on like nothing happened is all the confirmation I need that nothing will stand in our way.

I fall asleep in the car on the way back to the hotel. Completely exhausted, emotionally and physically, Talon practically carries me to bed. They strip me out of my clothes and climb into bed with me. But there isn't any sexual tension and I notice when they snuggle into me that they're content just to be near me, breathing me in. I fall asleep in their arms.

ARE YOU READY FOR BOOK 3?

Redeeming Kyle
Available March 31st, 2015
Pre-Order NOW!

Here is a look at Chapter One

chapter 1

When I wake, I know it's early, but I also know I slept a
long time. Not wanting to wake my men, I crawl out of bed
and head for the bathroom. I decide that I need a long soak
and this tub is far too big to go unused. So I fire up the
water and let it fill. I go in search of a hair tie. I don't know
why, but I look into the baggie and I see something strange
inside. It's a tie, or something that looks like one mixed in

with all the others. When I pull it out, panic races through my veins. Where did this come from? How did it get here? I sit down on the side of the tub very slowly.

"Breathe Addison." I tell myself. If this is in here, it's not in me, if it's not in me that means..."Oh god."

"Baby-girl?"

"Oh god." I groan. Panic rises and my breathing spikes.

"What's wrong Addison?" He kneels down in front of me.

I hold up the hand that has the ring, my birth control ring, in it. "Where did this come from?"

He shrugs and shakes his head, "I have no clue, where did you find it?"

"In with my hair ties. It's not for my hair."

"Then what is it baby girl."

Oh god. I don't know if I can tell him, god, I don't want to discuss this. "It's nothing." I say.

"You promised honesty Addison, you're lying to me right now."

I start crying, "not lying just, oh god Kyle, this is my birth control." I bat my eyes to try and slow the flood of tears flowing. Oh god, emotional, crying, bitchy, fuck.

"What do you mean 'birth control'?" he asks, completely innocent.

I look at him and fight the urge to scream as the panic continues to rise. "It's called NuvaRing." I say with a shaky voice, "it goes up there, it's full of hormones that act as birth control. I put it in and then three weeks later I take it out, I bleed and put a new on in. I need to know how long this has been with my stuff."

I can see fear and panic rising. "God Kyle, please, no, don't, damn it, don't. I need someone to be strong for me right now. Please don't panic, I can't, I can't handle it."

"Baby-girl, I'm sorry. I just, we haven't..." he falls onto his butt.

"Kyle, breathe. Please. I..." I have to tell him, "Kyle I have issues with my uterus."

He looks at me, praying for an explanation. "I'm on birth control only to regulate my periods. Without it, I bleed, maybe twice a year. I have cysts. Do you understand what that is?" He shakes his head. "They're little bubbles within my uterus that overtime can turn hard. These cysts completely block one of my fallopian tubes, which means eggs don't pass through. My other ovary only functions about twenty-five percent of the time. Without birth control I have a less than five percent chance of getting," I swallow hard, "pregnant."

"So there's no way..."

"I didn't say that. I don't know, it's all going to depend on how long this has been out of me. Which is why I need Talon. Can you go wake him for me? I don't think I can move right now."

I don't know how he does it, but he manages to pull himself together. He turns off the water behind me and leaves the bathroom.

I can hear him. "Talon, come on big man, Addison needs you to wake up."

"Huh, what's wrong?"

"Nothing, she just needs to talk to you, she's in the bathroom."

"Okay, give me a sec." Talon tells him,

I put my head in my hands while I wait for Talon to come into the bathroom. God, Kyle freaked out, I don't think I can handle Talon freaking out on me too.

"What's going on angel?"

I take a deep breath. "Do you recognize this?"

I show him the ring. "Yeah, I found it and put it into your hair ties bag."

Thank god, "When?"

"Oh, um, Vegas I think, when we packed you up."

Oh fuck. "Kyle, can you bring me my phone, please?"

"Angel, what's going on?"

"It's not a hair tie. It's actually called a NuvaRing, it's my birth control." I say softly.

He kneels down in front of me. "I don't understand."

"This goes inside of me, it releases hormones into my body, and then after three weeks, I take it out and within a few days I get my period." Kyle shows up with my phone.

"When were you suppose to take it out?" he asks me.

"Sunday morning, but I couldn't find it. Then with the Bryan Hayes thing, then yesterday and, I just forgot about it. I was going to have one of you help me, but everything just got so messed up. But I couldn't find it because it was gone and it's been gone..." I look at my phone, "for over two weeks." Panic flies once again.

"But we haven't used condoms." I put my hand on his cheek.

"I have problems, in my uterus, my likelihood of getting pregnant is less than ten percent."

"So you're not..." I can see the panic I feel reflected in Talon's eyes.

"I didn't say that, though I wish I could." I look back at my calendar, my period usually shows up Tuesday night, or sometime Wednesday. "I need a test, but it might be too early." The tears flow again when I see Talon with complete panic on his face.

Kyle kneels down behind Talon. "Talon, are you alright?"

He doesn't respond, he just sits there. His body is radiating panic and ready to freak out. I put my hand on his cheek. "Look at me big man." He doesn't look. "Come on big guy, I need you to look at me." Tears streak down my cheeks. I can't stand to look at his panicking face, I need him to look at me. "Come on angel, look at me." Finally his eyes meet mine. "Hi there." I smile. "You with me." He nods slightly. "Can you talk to me? What are you thinking?" He looks down again. "No, no, keep looking at me."

His eyes come up, meeting mine, they're thick with unshed tears. "I'm scared." He breathes.

"What are you scared about?"

"I'm not sure I'm ready to be a father." He says in a whisper.

"Awe, baby, we don't know that. We don't know one way or another. Until we know for sure, we cannot panic. Please, I can't." The tears flow harder and faster, "I can't stay strong for the three of us." I look past Talon to Kyle.

"Talon, no matter what, we're all in this together." Kyle says as he rubs Talon's back. "You're not in this alone, neither is Addison."

"What if it's yours?" Talon asks.

"Honestly, it doesn't matter to me whether it's yours or mine, if she's even pregnant, we're still all in this together. We've made a choice to be a triad, to be a threesome, everything we do involves all three of us, no matter what." Kyle says. His strength is like a shot of adrenaline straight to my heart.

Talon loosens up a little bit too. "Kyle's right. We can't make assumptions until we know for sure."

"How do we do that?" Talon asks.

I give him a small smile. "I need a pregnancy test."

"Where do I get one?" He's eager.

"Breathe big man. I will send Tori or someone else to get one."

"I'll go." Kyle says as he stands up.

"Relax cowboy. There is no guarantee that the result I get today will be accurate. A blood test is preferable, but I don't want to take the risk of it leaking to the media. So, if we're going to get one, I'll need at least two. I'll take one today and I will try another one on Thursday or Friday. My period usually starts on Wednesday after I take out my ring, but I only had it in about a week before it fell out. So my body is probably screwed up."

"Okay, let's get you a couple of tests." Kyle says.

I nod and look to Talon. "You feeling better?" He gives me a tiny lift of his lip. "I'm going to slide into this nice warm tub. I need to relax."

"Can I join you?" Talon asks. "I just want to hold you." He whispers.

I look up to Kyle who nods, "I'll go talk to Tori." He says.

"Are you sure?" I ask.

He leans down and kisses my forehead. "Absolutely." He says and leaves the bathroom.

I reach for Talon's hand. "Come on." He stands up with my help. I step over the the side of the tub and stand in the middle. Talon steps in behind me and slides down into the water.

"Come here angel." He says and I sit down in front of him. He wraps his arms around me, under my breasts and pulls me back, closer to him and he holds onto me like he needs air to breathe. I settle into him, his hold and his touch. Laying my head back on his shoulder.

About Zoey's

Zoey Derrick is a Best Selling Author of Contemporary, Erotic, Erotic Romance and Paranormal Romance from Glendale Arizona. She was once a mortgage underwriter and she now writes full time.

She writes stories as hot as the desert sun itself. It is this passion that drips off of her work, bringing excitement to anyone who enjoys a good and sensual love story.

Not only does she aim to take her readers on an erotic dance that lasts the night, it allows her to empty her mind of stories we all wish were true.

Her stories are hopeful yet true to life, skillfully avoiding melodrama and the unrealistic, bringing her gripping Erotica only closer to the heart of those that dare dipping into it.

The intimacy of her fantasies that she shares with her readers is thrilling and encouraging, climactic yet full of suspense. She is a loving mistress, up for anything, of which any reader is doomed to return to again and again.

Stalk Zoey on Social Media:

Facebook
Twitter
Pinterest
Website
Goodreads